PENGUIN B

MANDODARI

A feminist and a passionate mythologist, Manini J. Anandani is currently pursuing her postgraduate diploma in comparative mythology from University of Mumbai. She has previously worked in the hospitality, marketing, communication, banking and sales sectors, and as a corporate trainer. She lives in Mumbai with her husband, Jeetu, and her daughter, Anika. *Mandodari* is her first book.

Mandodari
QUEEN *of* LANKA

Manini J. Anandani

PENGUIN BOOKS
An imprint of Penguin Random House

PENGUIN BOOKS

USA | Canada | UK | Ireland | Australia
New Zealand | India | South Africa | China

Penguin Books is part of the Penguin Random House group of companies
whose addresses can be found at global.penguinrandomhouse.com

Published by Penguin Random House India Pvt. Ltd
7th Floor, Infinity Tower C, DLF Cyber City,
Gurgaon 122 002, Haryana, India

First published in Penguin Books by Penguin Random House India 2018

Copyright © Manini J. Anandani 2018

All rights reserved

10 9 8 7 6 5 4 3 2 1

This is a work of fiction. Names, characters, places and incidents are either the product of the author's imagination or are used fictitiously and any resemblance to any actual person, living or dead, events or locales is entirely coincidental.

ISBN 9780143442684

Typeset in Bembo Std by Manipal Digital Systems, Manipal
Printed at Replika Press Pvt. Ltd, India

This book is sold subject to the condition that it shall not, by way of trade or otherwise, be lent, resold, hired out, or otherwise circulated without the publisher's prior consent in any form of binding or cover other than that in which it is published and without a similar condition including this condition being imposed on the subsequent purchaser.

www.penguin.co.in

*To all the women in mythology—
the daughters, the sisters, the wives and the mothers—
known and unknown*

Ahalya Draupadi Sita Tara Mandodari tatha I
Panchakanya smarennitya mahapataka nasini II

Ahalya, Draupadi, Sita, Tara and Mandodari
One should forever remember the panchakanya—
the destroyers of sins

The Panchakanya shloka is a well-known Sanskrit hymn about the five iconic heroines of Hindu epics. All five women were married and though their lives were full of misery, they tackled the most difficult situations with courage. Orthodox Hindu wives remember the Panchakanya in their morning prayers. It is said that chanting this shloka washes away sins and provides valour, composure and ability to the woman who recites it.

PROLOGUE

Once an apsara named Madhura wanted to appease Shiva. She wished for the lord to either accept her as his second consort or bless her with a husband as great as he himself was. Hence, she took vows and adorned herself with jewels to please him. She reached Kailash when Shiva's prime consort, Parvati, was not around. Shiva was in deep meditation, unaware of any presence in his surroundings. However, the scent of the apsara's celestial body aroused the supreme god with lust. Shiva roused from his meditation and saw the beautiful-bodied Madhura. He made love to her and she willingly submitted, hoping to receive a boon.

When Parvati returned to Kailash, she noticed traces of ash from Shiva's body on Madhura's breasts. Frantic and full of anger, Parvati cursed Madhura to turn into a frog and live in a well for the next twelve years as punishment for charming and luring her husband into committing adultery.

Shiva calmed his angry wife and expressed remorse for his act. He consoled Madhura and gave her a boon: she would reincarnate as a beautiful woman and marry a great, valorous king—one of Shiva's own devotees.

Years after this incident, an asura king called Mayasura and his apsara wife, Hema, were performing months of penance in a nearby forest to seek Shiva's favour. Mayasura and Hema had two sons, Mayavi and Dundubhi. Unhappy with their roguish sons, the couple longed for a daughter.

It was a pleasant morning when Mayasura ended his penance and was walking through the forest to fetch some water. He heard a child crying nearby and started looking around. He realized the cries were coming from a nearby well and rushed to the child's rescue. Mayasura called out to his wife, who was still meditating. Together, they rescued a beautiful girl child from the well. Grateful to Shiva for answering their prayers and blessing their penance with the child, they adopted her as their daughter.

They brought her up as Mandodari.

ONE

I was getting dressed early that morning to join my brothers for hunting.

'You are not going anywhere,' said Mai while braiding my hair with flowers. 'You hurt yourself every time and I get an earful from the queen.'

Mai was the midwife assigned to my mother Hema and me. She was old, witty and took care of everything.

'But I can hunt better than my brothers, Mayavi and Dundubhi,' I argued.

'Princesses don't go hunting. Princesses are born to marry a handsome prince and . . .'

'Please stop putting these flowers in my hair, Mai,' I interrupted.

While my mother was a beautiful apsara and a celestial dancer, my father was the ruler of Mayarastra and a renowned architect. He was a father figure for the rakshasa, asura and daitya races of Bharatvarsh. He was also the designer and king of the three flying cities known as Tripura. He taught me about architecture on the different landforms of Bharatvarsh—mountains or heavenly plateaus known as *swarg*, plains known as *bhoomi* and deep valleys or the underworld known as *patala*. These terrains were collectively known as Triloka or the three worlds. The deva gana race occupied mainly the mountainous region of Bharatvarsh known as Devaloka. The plains were shared by the manava gana and the rakshasa gana. The underworld or the nether world was ruled by another race of asuras called the danavas.

Mai had once explained to me that we were asuras by race and others such as the devas and the manavas were very different from us.

As a teenager I always enjoyed playing outside with my sakhis. We would go hunting, compete in archery and often talk about marriages. We would gossip about princes and their affairs, and that's how I learnt about love. My sakhis shared numerous stories about love. Some were made up.

I grew up learning about the different buildings and mansions my father created for the rulers of the netherworld. It was said that his buildings and palaces drew envious looks from even deva Indra's Amravati. Sometimes he was visited by the devas too as there was barely a match for his design and architecture in Devaloka.

When I turned fifteen, my father started involving me in his ventures. I took a keen interest in construction and design as my father was a master of architectural illusions. Our palace was full of architectural wonders. My bedroom chamber was attached to a private garden, which had a small path connected to the main court of the estate. Our gardens were adorned with divine flowers and manicured landscapes that seemed like bright glittering emeralds during the day. Fresh waterfalls and supernal fragrance from the flowers made a remarkable combination of the natural world and illusions.

At the centre of the garden lay an illusory path towards the main court. It was made of fine crystals, which were transparent—walking on it felt like walking on the stars. We were devotees of Lord Shiva and hence a temple dedicated to him was built before the entrance to the main court. The temple was made at a height on a single-stone marble platform that looked like the mountain of Kailash. A huge Shiva Lingam of solidified mercury was worshipped in the centre. This temple had no roof, but trees had been planted around it in a way that they covered the entire temple platform. We believed that Shiva was neither a deva nor an asura. He took no sides. He favoured no one and envied no one.

The dome-shaped main court was centrally situated in the capital of Mayarastra. Visitors and guests were received in the main court first, and then directed towards the guest chambers or else towards the city exit.

One day, there was a very special guest expected at court. Mother told me about a young Brahmin boy who was going to visit father that day to seek his architectural advice on building temples in his kingdom. Rumours went around that he was a great scholar and also a Shiva bhakta like us. People called him Ravana.

Ravana was the son of the great sage Vishrava and the daitya princess Kaikesi. He was, thus, biologically a daitya and belonged to the caste of Brahmins. Mother told me that Kaikesi's father, Sumali, the king of daityas, wished for his daughter to marry the most powerful being in the mortal world so as to produce an exceptional heir. Sumali expected this heir to help develop the masses of his clan. He rejected the kings of the world as they were less powerful than he. Kaikesi took matters of her marriage into her own hands and searched among the sages and the scholars. She finally chose Vishrava, a Brahmin scholar and researcher.

Vishrava was an intellectual par excellence; he had earned great powers through *tapasya*. He was married to Ilavida, daughter of Rishi Bharadwaja, and she had given him a son named Kubera or the Lord of Wealth as assigned by the devas. Vishrava was performing a yagna in his ashram when Kaikesi stood in front of him. She was young; her features sharp and body well-toned. She approached Vishrava unswervingly for his seed to bear her a child who would improve the conditions of her clan.

Vishrava fell in love with Kaikesi and took her as his second wife. Although hurt and feeling rejected, Ilavida respected her husband's decision and abstemiously accepted Kaikesi as a part of her family and in the ashram. Vishrava fathered quadruplets through Kaikesi. The eldest son being Ravana, followed by Vibhishana, Kumbakarna and a daughter named Meenakshi. When Ravana was born, Kaikesi placed her crystal necklace around her firstborn to signify the superior destiny he would bring for her clan. The reflection of his mother's crystal necklace on his face created an ocular illusion of ten heads and so he was named Dashaanan, the one with ten heads.

Dashaanan learnt and mastered the four Vedas from his father at a very young age. He possessed a thorough knowledge of Ayurveda and astrology. He learnt music, arts, political science and occult science and became a renowned scholar of the six shastras.

He was named 'Ravana' by Shiva. It was believed that he once stood for months in tapasya to seek Shiva's blessings. He wished to carry the lord to Lanka so he would be close to him. He even tried to dislodge Mount Kailash on which Shiva was meditating. Shiva pressed the mountain down with his toe, crushing Dashaanan's forearm and his ego, clearly rejecting his move. Ravana then composed the Shiva Tandava Strotam to praise the lord and ask for forgiveness. Shiva acknowledged Ravana as his primary disciple—*parambhakt*—and also narrated a text on astrological predictions called 'Ravana Samhita' to him.

Taking advantage of his growing demonic powers, Dashaanan usurped his half-brother Kubera's throne in Lanka. Vishrava advised Kubera to let go of his throne as Dashaanan had greater powers and war strategies. After witnessing Dashaanan's disrespectful treatment of his older brother, Vishrava disowned his asura family and returned to his first wife, Ilavida.

Close family members and ministers of the court were invited to meet the renowned guest of the day. The dome of the main court was translucent and visible only to the people standing inside. I walked towards the main court realizing that I was late, or perhaps the others had arrived before time in their anticipation to meet Ravana.

There was music in the air. I stepped inside the court and saw a well-built man sitting right next to father's throne. He was playing the veena. Everybody's eyes were on him. He was tall, slightly tanned and sat with one leg crossed where he had placed the veena. He wore a tall golden crown, taller than father's. His earlobes were long and he wore gold earrings; he had shoulder length hair. His forehead was smeared with chandan paste in a symbol that signified his Brahmin caste. He wore an *upanayana* thread across his chest and a huge opal-pendant necklace. His perfectly carved abdomen was draped in a pure silk dhoti with a golden border. I couldn't take my eyes off of his arms, which were the most muscular arms I had ever seen. He had a royal blue-red velvet stole draped over his arm.

He kept his eyes shut while playing the veena. His aura was so magnetic that I could feel myself being pulled towards him even though I was barely paying attention to his face. My eyes were transfixed on him ever since I had stepped into the room, barely acknowledging the other people present there.

Suddenly there was rapturous applause, 'Marvellous! You play music better than a Gandharva!' praised my father.

He opened his eyes, placed the veena down, joined his hands in respect and smiled at my father.

'You are simply being generous in your appreciation, Asura Raj,' Ravana said.

'Oh . . . so beside your valour, you are also a modest man, Dashaanan? A rare quality to find in an emperor like you,' said father and they both shared a hearty laugh together.

'I believe my qualities were enhanced by my guru—the great asura emperor—Mahabali.'

Asura Raj Mahabali was the grandson of daitya king Prahlada. His reign was considered the most prosperous. The asuras believed that the devas envied him and planned his demise. It was not taken well by the asuras and that created constant wars between the two parties since then.

'Well, Asura Raj Mahabali would have been proud. He has trained you well and he made you a scholar.'

'Let me introduce you to my family now. I am so glad that you accepted my son Mayavi's invitation and we had the privilege of meeting a . . . a scholar like you,' praised father and turned him towards the court.

He glanced at the audience and then he looked at me. I felt a river running inside me.

Father introduced us to Dashaanan, his younger brother Vibhishana, and his royal adviser Malyavan, who had accompanied him. I don't remember the details of our first formal introduction. My eyes were lowered with some sort of embarrassment after he looked at me. He was meeting the other ministers of our kingdom and looked away from where I was standing. I could still feel his eyes on me, taking note of every movement I made. It wasn't that he was the first man I had ever been introduced to nor had I ever behaved this timidly with any other guest, but he was unlike any man I had interacted with before.

I couldn't sleep that night. I kept thinking about my brief moment with Dashaanan. I wondered if he too was thinking about me. He was staying with us that night and was put up in one of our luxurious guest chambers. Mother told me that the kingdom he ruled down south had walls made of solid gold. People called his kingdom the 'golden Lanka' and Dashaanan was also addressed as 'Lankesh'. Mother and Mai were concerned whether our guest chambers were comfortable enough for Dashaanan's stay. However, in my opinion, our guest chambers were lavish and Dashaanan didn't look like a guest who would come up with petty complaints.

I decided that if I happened to meet Dashaanan again, I would conduct myself more assertively. I tried to get his departure details from Mai. She said that Dashaanan would join the king for lunch and depart for his kingdom in his Pushpaka Vimana—a flying chariot that he had taken over from Kubera. Pushpaka was originally made by Vishwakarma for Lord Brahma and later given to Kubera. The vimana could travel between cities, kingdoms and overseas in a short span of time. Locals of Mayarastra gathered around the Pushpaka Vimana to gaze at the aeronautical wonder.

'Isn't Lankesh planning to join *bhrata* Mayavi for hunting?' I enquired from Mai.

'No, Lankesh said he doesn't enjoy games like hunting. A man with such profound knowledge and power must have outgrown such ordinary activities.'

I thought Mai was done admiring him. Father spent a lot of time with Dashaanan and I was doubtful of seeing him again. Mai hurried to my chambers in the evening, pulled me towards the window and pointed towards the Pushpaka Vimana flying high up in the sky. Even though I was accustomed to seeing all the illusory buildings and wonderful mansions my father had created, I was somehow still in awe at the sight of a flying vimana for the first time.

As a princess, I completed most of my education at the age of twelve. My tutoring mainly comprised physical training through yoga, a few Vedic texts for literary references, culinary arts, social science, and deva and asura history. I mastered engineering through my inclination towards my father's profession. I also learnt different languages. Unlike boys, girls were excluded from other lessons of chemistry, political science and warfare techniques. Asura men were fierce warriors and conquerors. There were many stories where asuras had successfully dethroned devas and conquered their kingdoms.

Mother had instructed Mai to teach me all the things that a perfect bride should know. I polished my culinary skills, acquired theoretical knowledge of politics and learnt an ethical code of conduct essential for a queen. I knew for sure that my life would change after marriage. I kept imagining the man I would marry. I kept thinking about the kind of values he would possess. Then I wondered whether my future husband would be an asura or a deva?

Or someday, would I encounter a Gandharva in the woods and fall in love with him? I remembered and relived my short meeting with Dashaanan every day. Four months had passed since I had last seen him.

Then one day Mai came running to tell me a new story of accomplishment she had heard about Dashaanan. Apparently, he was given a boon by Prajapati Brahma and was expected at Mayarastra to meet *Pitashri* regarding some matter.

A grand *Rajsik bhojan* comprising a variety of meats, curries and rice was being prepared for Dashaanan. Women were excluded from the lunch meeting as Pitashri had important matters to discuss. I stayed indoors and desperately waited to see Dashaanan again.

Next day, when I stepped out of my chambers to meet Mother, I saw several courtiers dressed in white and red robes standing with gold platters, which were covered by black velvet serviettes embroidered with gold lace; a motif woven on each of them—a golden veena. It was not unusual for us to receive such gifts and offerings, as Father often exchanged such gifts with other kingdoms in case of a victory in war, new establishments and achievements. Looking at the poise of these courtiers, I understood that those gifts came from some very reputable kingdom.

I went inside the room where Mother was busy talking to Mai; both looked very excited.

'Mandodari, we have some news for you,' said my mother.

'Mother, where are the gifts from? Looks like a big occasion this time.'

'Well, of course, it's the biggest occasion, or will be the biggest occasion Mayarastra has ever come across,' Mother and Mai smiled at each other.

'What is this all about, Mother?'

'These gifts are from Lanka, my princess. Lankeshwar Dashaanan sends them as a proposal. He has made a proposal to your father this morning and we are so honoured. He has asked for your hand in marriage.'

For some time I kept looking into my mother's eyes, waiting for the news to sink in. Mother and Mai embraced me and I couldn't think of anything to say. I wasn't expecting this at all and my heart kept pounding inside my chest, making me nervous.

'Princess, your father is waiting to meet you. He hasn't accepted this proposal yet as he wants to talk to you at first. You should go and meet him before Dashaanan leaves for Lanka,' Mai added.

'Mother, does Dashaanan really want to take me as his better half?'

'Well, of course! He sure does. We are very obliged, and certainly this means an ambitious alliance between Lanka and Mayarastra.'

I had dreamt about being with Dashaanan and couldn't believe it was really happening.

Father was pacing his chambers alone; it seemed he had a lot on his mind. He embraced me at once.

'*Putri*, I can barely express how proud your mother and I are to have a daughter like you. I am sure your mother must have told you about Ravana's proposal?'

Father had addressed him as Ravana for the first time.

'Yes, Pitashri. I am well aware.'

'So, what do you think? Your mother looks very happy. I want to know your thoughts on this union.' Father was very precise in his approach whenever he asked for my opinion. Whether it was about any design in architecture or matters of state.

'Pitashri, I have grown up with your teachings and values. I am certain you must have given profound thought to this proposal before asking me about it. If you think Lankeshwar is the ideal husband for me, I will walk with him with my eyes closed.'

'There is no doubt that I am fond of Ravana. He is a king with exceptional qualities, a great spirit with unlimited powers. But I also want you to know the other dark aspects he has acquired with his powers. With unlimited powers come unlimited disorder. You should be well aware of such consequences before you decide to get married to him.'

'What kinds of consequences, Pitashri? I thought you would be pleased with this proposal . . . '

'And I am, Putri. However, I merely want you to be prepared. There are a lot of people whom he has disappointed for his benefit. Every boon that Dashaanan has been blessed with threatens the existence of Devaloka. The consequences of such supremacy given to a man can be perilous.'

'Pitashri, you are making this more difficult for me. Do you really approve of this marriage or not?'

'At first I did not. When Dashaanan proposed his intentions of marrying you, I simply rejected the suggestion, stating that our standing is nowhere equivalent to his. And you know, Putri, I didn't mean this at all. I said this as I was afraid of denying Dashaanan's proposal straight away.'

'And how did Dashaanan react to this, Pitashri?' I was anxious to know what exactly had happened between them.

'He probably understood that I wasn't denying the proposal but denying him. He then convinced me by telling me how Mayarastra would benefit with its union with Lanka, always ensuring ultimate protection from external divine forces.'

'We are strong enough as a province. Do we really need an ally like Lanka to sustain us?'

'We don't, but I think Dashaanan was trying to imply that we might invite trouble if I don't accept the proposal. And in addition to this, he reminded me how we too are Shiva bhaktas and won't get a better match than him.'

'So, are you bringing this proposal to me out of fear of what Ravana might do or because you think he's a great match for me?'

'At first it was out of fear, but I have to agree with what Dashaanan said. You know you are no an ordinary girl; you are Shiva's blessing to us. I gave this proposal a lot of thought and I agree that you deserve an extraordinary husband like Dashaanan.'

I sighed with relief. Although I had feelings for Dashaanan, it was very important to me that father approved of my marriage with him. I wanted to be certain that I had made the right choice.

'You are destined to be the queen of Lanka. You are destined to marry a great king of these times.' Father had tears in his eyes already.

'I will miss you, Pitashri . . .' I sought his blessings. It was the last time we had a moment alone before my marriage.

Father ordered his ministers to prepare for a lavish wedding ceremony the following month. He ensured that my wedding remained a memorable one throughout the centuries. The ceremony was arranged in a nearby region and the mandap venue was named 'Ravana Chanwari' after Dashaanan.

TWO

A few days before the wedding, Malyavan, Dashaanan's royal adviser, paid a visit to our royal chambers. Malyavan was also the elder brother of Ravana's maternal grandfather Sumali. People in Lanka addressed him as Nanashri. I met him and his beautiful wife, Sundari, to accept the sacred clothes and trousseau they had brought for me from Lanka. Mata Sundari was the sister of Ketumati—Sumali's wife and Mata Kaikesi's aunt.

I was supposed to leave for Lanka in the royal robes sent by Dashaanan. His younger brother Vibhishana along with his wife, Sarama, had also accompanied Nanashri Malyavan. Vibhishana was nothing like Dashaanan.

I stared at him for a moment and found that although his features were quite similar to Dashaanan's, he lacked his brother's pride, aura and confidence.

Vibhishana was a man of few words. Later I thought I was being judgemental as he came across as a very pleasing, respectful and humble man. He paid his respects to my family and me and then swiftly left for Lanka to make arrangements.

I spent sleepless nights thinking about my wedding preparations. Father had invited all the neighbouring kings and royal families. He also invited a few devas whom he considered his closest associates. Heads of the asura, apsara and Gandharva tribes were part of the guest list too. Pre-wedding rituals and ceremonies lasted for three days. The fourth day was our wedding and on the morning of the fifth, we were scheduled to depart together for Lanka.

After a month-long preparation, my big day finally arrived. Post my bathing ritual, I headed towards the royal chambers to seek blessings from my parents. I wore a red-and-golden wedding robe; a veil covered my forehead and I was adorned with jewellery. My hair was braided with flowers.

The mandap looked nothing less than a garden in heaven. Its pillars were beautifully decorated with celestial flowers and four banana trees were tied at the corner of each direction. I acknowledged my immediate family who were present there. Nanashri, Mata Sundari, Vibhishana and Dashaanan's uncle, *Mama* Marichan, were the only family accompanying Dashaanan. Asura Guru Shukracharya, our priest for the wedding ceremony, was dressed in pure white and silver garments. He began reciting the mantras. Holding a garland made of cardamom buds and flowers in my hand, I glanced at the audience; everyone looked excited. Then there was a drum roll to announce Dashaanan's arrival. The crowd was cheering him with his most popular name: Ravana.

I stole a quick glance at Dashaanan and saw him climbing the stairs. My heart was racing and I felt nervous at his arrival. Once inside the mandap, I placed the garland around him and solemnly swore to accept him as the only man in my life. King or no king, rakshasa or Brahmin, genius or evil . . . he meant the world to me.

With a heavy heart the next day, I prepared to fly for my new home. I bid goodbye to Mother, Father, Mai, bhrata Mayavi and bhrata Dundubhi, and my sakhis with whom I had shared most of my time during childhood. Our vimana took off from the ground and headed south.

Lanka was an island and as soon as we crossed the ocean, I saw a land mass of bright yellow and green colour. As we descended to land, I figured the green patches were trees and vegetation whereas the yellow ones were buildings and mansions made or covered with solid gold. I remembered Mai's stories about the golden Lanka but one had to see it to believe it! This beautiful golden piece of island was designed and constructed by none other than my own father. My father, Mayasura, had built it for Kubera. Lanka was originally inhabited by the Yaksha tribe, ruled by Kubera, and later taken over by the rakshasa clan.

Dashaanan was very fond of advanced technology. He had constructed six operational airports in Lanka. He had named a capital in the mountainous part of the kingdom Trikota. The airports were equipped with navigational expertise as well as hangars for his flying vimanas. Other than Lanka, Dashaanan ruled a few other overseas kingdoms too. His empire spread over various lands, namely Balidweepa, Kalingadweepa, Swarnapura and Malayadweepa in the far east and also Angadweepa, Varahdweepa, Shankhadweepa, Yavadweepa and Andhralaya situated in the south of the ocean.

Our aircraft landed at one of the airports. As soon as we landed, we were welcomed by the natives of Lanka. Some were playing drums, some were dancing and the rest were showering us with flowers. At a distance stood Dashaanan's mother, Kaikesi. Signs of early ageing were clearly visible on her face and in her greying hair. As I approached her, she gently smiled at me and I bowed to pay my respects.

'Welcome to Lanka, rajkumari. I am fortunate to have such a beautiful daughter-in-law. May you be blessed with prosperity and happiness.' She sprayed coconut water on us to protect us from evil.

'*Bhabhi* Mandodari, no wonder your beauty has mesmerized my brother,' said Meenakshi, Dashaanan's sister and my sister-in-law. She had the most attractive eyes I had ever seen. Lined with kohl, her eyes resembled those of a doe. I paid my respects to her and she leaned forward to kiss my forehead.

I met other women of the royal family as well. Sarama and Kumbakarna's wife, Bajrajala, followed by their newborn daughters and sons. And some other women from the family with whom I merely exchanged a quick round of pleasantries. Then I met Anaala, the daughter of Nanashri Malyavan and Mata Sundari. Dashaanan had young cousins, namely Ahiravana, Khara, Dushana and Kumbhini.

'Welcome to Lanka, Bhabhi, I will guide you to your chambers so you can take adequate rest and be ready for the feast tonight. You will meet the others during the feast,' Meenakshi subtly cleared a path through the cheering crowd and took me to my chambers.

I barely had time to take in my surroundings. I rushed to my chambers and was introduced to several *dasi*s, maids and ladies-in-waiting. I was to have twelve ladies-in-waiting and dasis at my beck and call. At my father's palace I had three dasis for my personal chores and, of course, Mai. Each dasi in my chamber had an assigned task. Four dasis accompanied me to the bathing room and got me ready for the feast.

I walked towards the huge garden where the feast was arranged. Dashaanan stood at the centre of the garden where his *asana* was placed. As I approached the stage, he extended his arm to me. I sat next to him and together we acknowledged the joyous gathering.

'I introduce you all to my wife, Rajkumari Mandodari. She will be coronated as the "Queen of Lanka" tomorrow,' Dashaanan announced. 'Let the feast begin!'

I barely got any time to talk to Dashaanan. I waited for the moment when we would be alone after the feast. I met important dignitaries, ministers, army generals and guests. People in Lanka rejoiced and I could see how much Dashaanan meant to them. They loved him, blessed him and prayed to him like he was their god. Lanka was a flourishing kingdom. There was plenty of food, gold, skilled artists, promising technology, soldiers and the city was well-planned.

Suddenly the drummers played a different tune. People cleared the path and assembled at one side of the garden.

Dashaanan leaned towards me and said, 'Here comes Kumbakarna, my younger brother whom I love the most!' I saw pride and love in Dashaanan's eyes. I wasn't aware that Kumbakarna was closer to Dashaanan than Vibhishana.

Kumbakarna was a huge, muscled rakshasa, at least eight feet tall. Dressed in an orange dhoti, royal blue robes hanging around his shoulders, he leaned forward to greet us.

'My greetings to the newlywed couple! I wish you both a life of togetherness and prosperity,' he roared.

'My brother is as talented as I am, rajkumari. We have dealt with the toughest situations and challenges together. He has been my pride, my strength and my best adviser after Nanashri,' Dashaanan added.

The celebration ended in the wee hours. I headed towards my chambers for some rest; it was the day of my coronation.

※

Coronation in Lanka was a divine ceremony that raised a monarch to godlike stature. I was purified with divine waters from the five perennial rivers. I wore exclusive velvet robes and rubies. The ceremony was conducted in the main court of Lanka. After taking the solemn vows, Dashaanan's mother Kaikesi coronated me with a tall, gold crown and introduced me as Queen of Lanka. Dashaanan handed a royal seal to me, thereby declaring me as the empress of Lanka and all the other kingdoms that he ruled. A grand procession was conducted in the capital city of Trikota to honour my new title.

Later, we visited the temple constructed in the honour of the legendary Lankini Devi of Lanka to seek her blessings. She was a deity believed to have guarded the coast of Lanka for many years. She was an original inhabitant of the island. It was believed that Devi Lankini protected Lanka from robbers and thieves; and for a certain period managed overseas trade at the ports of Lanka. We prayed to her for a prosperous future.

That evening, I was expecting Dashaanan in my chambers. It was going to be our first time together as a married couple. The entrance was decorated with flowers to welcome him. Aromatic candles and lanterns brightened my palace corridors. My round bed was carved out of marble with a crystal base. It was covered with soft satin sheets. One of my chambermaids cued me about his arrival. Surprisingly, I wasn't nervous or anxious. My marriage had brought about a change in my personality.

He entered my room and the doors closed behind him. I bowed to greet him and he held my arms in his.

'I was longing to spend time alone with you, my queen.'

'And I feel like I have waited my entire life for this moment, my lord.'

He kissed my hand and held me close. I had often wondered how our first night would begin. Would he show me the stars in the sky before he held my hand? Would he narrate a story? Dashaanan, however, was a complete natural at expressing love. He didn't need any pretext to begin with on our first night.

'You know, Mandodari, I wasn't born royal. I have fought various battles, won different titles and worked very hard to reach where I am.'

'I am proud of you, my lord. You are a self-made man.'

'Yes, and it wasn't easy. I made more foes than friends; I made more errors than successes. And yet, I believe you will accept me the way I am.'

'I am honoured to be by your side. I accept all your enemies and friends, flaws and strengths.'

'Lanka is everything to me. Its people are like my family. Very few people know that Nanashri Sumali and Malyavan ruled Lanka before my half-brother Kubera. But, they made some wrong decisions and as a result were overpowered by the devas. Kubera at that time ruled the Yaksha tribe that brought him enormous wealth and he soon seized the throne of Lanka. I have conquered this kingdom with a great deal of endurance and effort. I have changed the destiny of this kingdom. I have brought huge development with the knowledge I possess. And I shall continue to do so.'

'This kingdom and its populace are very fortunate, my lord. I have seen the way they love you, respect you and honour you. Let me be a part of it.'

He smiled and moved closer to me. 'Mandodari, this journey of our life might not be easy for you. You were a princess, not a stranded offspring who was always given half-caste treatment. You may find it difficult to understand me at times but you have to trust my goals.'

'I will not disappoint you, my lord. I am your wife; I will always stand by you.'

'The first time I saw you, I realized you were made for me. I was in awe of your beauty. And now that I have you, I will win the world with you.'

It was the first time we were truly alone, the first time I could talk to him without a third person around. He slowly took off my ornaments and bent forward to kiss me—my first kiss ever. Everything else came to a standstill. We kissed for a long time, neither of us wanted to stop. We looked into each other's eyes; a warm feeling engulfed us and I felt a sudden rush of blood to my face.

'Why have your cheeks turned red, Mandodari? Have I embarrassed you?'

He tenderly undressed me and we made love till dawn.

Dashaanan was a passionate lover. But he was also gentle and tender and knew how to make a woman fall in love with him. The next morning he was up early.

'You should probably take a look around the palace today. Explore your kingdom.'

'Yes, my lord, Vibhishana has planned a short tour for me today.'

'That sounds good. I shall see you in the evening then,' he kissed my forehead and left.

Vibhishana, along with a few courtesans, took me around the palaces of Lanka. No matter what I saw, or where I went, I kept thinking about my night with Dashaanan. I replayed it in my mind and relived each moment spent with him. I was in love.

Noticing my forlorn state, Vibhishana exclaimed, 'Bhabhi Mandodari, you look a little tired. Do you wish to see any other places today or should I escort you to your palace?' I excused myself and rushed to my room for blissful sleep. It was the result of zealous lovemaking the night before.

※

I was living the perfect marital dream. My routine consisted of getting dressed, taking a tour of Lanka, seeing different places and sharing my opinion for improvements in construction. Every day, I accompanied Dashaanan and the ministers to court. As queen and regent, I judged matters of the state.

We had been married for a month. My mother had sent various presents along with my brother, requesting my mother-in-law to allow me to visit Mayarastra for a few days. I was excited to meet my parents and visit my home. I had a lot of stories to tell, a lot of observations to share. I prepared to leave for the journey but it was difficult to stay apart from Dashaanan.

'Rani Mandodari, you look prepared to leave for Mayarastra already. Leaving me all alone, by myself here.'

'No, my lord. I'm only going for a few days, I assure you. I wish to see my parents and will be back in no time.'

He smiled and caressed me. 'Take my vimana. The guards will be at your service for your safety and comfort. I wish you a safe journey.'

I kissed him and left for Mayarastra. Indeed, it was very difficult to part now that I was so used to him. He cared for me, pampered me, made me laugh, and above all, he loved me. He loved me like no one ever.

A large group of royal guards and maids accompanied us for the journey. I had left Mayarastra as a princess and was returning as a queen. Father extended me an elaborate welcome. I had never thought that I would miss my family so much after marriage. No matter what I became in life or where I went, I was deeply connected to my roots.

THREE

No sooner had I reached Mayarastra than I started planning my return to Lanka. After a few days, I had started missing Dashaanan and wondered what all must have changed in Lanka since my departure. I wrote numerous letters to him, but every time someone else would reply on his behalf informing me of his whereabouts. It was strange that my loving husband, who otherwise couldn't stay one evening without visiting me, didn't even care to ask me how I was doing. He had looked visibly upset when I was about to leave for Mayarastra and I had thought he might come to take me back with him after a few days, but no such thing happened.

After a month of my return, father and mother loaded my palanquin with gifts. They bid me farewell, and soon after the send-off, my soldiers and servants marched towards Lanka. When I reached Lanka, a crowd gathered to welcome me. Mother Kaikesi emerged from the crowd to shower her blessings. She seemed a little reserved; she spoke a few words and returned to her chambers soon after.

I was expecting Dashaanan to receive me too but he was nowhere in sight.

I sensed something had changed by the way people were avoiding conversation with me. Or maybe I was too tired and was overthinking? I walked towards my chambers and took a day's rest, hoping to see Dashaanan in the evening but was informed that he was on a political tour and would return after three days. I was rather upset that my husband hadn't even cared to inform me about his absence. Unlike me, he wasn't eager to meet me.

Bored and restless, the next day I took a tour of the project area where different towers were under construction. As I was exploring the area, I met Nanashri Malyavan.

'Welcome back, Rani Mandodari. How was your stay at your parents's house?'

'I stayed very peacefully, Nanashri. However, I feel a lot has changed during my absence,' I replied.

'And may I ask what changes have you observed?' Nanashri enquired defensively.

'I am not completely certain, Nanashri. It's just that no one's been talking to me very much since my arrival here. Anyway, how is the progress on the planetarium?' I wanted to change the subject of our conversation as I observed Nanashri was not comfortable talking to me as well.

'Progress is good; I shall show you around if you wish.'

I simply smiled and followed him, looking for an opportunity to ask about Dashaanan's exact whereabouts.

While we were taking a stroll, I noticed a huge construction site in the distance where something that looked as grand as a palace was being built.

'Nanashri, which building is that?' I asked carelessly.

'That would be the ladies' palace, the *antapura*, which will house all the women belonging to the royal family.' Nanashri answered without any further explanation.

'Why would we need an antapura?'

'Dashaanan's travel to the north-western lands has inspired him to have a harem. He described how women belonging to the king were kept together in a separate section; it is forbidden for men other than the immediate family members to enter those quarters. It ensures their safety. The concept is getting popular; Indra's capital city Amravati also houses an antapura famous for its apsaras.'

'We already have a lot of chambers for the royal family, and what do you mean by women belonging to the king?'

'Well, Mandodari, all those chambers are almost occupied,' Nanashri replied and saw the look of surprise on my face. 'I am not certain if I should be the one to give you this news . . . but . . . Dashaanan has taken another wife, she is a princess of one of those tribes that is now headed and ruled by him.'

The news shook me and I could barely stand on my feet.

'And this happened during my visit to Mayarastra?'

'Yes. Lankapati wanted to leave for a political tour to the western deserts and the marriage proposal was made by the tribal head himself. This marriage was a political advancement adding to our alliances. Dashaanan now heads ten tribes of Lanka.'

'And for the sake of his political advancement he may decide to take as many wives as he wishes!' I was suddenly enraged at the explanation provided by Nanashri. I still didn't know if I was supposed to respond like a queen—calm and collected—or if I could scream like an angry wife who had been betrayed.

'Rani Mandodari, I understand how you might be feeling. But this is a marriage made for political advancement and strengthens the rule of the emperor. It is a negotiation done for diplomatic reasons.' Nanashri tried convincing me.

'No matter how diplomatic the reasons, such actions should have been discussed and shared with the queen well in advance. I presume my husband is ashamed of facing me now.' I gathered my emotions and returned to my chambers.

I didn't see anyone from the royal family for the next few days. It was taking me time to get over this political marriage of my husband's, and to save myself from further embarrassment, I stayed indoors. I waited for him to return so I could express my disappointment to him in person.

Mother Kaikesi came to console me. She took my hands in hers and gently tried to explain, 'Mandodari, I have no words to calm the rage inside you at this time. I understand how it feels to share your husband with another woman. I want you to face this situation like a queen, and once you do that, you will see the anger inside you subsiding.'

'Why didn't he tell me about this marriage, Mother?' I cried out loudly.

'Putri, there are a lot of things Dashaanan is involved with currently. Much more than you know. There is no doubt he loves you a lot. You are and will always be his prime queen.' She expected me to be happy as a prime queen? It sounded like a compensation.

'Dashaanan is not just your husband, he is also an emperor, and in the coming years he will be the most powerful king of all.' She tried her best to comfort me.

'But, Mother, just because my husband is so ambitious and aspires to be the most powerful ruler, I cannot be treated like this. I also cannot be expected to simply face everything like a queen!'

'He has done nothing to disrespect you. And yes, a queen has to make a lot of sacrifices for her king. I am not trying to scare you, Putri, but you will have to make certain choices as a queen, leaving your personal aspirations behind. Take some rest and think it through. Dashaanan is expected to arrive the day after tomorrow. You can talk to him about it.' Saying so, she left my chambers, leaving me to think about my next course of action.

I knew then that my marriage was going to be anything but ordinary.

༄

A reigning queen should gracefully accept other wives taken by the king, so said the standardized code of conduct for queens. So I spent an entire day pondering on my disappointment, and then sent gifts to my husband's new wife as a token of acceptance. I couldn't make her the victim of my disappointment. She was housed in one of the guest chambers of the queen's palace until her permanent chambers were ready. My dasis elegantly presented my gifts to the tribal princess and in return the princess asked permission to see me in person. I agreed and asked my dasi to arrange for a meal for us in my chambers.

It then suddenly struck me that Nanashri had mentioned the huge ladies' palace being built for the women of the royal family.

I was lost in thought when one of my dasis announced, 'The princess has arrived, your majesty.'

Standing in front of me was someone who looked like a twelve-year-old girl. I had been curious to see my husband's second choice, but once I saw her, I could tell that she was not his choice at all. She was slender and had many piercings. There were tattoos on her hands and near her eyes—she was too young to be anyone's wife!

She stood with her chin down and hands joined to greet me. With an innocent look in her eyes, she bowed low. I was not sure if this was due to respect or the guilt from marrying my husband.

'Please seat yourself,' I gestured towards the sitting area.

'Rani Mandodari, thank you for the warm welcome. I am Dhanyamalini, a tribal princess. Irrespective of our relationship, you have shown respect towards me and, therefore, towards my tribe. Despite our complex relationship, I promise I will be like a sister to you.' And I smiled after many days. Dhanyamalini, the tribal princess, was warm and smart in her conversations.

After meeting her, I kept my prejudices aside and concluded that I had overreacted about my husband's second marriage. I was pacified thinking Dashaanan hadn't talked to me about it because he probably didn't feel it was important enough to be discussed. I also concluded that this marriage was clearly a political alliance, and not one borne out of love.

I offered her drinks and delicacies and smiled at her to make her feel comfortable. In return, she kept smiling innocently at me; however, she kept her eyes lowered as a mark of respect. She was talkative, respectful and humble and knew how to behave in the presence of a queen. After our meal, she gently bowed and left. I slept peacefully that night.

We were expecting Dashaanan's arrival the next day. I dressed vibrantly and got my chambers decorated with beautiful pink flowers. Dashaanan headed the tribes of Lanka. As a token of their love and respect and to signify their union, the tribal natives had made a ten-headed crown of gold for him.

As soon as Dashaanan alighted from his vimana, we showered him with rose petals. He acknowledged everyone present to welcome him. Then he looked at me and gave me a warm smile. I was delighted to see him after such a long time and felt like running into his arms immediately, almost forgetting the entire turmoil of his second marriage.

Dashaanan then extended his arm to help someone step out of the vimana. She was an elegant woman—more a nymph than a woman—and was beautifully dressed like an apsara in a golden dhoti. Her eyes were lined with kohl, her slender waist and hands were decorated with gold dust. Her hair was unusually straight and she wore a headgear with a small golden serpent on it. Everyone was in awe of her beauty. He introduced her as the daughter of the pharaoh, the king of the desert land where he had been on tour.

This was no ordinary woman. As she stepped on the land of Lanka, she ruined all hopes I had for my marriage. She was my husband's new concubine.

FOUR

Dashaanan was now spending most of his time with the new women in his life. He enjoyed Dhanyamalini's company as she was talkative. Mata Kaikesi didn't try to console me this time. She presumed I could handle it all by now. Soon, the pharaoh's daughter became the latest topic of discussion. Her unmatched beauty and charisma not only mesmerized my husband and the other men around her, but also caused jealousy among the women. Marriage was not customary in the land where the pharaoh's daughter came from, and so Dashaanan didn't marry her as per the rituals. She was merely a beautiful gift that my husband got on tour, and which kept him busy during the nights too.

With Dashaanan engaged, I felt lonely in my chambers but I avoided going out to save myself from embarrassment. I missed my mother during those times and felt like running back home to Mayarastra. Bajrajala became a regular visitor to my chambers in those days. Though Kumbakarna had taken other wives, Bajrajala maintained her poise and composure at all times. I felt she was the only one who could relate to me, hence, we soon became friends. She seemed very discontent with her married life. She had been married to Kumbakarna only a year before my wedding. He was married to two other rakshasi women. Due to his abnormal height and strange sleeping pattern, Bajrajala was married in a rush and barely got to spend any time with her husband.

She took my hand in hers and asked me a very unusual question, 'Have you ever loved anyone more than your husband, Bhabhi Mandodari?'

I looked at her in surprise. Except for my parents and brothers, I had never loved anyone as much as I loved Dashaanan.

I hesitated to answer. She smiled, 'I understand how difficult it must be for you to share your love with other women. In my case, I tried loving my husband, but as soon as I managed to develop a strong affection towards him, something or the other kept coming between us. My husband has taken other wives too. Now I have children who keep me busy. But I can still conclude one thing for sure: Lankeshwar really loves you the most.'

I said nothing in return to her kind and gratifying words. Bajrajala wanted a heart-to-heart, but I had passed that moment where I could take comfort in our shared predicament. I was busy building a strong emotional defence for myself.

Dashaanan paid a surprise visit to my chambers that evening. He was drunk and looked as if he had not slept for a long time. I felt like I didn't want to see him at all; I was angry, upset and wanted to hurt him. I told my dasi to make an excuse and tell Dashaanan that I was asleep. But he dashed into my bedroom ignoring her.

'Lankeshwar, you look very tired. Is everything all right?' I asked out of concern. I wasn't expecting him to visit me in such a state. He couldn't even stand on his feet and kept losing his balance.

'Lankesh is god, Mandodari. How can everything not be all right with him?' He kept saying. I chose to ignore him because he was clearly not in his senses.

'Aren't you happy about your husband's achievements? You should be proud that I have conquered the planetary mentors of Devaloka, the *navagraha* gurus, and made them my slaves! I conquered the underworld! Your husband rules the oceans and lands beyond,' he said and stumbled.

I helped him up and made him sit on the bed. 'I am very proud of you, Lankesh. But how do you expect your wife to be pleased when she has to share you with other women? How can I be pleased when you didn't even inform me about your second marriage? And now this third woman? It hurts me when I imagine you with this other woman in your bed.'

'Mandodari, you don't have to worry about the other women. You know I love you the most,' he said as he reached out to kiss me, his breath reeking of alcohol.

☙

I was taking a stroll around the newly built antapura, the ladies' palace, where I was told that the pharaoh's daughter was going to shift soon. I saw Vibhishana around the astronomy tower. As usual, he looked busy assigning tasks on behalf of Dashaanan. Access to the astronomy tower was restricted to very few people, and Vibhishana was in charge of its security. Dashaanan had influentially housed the navagraha gurus in that tower. He believed that they could control the planetary positions for his benefit and that keeping them under his direction could save him from facing any political defeat.

The navagraha gurus were considered lords or demigods of Devaloka. It was believed that they had mastered the knowledge of each planet surrounding earth. They predicted eclipses through their understanding of astronomy. It was also rumoured that through their *siddhi* and meditation, they controlled the movements and temperament of planets with their minds. Hence, the commoners worshipped them as deities and pleased them with different offerings.

Surya, Budha, Shukra, Mangal, Guru, Shani, Chandra, Rahu and Ketu were the nine gurus. Except for Surya, Chandra and Guru Shukracharya, Dashaanan held the rest captive. Our marriage was also made possible after he calculated the favourable planetary positions of our horoscopes.

Women of the royal family gathered that evening to celebrate the completion of the newly built palace. We exchanged a brief round of pleasantries with each other and Mata Kaikesi inaugurated the new building. Meals were brought in and our dasis began to serve the ladies of the royal family. Trijata, one of the rakshasi dasis assigned to the queen's chambers, looked awfully pale and I couldn't help but ask her if she wasn't feeling too well.

'Your majesty, I am undergoing Ayurvedic treatment. I had two miscarriages before, and since I am pregnant again, the physician has suggested that I keep my treatment mild so it does not affect the health of my child,' answered Trijata.

'In that case, Trijata, I suggest you quit all your chores for a few days and take some rest.'

Trijata mainly supervised the chambermaids attending to the ladies of the royal family. She was highly trusted and all the women would confide their secret affairs, desires and quarrels with their husbands in her. Vibhishana treated Trijata like a sister as she was nearly his age. Even Sarama treated her like family.

My eyes fell on the pharaoh's daughter and her maids who were seated in one corner; her presence was always disturbing to me. Bajrajala saw my reaction and tried to divert my attention. 'Bhabhi Mandodari, what has been keeping you busy these days?' she asked.

I was still looking at the concubine. 'I am married to an emperor and I think I have accepted the fact now. I used to think I am the only woman he loved and married. But I've now realized that there are marriages made in the interest of the state, marriages for political reasons and marriages for gaining allies.'

'It is better than having a husband like mine, who is asleep most of the time,' said Bajrajala.

I could never win an argument with Bajrajala. I looked at her empathetically and she smiled. 'I have heard about bhrata Kumbakarna's *nidravasta*. But I've never asked you how it happened. Were you married then?' I enquired.

'I was married to Kumbakarna three years after he got his sleeping boon. Although I am not sure if it's a boon or a curse,' said Bajrajala, and then she narrated the episode when Dashaanan and Kumbakarna received their boons from Prajapati Brahma.

Dashaanan, Vibhishana and Kumbakarna were travelling to the northernmost mountain to please Shiva. After months and months of tough tapasya, Dashaanan was successful in obtaining the Chandrahas sword from Shiva as a boon. After this, he and his brothers travelled south and took vows to please Brahma, their great-great-grandfather.

Dashaanan and Kumbakarna spent months and months in tapasya, with Vibhishana ensuring that they were not disturbed by any external force or being. Come winter, rain and summer, they stood on a single foot at a time with their palms joined in respect. They chanted mantras to invoke Brahma.

Their penance not only invoked Brahma, but also disturbed the leader of the devas—Indradeva. Indradeva knew that after defeating his brother Kubera for wealth and estate, Dashaanan had his eyes set on Indralok—Indra's kingdom situated in the mountains, also called heaven on earth for its scenic beauty. Indradeva had introduced irrigation projects to save his people from drought and famine. His designs brought rains and water to their land, which was now prospering and flourishing.

When Indra saw the brothers in meditation, he was alarmed by the danger they could pose to his kingdom. He, thus, returned to his kingdom and summoned Goddess Saraswati in his prayers. Saraswati was one of the most powerful faces of Shakti and was considered the goddess of knowledge in totality.

Indra requested the goddess to help him save his kingdom. Indra knew that Dashaanan and Kumbakarna would aim for Indralok so he asked Saraswati to manipulate their minds whenever they ask for Indraasana—the throne of Indralok.

The brothers were determined; pleased with their severe tapasya, Brahma appeared in front of them at dawn and offered them a boon.

'You both have astonished me with your dedicated tapasya. What is it you wish to gain, sons?'

'You are not only the creator of this universe but also our great-great-grandfather. We are the third generation in line to your son Prajapati Pulastya. Our father Rishi Vishrava is Prajapati Pulastya's son,' explained Dashaanan.

'I am overwhelmed by your tapasya. You may ask whatever you wish for. As for our relationship, my son, I am related to every being on this soil,' said Brahma.

Dashaanan took a deep breath and said, 'Oh creator, make me immortal so I can change the course of this world.'

Brahma replied, 'I can grant you no such boon, son. Every life on this earth has to end. Ask for something else and you shall be granted that.'

Dashaanan then asked for absolute invulnerability and superiority over the gods, heavenly mountainous spirits, demons, serpents and wild creatures. He asked to be invincible before all deva, asura, yaksha, rakshasa, pisacha, apsara, gandharva, vetala and preta races.

Brahma granted him the boon and also provided him with great strength by way of sorcery and knowledge of the divine weapons. He also gifted him a divine arrow as a symbol of superiority.

Brahma then turned towards Kumbakarna. 'You have always followed your brother's directions without any hesitation. Although you both are of the same age, you trust his judgement solely and give your best to stand by him. Ask, and your wish shall be granted too.'

Kumbakarna joined his hands and wished, 'Dear lord, I ask for my brother to be seated on the chief throne in the heavens of Devaloka.'

'Dear son, your brother has already asked for a boon for himself. You shall achieve a boon for your tapasya now,' said Brahma.

Till then, Indra had concluded that Kumbakarna would ask for his throne. He beseeched Saraswati, and the goddess made Kumbakarna anxious. It is believed that she sat on Kumbakarna's tongue and twisted it a little, thereby influencing his speech.

'Tell me son, what do you want?' asked Brahma.

'Nidraasana,' said Kumbakarna with his twisted tongue instead of saying 'Indraasana'.

'*Tathastu*! So be it, son,' said Brahma as Goddess Saraswati released Kumbakarna's tongue.

Kumbakarna felt a sudden change in his body. His limbs felt weak and his eyes droopy with sleep. 'Oh, how do I feel so different, my lord?' asked Kumbakarna.

'Dear son, you have asked for Nidraasana. It is a boon to sleep throughout your life,' explained Brahma.

'But, my lord, I asked for Indraasana, the throne of Indralok.' Kumbakarna panicked and realized that he had unknowingly mispronounced the name.

'You got what you asked for, my son. And to remind you, I can only bless you with a single boon at this time,' said Brahma.

'But I haven't asked for the sleeping boon, my lord. Please eliminate the effects of this boon. Don't let my tapasya be in vain.' Kumbakarna felt the urgent need to go to sleep. He felt tired. It was as if his body was not in his control any more. Brahma realized that Kumbakarna's error in asking for the boon was not out of his own wish.

'All right, son, I can limit the effects of this boon. You will now sleep for two moons at a stretch and for the rest of the months, you may lead a normal life,' said Brahma.

※

'Along with these two boons, there was a third boon that Brahma gave that day. He also blessed bhrata Vibhishana for unconditionally supporting his brothers. Vibhishana's era of reign will observe peace, and righteousness will be established,' added Bajrajala.

'Bhrata Vibhishana's era of reign? Does he rule any of the kingdoms currently?' I intervened.

'Not yet, bhabhi, but since he handles most of the administrative assignments in Lanka, Lankeshwar may assign him a few projects or regions for complete supervision.'

I realized that Bajrajala was the closest person I could freely talk to about such matters. I barely shared such a bond with anyone else. Our status was different but our situation was the same. Only empathy was what we could give each other.

FIVE

Dashaanan got bored of his concubine in just a few months. He limited his visits to her palace and spent most of his time planning new projects with Nanashri. Nanashri would never discuss anything personal with me but I knew he was happy when Lankesh concentrated more on his projects than on women. He also encouraged Dashaanan to spend more time with me. After court hours, Dashaanan visited my chambers regularly for afternoon meals. I was beginning to believe that my marriage was back on track. I had vowed never to leave my kingdom or Dashaanan for such a long time again.

We would talk for hours in the evening. Besides afternoon meals, he also started spending most of his nights with me.

'Rani Mandodari, I see a certain glow on your face. Is it the result of my sweet talk or the wine from the grapes?'

'When a woman gets all the love that she deserves from her husband, it's all she needs to glow.'

Dashaanan laughed out loud, 'You seem to have mastered the art of mockery.'

'No, my lord, I use no mockery against you. However, I promise that I shall never leave you alone henceforth. It was the distance between us that led to such differences. I am never leaving you alone again.'

There were tears of regret in my eyes.

'You will always be my first choice, Mandodari. Do not compare yourself with other women.'

'With all due respect, my lord, how would you justify your relationship with the princess of Misr?'

'Ah, Mandodari, she is merely a gift from the pharaoh. I am what I am with you. And you are well aware of that. I am a different man with you, and no woman can take your place.'

I smiled at the way Dashaanan was trying to convince me. His justifications were flattering and I felt like I was an easy prey for his smooth talk.

'I have something important to tell you. I will be discussing this with Nanashri and Vibhishana tomorrow.'

'What is it, my lord?'

'After all my years of research and learning, I have successfully created an elixir that would reverse the ageing process for me. With the use of this elixir, my body will not grow old; also, it will boost my overall immunity and provide strength.'

I didn't know much about chemical potions and herbs, but I knew that Dashaanan had mastered the use of herbs and chemicals through the Vedas.

'What kind of elixir is this? Are you referring to the nectar of amrita? And why do you really need it?'

'Yes, I have created amrita! Asuras and devas have fought over this potion for years. Why is it that consumption of amrita and the right of its possession is restricted to the devas?'

'I understand that, my lord. But how can you create amrita? I thought that the nectar is preserved by the supreme gods.'

'Devas have kept the chemical compositions of amrita a secret for decades. But I have tested different chemical compositions and the results are similar. The antioxidants in the potion will make it work in the same way as amrita. I will have power over my age; I can conquer time and age.'

'What will you do with such power, my lord?' I was worried about Dashaanan's new experiment and its consequences.

'The question is, what can I not do with such power?' said Dashaanan and smirked at me.

I had no idea what he had planned if his experiment turned out to be a success. The navagraha deities were already captive at Lanka. I didn't know what he aimed at doing next.

'My lord, I am worried about the consequences of this experiment. What if the effects are not the same as you have calculated? What if it turns out to be harmful for your health?'

'You are panicking for no reason. This is not any careless experiment. It will help me extract all the nutrients of the elixir once the surgery is complete.'

'A surgery? You will have to undergo a surgery for this?'

'Well, yes! The only way to consume this elixir is to place it directly behind the navel through an incision in my abdomen.'

'Why so, my lord?'

'I will not be able to drink it because this amrita has been created through a chemical process. And umbilicus is centrally placed in one's body; it is the beginning of life, the only strongest part of a child that is connected to the mother's womb. Hence, once I place this amrita behind my navel, it will revive my body with extra life.'

'What if something goes wrong, my lord?'

'That is enough, Mandodari!' Dashaanan was getting irritated with my constant questioning. 'You should be aware that I have skilled people to perform the surgery. And nothing can go wrong when I have done my research accurately.'

'No, my lord, I apologize for my behaviour. I am only worried about your health and well-being. I may not sound supportive, but as your wife I stand by your decisions.'

After a long time, we shared a strong bond with each other. I was concerned that my continuous objections and questions would annoy Dashaanan. I didn't want to infuriate him any further lest he stopped seeing me. Hence, I had to blindly support him in most of his decisions.

After a few days, a team of skilled vaidyas performed the surgery on Dashaanan and put the elixir inside his abdomen. He was advised to take complete rest for two full moons. The vaidyas said that the elixir would take time to settle down in his body. They warned us that there would be sudden changes in his behaviour and temperament.

Until Dashaanan's recovery, I supervised most of the tasks and acted as regent in court. Vibhishana and Nanashri managed the rest of the affairs. I assigned a few of my dasis to tend to Dashaanan's needs at his palace. He was bed-ridden until his wounds healed. Mata Kaikesi visited him every morning while I narrated the court affairs to him every evening.

There was rapid change in Dashaanan's condition during the recovery phase. The change was also much more than we had anticipated. He would suddenly feel very hungry and thirsty and would end up eating twice as much as he did earlier. He also started consuming more alcohol than before. Some days he would look extremely pale and on some he would look completely rejuvenated. I consulted the vaidyas about this condition; they pacified me saying these were natural after-effects of the elixir and there was nothing to worry about.

It was not just his temper or appetite that was impacted. Some days he would feel extremely sexually aroused and it was getting tougher to satisfy his desires. With each passing day, his desire for spicy food and rough sex was increasing. Mata Kaikesi and I tried to divert his mind with music. We asked the musicians to play soothing music outside his chambers. We also placed a veena in his chambers so he could play music on his own. However, all our efforts were in vain.

Dashaanan wanted to be entertained in his chambers, and would call upon dancers and courtesans to perform there daily. I wasn't pleased on hearing this. Bedroom chambers were our sacred space—something only he and

I shared. One day when I walked in, I saw him making sexual advances towards a dancing courtesan. Seeing this, I lost my temper and commanded the guards to stop allowing courtesans inside the chambers henceforth.

I asked Dhanyamalini to join me during my evening visits to Dashaanan. Since she was a good talker, I thought it would help me divert his mind from sex towards other things. This trick worked for a few days and I started limiting my visits from daily to alternate days. But Dashaanan wasn't so easy to tame. He forced his fantasies on Dhanyamalini and the submissive girl agreed to everything he demanded.

He resumed court after two months. As far as his temper was concerned, it didn't look like it was going to settle down. His court ministers were scared to approach him; his guards were always at attention and we, as a family, were terrified of him. Not only had he risked his life with that experiment, but he had also ruined his relations with the people closest to him.

As his wives, Dhanyamalini and I would give into Dashaanan's demands to avoid quarrels. He would storm into our chambers any time during the day and insist on wine, food or sex. Failure to give him what he wanted would result in offensive charges against all of us or against any of the dasis present. He would call any of our dasis into his chambers whenever he felt like it. Although the dasis tried to hide it, we were aware of his mistreatment but couldn't do anything to stop him.

When one of Dhanyamalini's dasis protested against Dashaanan's behaviour and denied his sexual demands, he threatened to kill her husband. The dasi was frightened for her husband's life but refused to give in to his demands. An irate and incongruous Dashaanan took it as an offence and ordered his guards to kill her husband and feed his head to wild animals. She came crying to us, asking for our help to secure her husband's release—we were nothing but embarrassed for Dashaanan's actions. I knew my husband was ambitious and short-tempered but I never expected him to be so cruel to a woman.

Once again my heart was filled with rage and despair. I felt sorry for the helpless dasi. I marched straight towards Dashaanan's chambers and entered his room without announcement. He was standing at a window with his back towards me; he looked drunk and had another glass of wine in his hand.

'Ah, Rani Mandodari, the queen of my heart! I could sense you were coming from a distance. Your fragrance has filled my entire room.'

'So you would have sensed the reason I came here too, my lord!'

'What is the matter? You look annoyed. Or is it your husband's longing that has brought you here?'

'Lankeshwar my lord, I have accepted you with all your shortcomings. I know at times I have asked you a lot of questions, at times my objections have turned into quarrels and at times I may have set many limitations for your benefit, but today you have humiliated the woman in me. You have abused all the women of Lanka.'

Dashaanan turned around at once. 'What are you talking about?'

'You know what I'm talking about, my lord. Today you ordered to kill someone simply because his wife would not sleep with you!'

'Mandodari, I command you to leave my room,' he screamed and turned away from me.

'Lankeshwar, I am not leaving this room until we talk about it. You are the king of Lanka but don't forget that I am its queen. The people of Lanka have certain expectations from you, my lord, and so do I. Your people have faith in you as well as in me. Hence, with all my rights in this kingdom, I am asking you to provide justice like a king!'

'What justice?' he was furious with me.

'Justice for the women of Laṅka, my lord. We cannot undo what has been done, but I request you to stop your guards from killing the dasi's husband.'

'Did she come crying to you?'

'Yes, my lord, she came to me. I have accepted the changes in you due to that experiment. But this is not you! You can lust after a woman, but you were never so cruel! What is it that makes you so pitiless?'

I had tears running down my face. Dashaanan stood still for some time and I fell on my knees. He was quiet and looked remorseful.

'Have you ever wondered, my lord, how I feel when you share that bed with other women? How would you feel if I spent the night with another man?'

'Decorum, Mandodari!' Dashaanan yelled. 'Maintain decorum when you speak to me.'

'When you cannot even talk about me committing adultery, then how do you expect me to live with it? Until you regret your actions, we shall not see each other.'

Saying so, I prepared to leave but he held me.

'Stay, Mandodari. I have caused you a lot of grief and I regret it. I have brought you shame and humiliation throughout this marriage, but you have always stood beside me through thick and thin.'

'My lord, I cannot bear anyone pointing a finger at you.'

'I have failed as a husband somewhere. I am successful as a king but I am unable to keep my wife happy as a husband.'

'No, my lord. I don't feel you have failed as a husband. But what makes you get involved in adulterous relations with other women? What makes you so angry that you give the command to kill someone's innocent husband? What makes you so proud that you don't value anyone's sentiments any more?'

'You're right. I may come across as cruel and insensitive, but I feel like conquering more than ever before—even if it is beauty in the form of a woman.'

'The elixir you consumed is responsible for every change in you, my lord.'

'Don't blame the elixir! Can't you see the power of that potion? The healing ability of my skin has increased tremendously. In a few years, I'll stop ageing. No other asura on this earth has held nectar in their body before. No one else was successful in producing amrita the way I was.'

'But, of course, my lord, I blame that so-called amrita you produced. It is nothing but a poison in you—it may give you a long life, my lord, but it is has taken away the very essence of your character.'

'Whether you blame the elixir I created or you blame me, in any case it is a part of me now. And I don't have any alternative but to live with it. I accept your charges, my queen, because you made me realize that my actions are not ethical. And as your husband, I promise I will be careful about my actions.'

'Promise me, my lord, that you will do nothing to destroy the faith that your people and family have placed in you.'

'I promise you, Mandodari. I promise you with all my love for you.'

The surgery and the use of nectar was kept a secret from everyone except close family members. The people who were aware of it were Mata Kaikesi, Vibhishana, Kumbakarna, the vaidyas who performed the surgery and I. Soon, Dashaanan continued on his journey of exploring other lands looking for possible allies. As promised, Dashaanan controlled his temper and for a few weeks we went on with our lives as usual.

Kumbakarna visited Dashaanan to congratulate him for his success in producing the nectar. He also instigated Dashaanan to put himself to a robust test by challenging their perpetual rival—Indra of Amravati—to a duel. Kumbakarna's grandfather-in-law, Virochana, was defeated and killed in battle by Indra. Since then Kumbakarna had wanted to defeat Indra and take revenge. There was no end to Dashaanan's aspirations. Together with his brother, he planned to challenge Indra. The next day, I got news that he had already left for Amravati.

He returned after two weeks and met me as soon as he landed. The victory melody was played by musicians as an indication that Dashaanan had been triumphant. I could see it clearly written on his face. After their battle, when Dashaanan detained Indra, Prajapati Brahma sent his disciples to request Indra's release. Although Dashaanan's arrogance was at its peak, he released Indra on Brahma's request.

The inebriated feeling of victory kept Dashaanan thrilled for a few days. His ego was satisfied. Kumbakarna was pompous about it too. A few days later, Dev Rishi Narad came to meet Dashaanan. This son of Brahma's was a devotee of Lord Vishnu. It was believed that he could travel to distant worlds and realms. He was known for being dishonest, but nobody stopped him from entering any court, meeting, celebration or sacrifice.

Mata Kaikesi welcomed him at court and offered him a seat close to Dashaanan's asana. Although I had heard a lot of anecdotes about him from Mai, this was the first time I was seeing him in flesh.

Dashaanan entered the court and greeted Narad by bowing low. Rishi Narad responded by bowing lower and Dashaanan was surprised.

'Don't be surprised, Lankesh. People of the three worlds are talking about you,' said Narad Muni, and Dashaanan's heart swelled with pride.

'Good to see you, dev rishi. Tell me, what is the purpose of your surprise visit today?'

'I came to congratulate you on your victory, Lankesh. I heard how you defeated Indra. He was terrified for days,' Narad Muni said with appreciation in his voice.

'I am grateful for your appreciation, dev rishi. It has been quite a few days since that incident,' replied Dashaanan.

'Oh, I am aware, Lankesh. And I would have come sooner to congratulate you.' Narad Muni smiled silently.

'So what delayed your visit, dev muni?' asked Dashaanan.

'Well, I was delayed by a vanara.' said Narad Muni.

Dashaanan looked at him in surprise, 'A vanara?'

'Yes, Lankesh, I was on an excursion near the region of Kiskinda and this vanara named Vali, who happens to be the king of Kiskinda, insisted that I stay there as his guest so he could talk about his adventures. I told him I was on my way to meet you but I was surprised when he said he hadn't heard of you.'

Vanara was a forest-dwelling tribe headed by humans that included apes and monkeys of the forest too. The monkeys and apes were trained by the male head of the humans. Men of the vanara tribe proudly displayed monkey-like characteristics in their clothing and habitations.

'You say that the vanara hadn't heard of me?' asked Dashaanan.

'Oh, I was surprised too, Lankesh. Everyone around the three worlds is talking about your valour and victory over Indra but this mighty vanara seemed too proud of himself.'

'Is that so?'

'Yes, Lankesh, he has fought and won many battles alone. And he is famous for his boon too.'

'What kind of boon, dev muni?'

'That anyone who fights Vali in single combat would lose half of his strength to him. He is invincible to any enemy.'

Dashaanan was stunned to hear that. He didn't blink and kept staring in the distance; various thoughts were running through his mind.

'Lankesh . . .' Narad Muni called out, 'What are you thinking about?'

'Where did you say this vanara lives, dev muni?'

'In the Kiskinda region of Bharatvarsh. He has an army of monkeys. And do you want to know who Vali's father is?'

Dashaanan nodded.

'None other than Dev Raj Indra!' said Narad Muni.

Dashaanan rose from his asana. 'Vali, son of Indra! And you say he doesn't know what happened with Indra recently?'

'I am not sure, Lankesh. Or he must have heard about it but he doesn't care much. As I said, he is too brave and too proud.'

I was not sure if Dev Rishi Narad's purpose of visiting Lanka was to simply congratulate Dashaanan or if he wanted to sow the seeds of wrath in his mind. I remained seated as I didn't want to interfere in their conversation and face Dashaanan's anger.

'Well, dev rishi, in that case, this vanara should hear about me soon,' claimed Dashaanan.

Narad Muni smiled, 'What do you plan on doing, Lankesh?'

'I am not sure now. But very soon he will learn about me.' Dashaanan's voice echoed.

'I shall take your leave now, Lankesh. Narayan Narayan!' said Narad Muni and left.

SIX

Dashaanan was fighting unrest within himself after Dev Rishi Narad's visit. The thought of the vanara kept him awake for nights. Then one day, he took his vimana and flew towards Kiskinda to challenge Vali in combat.

He returned after several days. When he stepped out of his vimana, he was limping on his left leg. He had scars on his face and arms. He looked dreadful. The guards took him to his chambers and his injuries were well-tended to. I didn't allow anyone to meet Dashaanan till he had completely healed.

'My lord, what took you so many days to return?' I asked.

'You know I was in Kiskinda.'

'Yes, what happened? How did you get injured?'

'When I landed at Kiskinda at sunset, I saw a huge moving rock at a distance in the river. I walked towards the river and learnt that that rock was actually a vanara. He was none other than Vali. I misunderstood the brown hair on his body for a rock. He facing the west, saying his evening prayers. When he came out of the water, I introduced myself and challenged him to a duel.'

Dashaanan went quiet suddenly.

'What happened next, my lord?' I asked him.

'That vanara paid no attention to my challenge. Instead, he smiled at me and said, "Go back to where you came from or else I will crush that vimana you flew into my kingdom." I got angry and attacked his tail first. I thought his tail was probably the weakest part of his body and I could drag him with it. But when I tried lifting his tail, to my surprise, I couldn't move it at all. He got angry and coiling his tail around my body, locked my arms and threw me into the river. I have never been insulted like this before, and that too by a vanara!'

His eyes went red while he narrated the incident. I felt sorry for him. He had allowed himself to get carried away with his recent fame and had gone after that vanara unarmed and without any royal guards, merely to show off his courage.

'I got up again. With all my strength, I ran towards him and tried lifting his legs to make him fall on the ground. Once again he coiled his tail around me, lifted me and dropped me on the ground forcefully. The third time I went close to him, he tied me up for an entire night. I tried to get out but in vain. No matter how hard I tried, I couldn't even release my hands. He waited for me to give up. This took all night and soon it was time for sunrise.

'"You don't look like an ordinary person. Who are you? Where do you come from?" he asked. I introduced myself again and he simply nodded.

'He then invited me to stay in his palace as a guest for one day. "Lankapati Ravana, you have fought with all your strength today. I respect you for that. If you wish to challenge me again, then I suggest you stay in my palace as my guest for a day. After all, you are a king too and I would like to give you a welcome in my kingdom. Take proper rest, eat and sleep for a night. We shall combat again tomorrow."

'I was tired but I wanted to challenge him again. So, I had no choice but to accept his invitation.'

'You accepted his invitation?' The whole incident was sounding a little strange to me. How could Dashaanan have lost against a vanara and why did he accept the enemy's invitation?

Dashaanan looked at me and said, 'I was amazed that someone in a battle situation could invite his enemy over to his palace. He was mighty, courageous and also very hospitable. Even though I lost in combat, he treated me with great respect as a king would treat another.'

'But, my lord, I thought you were blessed with absolute invincibility. Prajapati Brahma blessed you with that boon. Then how could you lose against a vanara?'

'I thought about the same thing the entire night. Then I realized that while asking for the boon from Brahma deva, I hadn't ask for invincibility against any vanara. I never knew a vanara could be so powerful. I didn't mention them because I didn't think any vanara could stand a chance against me. You can call it my ego or my negligence,' answered Dashaanan.

'What happened the next day?' I probed him.

'The next day we started after dawn and the battle went on till sunset. I lost again. Finally, I concluded that I could not win over Vali. I had to put an end to our battle. I bowed and accepted his victory over me.'

It was unbelievable. Finally there was someone who could defeat Dashaanan! At first I felt bad that my husband had lost in battle against a vanara. It took him time to overcome the despair of his defeat. He was upset that his boon of invincibility was incomplete and that his entire tapasya had been somewhat worthless. But later I realized that the incident had made him wiser than before.

'Vali offered his friendship to me. I accepted, not because he defeated me, but because he was exceptionally courageous and generous at the same time. There was no alliance this time, but in future I may offer him that too. I couldn't win the battle but I won his friendship,' said Dashaanan.

'My lord, this incident with Vali has brought about some good changes in you. I have never seen this side of your personality before.'

'I don't know if the changes are good or bad but I am glad I encountered someone more powerful than I. I was under the impression that I was invincible, and this encourages me to improve myself more.'

Soon Dashaanan became occupied with research work. Then one day, Shardula, a spy of Lanka, reported with news at the court. Dashaanan had appointed several emissary spies to ensure the safety of his immediate family and also to gather information in case of any threat to the kingdom from outside forces. This time the news was concerning his sister Meenakshi. She had reportedly secretly married Vidyutjihva, a danava prince of the Kalkeya clan of which he was the head. Kalkeyas were Lanka's avowed enemies since ages, and Dashaanan was furious to learn of his sister's involvement with his enemy.

Dashaanan commanded his guards to present Meenakshi and Vidyutjihva in front of the court. He blamed the women of the family for being negligent.

'Mata Kaikesi, can you explain how Meenakshi met the danava prince? Had you no idea about her secret marriage? And Mandodari, surely your supervision of the queen's palace needs more focus. With so many women around, you have to know their whereabouts! Bhabhi Sarama and Bajrajala, you are equally responsible for what goes on in the palace. When Mandodari is occupied, can you not take over her responsibilities?' he screamed at everyone and no one dared to answer him back.

'My lord, we should give Meenakshi a chance to explain herself,' I said in the softest tone possible.

'What explanation? That she is young and got carried away? She has proved she is a fool!' screamed Dashaanan.

'Calm down, my lord. Perhaps she loves him? And what can we do if she is married now? We have to accept him as her husband.'

'I will not accept him . . . come what may.'

'Don't say such words, my lord. I request you to forgive your sister. It is possible that she may have been scared that you would reject her decision.'

'I cannot forgive them!' declared Dashaanan and stormed out angrily.

Mata Kaikesi and I tried our best to convince him. At last, he agreed to forgive them and accepted their marriage because of the affection he had for her. However, he was still angry with her husband for getting married secretly without taking the consent of our family.

The next day Meenakshi and Vidyutjihva were presented at court. Meenakshi fell at Dashaanan's feet, seeking his apology.

'Bhrata Dashaanan, forgive me if I have hurt you. I have done nothing wrong . . . '

'You may not have done anything wrong, but you have certainly done it the wrong way,' said Dashaanan.

Still sounding offended, he turned towards her husband and said, 'Kalkeya kumar, if you have the courage to marry my sister, you should have shown the courage to face me and ask for her hand in marriage. I would have appreciated your bravery. Not only that, I would have happily given her to you, even forgetting the fact that our families have never really got along very well. Because of my affection for her, I accept you as a member of my family. But I will never forget that you have an evil mind that brainwashed my sister into doing something against her family's wishes. In Lanka, you will henceforth be known as Dushtabuddhi.'

Meenakshi looked upset by the new name given to her husband but refrained from saying anything.

⚘

Dashaanan took a sea voyage to monitor the progress of the other islands ruled by him. In a way, he wanted to escape the ongoing turmoil over his sister's marriage. Any sea voyage would usually take around a month or more before he returned. I was concerned about him this time. He had left abruptly without saying much.

One night I woke up, suddenly feeling very worried about him. I hadn't had a nightmare but something had made me restless the whole night. The next day my uneasiness increased and I was sure it had something to do with my husband. I met Nanashri to talk about Dashaanan's absence.

'Nanashri, a month has passed and there is no news of Lankeshwar's exact whereabouts.'

'I understand your concern, Mandodari, but Dashaanan should be fine. He is travelling towards the east of Bharatvarsh to meet with one of our allies. He might also meet his Mama Marichan and cousins. Don't worry,' he assured me.

'Still, I insist you send a few guards to ensure his safety. I have never felt this way before. I am afraid Lankeshwar is in some kind of trouble,' I added.

'We are talking about Ravana here—the mighty emperor who scared Indra with his supremacy. He is in no trouble. But if you insist, I will send a group of guards and a spy for his safety.'

Nanashri sent a few guards off to sea with a message for Dashaanan. I was growing restless with each passing day. I started seeing visions of a young woman standing inside my chambers. She was dressed in tree barks; her hair half matted like a yogini. She would keep staring at me as if she wanted to communicate. I was scared that my lack of sleep was resulting in such hallucinations. In a few days, thankfully, my visions discontinued.

Shardula, the chief spy and other guards reported back after some days. Nanashri summoned me to a restricted area below the court where most confidential matters were discussed. He was accompanied by the leader of the guards. He looked tense.

'Rani Mandodari, thank you for joining us on such short notice,' said Nanashri.

'Is everything all right, Nanashri? Did Lankesh send any message with our guards?'

'Lankesh will be back in a few days. Apparently, the guards have some news for us . . . '

'What is it? Did you meet Lankeshwar or not?' I asked Shardula.

'I did meet him. He said he will be back in a few days and commanded me to return. He has sent no message,' answered Shardula nervously.

'Then what news did you want to give me? Where did you find him? Is he all right?'

'He is all right. However, he has encountered some misfortune while he was on his way to the east of Bharatvarsh. After meeting his uncle, Marichan, he had landed his vimana in the forest of Pushkara to find some water. There he happened to meet Vedavati, who was deeply meditating near a river. She was the daughter of Brahmarishi Kusadhvaja. It is believed that Vedavati set herself on fire because of Lankeshwar.'

I could barely believe what I was hearing.

'What do you mean because of Lankeshwar?' shouted Nanashri. He was stunned too.

'A few natives of that region who were doing their daily chores near the river heard some noises and saw fire in the woods. They ran and found a woman standing with her eyes shut in the middle of the fire. They saw Lankeshwar trying to get back to his vimana as the fire had spread to the nearby trees. They knew it was him due to the Pushpaka Vimana.'

'Is she . . . is she dead?' asked Nanashri.

'Yes, the natives could not extinguish the fire. It had consumed her body completely.'

'But how is Lankeshwar responsible for her death?' I cried.

'Mandodari, please remain calm. Dashaanan is unharmed, the guard met him and he will be back soon,' Nanashri tried to console me.

'How can I remain calm? My husband is being held responsible for a woman's death. What could be the reason that provoked her to set herself on fire?'

'When you met Lankesh? Did he tell you exactly what happened in the forest?' Nanashri asked the spy.

'He didn't tell me what happened when he met Vedavati. He said he was performing penance to overcome the sin of Vedavati's death and will return when he is done,' answered the spy.

Tensed and concerned, we waited for Dashaanan's return.

I performed secret penance and prayed for his safe arrival. He didn't return for one more month. I had many questions, many regrets and more than anything, I was full of rage. I was angry that he chose to remain absent in order to hide the incident.

Dashaanan returned unannounced after a month and my dasi informed me about his arrival. He went straight to meet Mata Kaikesi and Nanashri. Then late in the evening, he came to meet me.

I sprinkled rice and saffron on him when he entered my palace. 'Welcome home, my lord. How are you? And what kept you away from us for so long? Your absence has raised many questions in the minds of your people and your family,' I asked him with tears in my eyes.

'Mandodari, I am not ashamed to admit to you that I have committed a sin. I was away for a long time in order to perform penance.'

I smirked at him, 'When did it become so easy for Lankesh to admit to his guilt? Have you ever thought how I pay the price for your sins? You have made my life miserable, my lord.'

'Please don't say this. I have suffered a lot and the last thing I want to see is hatred in your eyes. I couldn't face you any sooner. Please forgive me.'

'I have lived a desolate life since that guard returned after meeting you. Tell me what happened? How are you guilty of that woman's death?'

'It was an unfortunate incident. I don't want to remember it.'

'What is it, my lord? You say you don't want to remember it but are you scared to narrate it?'

'I am not scared. The sooner I forget it, the better I will feel. I regret whatever happened. I made myself suffer too.'

'Your suffering cannot bring her life back! You need to tell me what happened, my lord. Let me help you.'

'I landed my vimana in the forest to find water. As I walked towards the sound of flowing water, I heard a beautiful voice chanting a mantra. I walked towards the sound and saw a beautiful young woman lost in meditation. Even though she was dressed like a rishi, I had never seen such a raw form of beauty before. Her eyes were closed in meditation; I couldn't take my eyes off of her. I saw her fair skin—she was wearing the hide of a black antelope—her full lips and her young body could bring any god down on his knees. I wanted her to open her eyes, so I walked closer to her. As I moved, I stumbled upon a Kamandal and accidently splashed some water on her face. She opened her eyes at once . . .

'"Stay right where you are standing! You have interrupted my tapasya! Who are you?"

'"I am Lankesh, Lankapati Ravana. I was going to the river when I heard you chanting. If I may ask you, why is a beautiful young woman like you dressed as a rishi? And it is nearly time for sunset, what are you doing in this cruel forest?"

'"I am Vedavati, daughter of Brahmarishi Kusadhvaja. My father wants me to have Lord Vishnu as my husband, hence I am performing a tapasya to win him over."

'"You are not made for tapasya. This forest will ruin your beauty with its cruel nature. And mind you, there are wild animals in the forest that can attack you in the dark. You should get back to your shade. Or you can climb on to my vimana and I will take you to a better place."

'"Don't worry about me, Lankesh! I was born in this forest. You should leave now," she said sternly.

'"Oh, Vedavati, there has to be some reason why I found you in this forest. You are wasting your time trying to please Vishnu. If he had any interest, he would have already given into the charms of your beauty till now." I moved closer to her and she got up at once.

'"Enough, Lankesh, please don't come any closer. I cannot allow any man except Vishnu himself to come that close to me. You are crossing your boundaries. I request you to leave!"

'"Why don't you come along with me? I am captivated by your beauty. I am a powerful king of a prosperous land. Come with me and be my queen!"

'"Have you no honour? I have no interest in your power and prosperity. My life is devoted to the holy one, and if I take a husband in this life, it would only be Hari! Now, please leave before I curse you," she screamed.

'"You are not listening to me, Vedavati. If Vishnu wanted you in this life, he would have never let me find you in this forest. Maybe it's an indication that he has chosen me for you," I said taking her hand in mine.

'"Don't you dare touch me again, Ravana! Or I shall be the reason for your death!" she yelled.

'I couldn't bare the rejection. "No woman has ever rejected Lankapati Ravana!"

'She was stubborn and I wanted to teach her a lesson. I grabbed her by her hair and pulled her towards me. She took out a sharp blade that was hidden in her bosom and cut off the section of her hair that I had grabbed.

'"You have ruined my tapasya! You have stained my aura by touching me," she screamed. I didn't think she would get so angry. All I wanted to do was teach her a lesson.

'"Listen to me, Vedavati. There is no reason to get so upset," I tried to calm her down.

'"Don't say another word. You think no woman is powerful enough to reject you? You have corrupted my body with your touch and I shall burn it to the ground. But remember, I will return in a new life! A woman will be the reason for your death and that woman will be me! I shall be born again for your destruction!"

'Declaring so, she used some kind of sorcery to invoke fire! I tried to stop her but I couldn't control the flames. I saw Vedavati's body burning in front of my eyes and I couldn't do anything about it.'

'What have you done, Lankeshwar? It's a curse! She was a hermit; you shouldn't have troubled her.'

'I tried to stop her.'

'And you didn't succeed!'

'Trust me, Mandodari; at first I was curious to know who she was and what a woman like her was doing alone in that forest. But when she rejected me, it made me angry. And I wasn't wrong about her sacrifice going in vain. "Hari" didn't wish to marry her in this life . . . '

'How can you defend yourself, Lankeshwar? She was a *tapasvi*! You didn't just criticize her tapasya but you took away the very reason she lived for.'

'I performed rituals after her death. I mourned for her. I did whatever I could to get absolution. But I still have nightmares. I feel her angry soul around me all the time.

Now I think I have mourned enough. She chose the way she left this world; I was merely a medium and not the reason,' declared Dashaanan and walked out.

SEVEN

Even though Dashaanan was back, I spent sleepless nights worrying about Vedavati's curse. I decided to meet Mahanta—the chief priest at Lanka—to ask what he made of the curse.

Mahanta was an old man; he could only see during the day and at night it was believed that he had mystical powers to visualize prophecies. Some people also said that he was a sorcerer. His predictions were said to never go wrong. He was the one to predict Dashaanan's triumph over Kubera. I took my trusted dasi along with me and paid respects at the Mahanta's abode.

'Respected Mahanta, I seek your guidance. I am worried about my husband's future. Tell me, how can I protect him? Show me the course.'

'Hmmm . . . I see you plead like a wife and not like a queen! What is done cannot be undone! Your husband has disturbed a chaste soul. Only another chaste soul can protect him. And that would be you!'

'Mahanta, we have done a lot of penance and my husband regrets his actions. But he carries a curse on him. Is it going to be true?'

Mahanta smirked, '"Regrets his actions?" Then why isn't he here with you? Or doesn't he really care what this aged moron has to say?'

I tried to answer and cover up for him, 'He . . . he . . . '

'Who are you fooling, queen? As far as the curse is concerned, it will come true; she will be the reason for his end.'

'How . . . how can I prevent that from happening?'

'You couldn't prevent the past from happening nor can you prevent the future. You will be the mother of a very courageous son. He will be as great a warrior as Shiva! He will be called an *atimaharathi*, but your firstborn will be a threat to your husband's reign and life.'

'My firstborn? My son? What kind of a threat, Mahanta?' I wanted more answers but he closed his eyes. I waited for him to talk to me. But he sat there motionless in deep meditation. He had said a lot of things but none of them made complete sense. I was left even more restless and perplexed than before.

Lanka gained a lot of popularity in the next one year. Dashaanan had conquered various lands and captured their wealth and women. He brought women of various races from various kingdoms. He filled the antapura with seductive women of the Naga tribe of Bharatvarsh, gandharvis from the north, deva women, dark rakshasi and asura women. Some were the daughters and wives of kings whose kingdoms he had conquered. There were women of Kinnara tribes from the east of Bharatvarsh.

With the growing wealth and number of women, Dashaanan's greed and lust also increased. He started spending most of his nights with the other women in the antapura. In the past few months, I had lost count of the number of women he kept there. Nanashri and Mata Kaikesi turned a blind eye to his activities in the antapura. Night after night, the antapura started becoming famous for its drunken orgies.

To my surprise, Dhanyamalini never objected to Dashaanan's involvement with other women. Such practices of polygamy were common in her tribe. She herself willingly got involved in all the drinking, gambling and sex. I had nobody to blame as I was the only one who felt disconnected.

It was four months since Dashaanan had last visited my chamber. Every night I yearned for my husband. I was lonely. Apart from the daily chores at court, I had nothing to do the whole day. Some nights as I would lie alone in my bed listening to the insane noises coming from the antapura, I felt envious. At times I heard screams of pleasure, laughter from wines they consumed and that made me feel even more lonesome.

☙

Monsoon clouds filled the skies. The season had slowed all construction work due to heavy rainfall. Dashaanan came to see me one morning. I assumed it was something very important as he was visiting my chambers after a long time.

I thought I would welcome him with a smile, but when I finally saw him, all I could feel was anger.

'Welcome to the old mansion, my lord. What can be so urgent that Lankeshwar has been reminded of this chamber today?' I asked sarcastically.

'Why, Mandodari, you don't look very pleased to see me here.'

'I am just surprised, my lord. My husband has visited this room for the first time in four months, which is as frequent as taking a tour of your neighbouring allies.'

'Which is why you should be happy and not mock your husband.'

'Should I be happy, my lord, that you visit this room like a guest?' I asked. Dashaanan looked infuriated by my constant mockery.

'I presume that I should see you some other time then, Mandodari. This is definitely not the best time to talk,' Dashaanan rebuked and turned around to walk out of the room.

'There will be no better time than this, my lord. I suggest you complete what you had to say.' I stood in front of him again and peered into his eyes. 'Tell me, my lord, how can Mandodari be of any help to you?'

'I have received a proposal from the northeastern land of Bharatvarsh. The king wants to be an ally. In return, he proposes his daughter's hand in matrimony.'

'And what have you decided, my lord?' I asked.

'I have decided to marry his daughter. I shall be back in five days,' declared Dashaanan and prepared to leave.

'If you have already decided, Lankeshwar, then why did you come to me?' I asked with disappointment.

'Because last time you were unhappy that I hadn't informed you! Hence, this time I wanted to notify you in advance. May I remind you that I am doing this to form an alliance with that kingdom.'

I mocked him, 'Why are you trying to hide your true intentions, Lankeshwar? One more marriage is simply like one more feather on your crown. Whether you marry another woman or not, it does not clear you of committing adultery with hundreds of other woman in the antapura.'

'Why do you keep saying that?' he raised his voice.

'Because it hurts me, my lord! It hurts to see my husband lying around with other women every night! Till when will things continue like this, my lord? Haven't you had enough? If you had to ignore me like this, why did you marry me? My father didn't propose an alliance with Lanka! It was you who convinced him for our marriage . . . so why? To hurt me like this?'

'I married you because I fell in love with you, Mandodari. And I still love you,' answered Dashaanan. 'I shall be back in five days. Make necessary arrangements for accommodation in the antapura.' Saying so, he left me weeping.

I spent days in regret. I was angry with myself. On the one hand, I was upset that Dashaanan didn't visit me as often as I wanted him to, and on the other, when he did visit me, I behaved like a little child. On one of those days during Dashaanan's absence, we were expecting a guest named Gritsamada. He was a rishi belonging to the Bhrigu family of saptarishis. He was on a voyage and needed to rest for a few days near the shore of Lanka. Mata Kaikesi had invited him to stay in our guest chambers but he requested a more modest place of accommodation.

'I offered him to stay in Dashaanan's silent chambers as nobody uses them. I need you to make the necessary arrangements for his stay,' said Mata Kaikesi. I sensed pity in her eyes for me. She wanted to talk about Dashaanan's new marriage.

'I will certainly get everything done, Mata. Is that all?' I asked politely.

'Well, I also wanted to know if you need any assistance for making arrangements in the antapura,' she asked.

'Mata, if you are concerned about the accommodation arrangements in the antapura, then you can rest assured, I will have them ready before my husband's new wife arrives. Now allow me to leave, I shall visit the palace,' I replied and prepared to leave.

'Please stay, Mandodari. I am not sure how to say it, but regarding Dashaanan's marriage, I understand how you must be feeling at this time.'

'You won't understand how I feel, Mata, because you were the other woman in your husband's life and I believe only his first wife can tell you how I feel!' Mata Kaikesi had no answer to my daring statement. She seemed sickened by my hurtful comment. Yet she thought better than to protest.

'I remind you that Dashaanan's third marriage is intended for the same reason as his second marriage—to form strong allies for Lanka!' she clarified.

'I certainly understand—for the interest and benefit of our kingdom. I have heard it several times! And in the bargain to form strong allies, it doesn't matter if relations within Lanka fall apart!'

'You are taking this the wrong way.'

'It is clear that Dashaanan is influenced by your opinion when it comes to the benefit of Lanka and making allies. And I don't wish to challenge your influence.'

'Why do you think I have influenced Dashaanan to get married?' She was offended. 'I brought Dashaanan in this world for a purpose. He has changed courses. He has brought honour and liberation to our daitya clan.'

'The purpose of bringing him into this world has been duly fulfilled. The purpose he has now is far more than passion and ambition. He challenges nature, aspires for supreme powers that are not meant for mortal beings. I am surprised no one else sees the hazards involved. No one else is concerned about the outcome.'

'You think I am not concerned about my son! I have sacrificed my life, my youth and my marriage to get Dashaanan into this world. I was younger than you when I was married off. I held the entire tribe's responsibility on my shoulders. I gave my virtue, my youth to a man almost my father's age so I could provide a perfect heir to my clan. I knew Dashaanan's father could not assure me an ideal married life. I managed four kids at a time; constantly struggling to ensure they got their basic rights as they were not considered Brahmins for superior studies. And yes, I influenced my son mainly because I know he deserves more. It is easy to point fingers at me, Mandodari, but you will never understand all that I have gone through to get Dashaanan to this position.'

'I respect your struggle and all that you have done for him. However, it is high time you realized your struggle already paid off. His strife for more and more is turning hazardous. You may not see that now because you are blinded by the efforts in your past and the prosperity of your present. Anyway, I should take your leave now. I will visit shanti bhavan and ensure proper arrangements for our guest.'

I left her chambers realizing that I had quarrelled with a woman who was exceptionally proud of her son. Her life had been lonely, burdened with an unwanted responsibility at an early age. Her life revolved around her children and she was merely trying to make the most of it. I felt more for Mata Kaikesi that day.

※

When it came to sages and rishis, Dashaanan didn't have a good history with most of them. During their adolescence, Dashaanan and his siblings suffered constant mockery and condemnation at the hands of Brahmin sages who didn't consider the half-daitya siblings eligible to read and learn from Vedic texts meant only for Brahmins. Later their father Vishrava, upon seeing the thirst for knowledge and aptitude of his children, reminded the Brahmins that children primarily acquired the caste of their father and hence his half-daitya children had full rights to their education. However, in the interim, Dashaanan had grown hateful towards the sages. And this hatred grew even more when the Brahmins and other wise men started a civil war to abolish the rights of the daityas.

Dashaanan and his siblings were taught mainly by their father. Education and knowledge empowered them. They learnt advanced skills that even the most learned sages failed to master. And then Dashaanan began to eradicate most of the sages to prove his valour. Rumours went around that he would store the blood of the sages he killed in a large pot.

No matter how bad Dashaanan and his siblings' history had been with sages and Brahmins, we had to serve them if they were housed as our guests. I briefed the attendants and the guards of the palace regarding our guest. As informed by Mata Kaikesi, Rishi Gritsamada desired complete peace and silence during his stay. The guards announced my entry into the shanti bhavan premises and I went inside to welcome him.

'Oh, divine rishi, I welcome you. Accept my warm greetings. I am Mandodari.'

'Mandodari, the daughter of Mayasura and the queen of Lanka!' he said, turning towards me.

It had been a long time since someone had addressed me by my father's name. I was reminded of my second identity besides being Ravana's wife.

Rishi Gritsamada was not as old as I had imagined. He was tall, had a fair complexion and a muscular body. He wore beads of rudraksha around his arms and neck.

'You don't need an introduction. People in Lanka have been kind to me. I thank you for letting me stay here. I am performing some rites and needed to halt for a few days,' he said.

'Please don't thank me, oh great sage. We are truly honoured by your visit. Must you need anything with regards to your accommodation, feel free to ask.'

He smiled at me. 'That is very noble of you. I didn't imagine the queen of proud Lankeshwar to be so kind.'

'If I may ask you, oh rishi muni, what kind of rites are you performing?'

'I am surprised you asked, your majesty. Lankeshwar and his brothers are known for their tough tapasya and my little experiment may not really interest you.'

'It's all right if you do not wish to tell me. I shall take your leave now. The guards have been briefed about your privacy.'

'Is it true that Lankeshwar stores the blood of sages in a large pot as a mark of his revenge against them? Have you seen it?' he asked as I turned to leave.

I didn't know how to answer the question. Certainly he must have heard of Dashaanan's dispute with the sages and the story of their blood being stored.

'Ah, well, I am not sure about that. I haven't seen any large pot filled with blood in the palace.'

'Yes, you have. That pot is housed in the veranda of this palace. I saw it while passing through the inner corridors. That is the area where Lankeshwar practices archery, I was told,' he added.

'Well, I've seen the pot but I haven't seen what it contains. And now, if you'll excuse me, I am needed at the court.'

'Sure, your majesty, I don't intend to keep you. I would need a similar large pot for my tapasya. Is that possible?' asked the sage.

'Yes, I will ask someone to arrange one for you. Have a comfortable stay,' I said and quickly left before I could be asked more uncomfortable questions.

EIGHT

Dashaanan was expected to return with his new wife. I did all that was asked of me. I arranged for an accommodation, servants, trousseau and a feast. The courtiers announced the sighting of Dashaanan's vimana and everyone gathered to welcome him with his new wife. Sarama willingly took the responsibility of performing the necessary rituals. She knew I would never have the heart to welcome another woman to share my husband. I wanted to make an exit as soon as possible.

We waited for the vimana to descend and as it landed, the crowd started cheering loudly. The guards stepped out, followed by Dashaanan with his ministers, and then came the much-awaited new wife of my husband. I avoided looking at her face; I am not sure whether it was out of anxiety or jealousy. Dashaanan introduced his new wife to Mata Kaikesi and Nanashri. Then they turned towards me, and I looked from Dashaanan to the woman who was accompanying him. She was smiling, graceful and poised; she bowed in respect.

No matter how jilted or hurt I felt, I couldn't let another woman bear the brunt of my husband's misdoings.

'I welcome you to our kingdom,' I said with a heavy heart. 'Bhabhi Sarama will escort you to your chambers.'

She caught my hands in hers and said, 'Thank you for accepting me. I have heard a lot about you.' Dressed in fine satin robes, she also wore a tiara as a symbol of her royal identity. She was fair; her hair was black and fell straight down to her hips. I simply smiled at her and gestured Sarama to take over.

'Welcome to Lanka. What is your name?' asked Sarama.

'Bhabhi Sarama, she is as white as milk, sprightly like a doe in the wild forest. She is attractive and it's not easy to take your eyes off of her pretty face. I have named her Nayanadini,' announced Dashaanan and everyone applauded for the newlyweds.

'Very well said! I now seek your permission to escort Nayanadini to her chambers,' said Sarama and for a moment I wasn't sure if I was needed. I walked towards the palace thinking if I was really required anywhere that day. I couldn't speak to Dashaanan as Nanashri and the other ministers had surrounded him. Mata Kaikesi was not someone I wanted to be with at this time and nor was I required at court.

I found a quiet spot in a garden near Dashaanan's palace and waited for him to return. I wanted to apologize to him for my behaviour. More than that, I was lonely and I only wanted to speak to him for some time.

'Looking for company, Rani Mandodari?' I turned to a familiar tone that I didn't find very pleasing.

'Is there something you need, rishi muni?' I asked.

'Nothing, but I think you are in dire need of good company. You seem very displeased today. Is your husband the reason for your apprehensions?' said Gritsamada.

'This is coming from a sage who barely knows me or this kingdom. You are our guest, rishi muni. I expect you will maintain etiquette in order for us to respect you,' I answered.

'I meant no offence. Don't take me wrong here but I know your father very well. I had seen you several times at Mayarastra before you were married. We haven't met but you seem like a changed person.'

'Well, of course, I have changed, from being a girl to a woman. You must have seen me but you definitely don't know me.'

'And what will I not know, Mandodari? You are not good at hiding things, are you? It is very obvious that you do not approve of your husband's other marriages and his relations with other women disturb you. You married an overambitious man who doesn't care for your presence in his kingdom any more.'

'Mind your words, rishi; this may cost you your life!' I objected.

'Cost me my life, Mandodari? For speaking the truth or will the great Ravana spare no opportunity to slay one more sage for his ego?'

'Listen carefully, rishi, I may not approve of my husband's affairs but I cannot bear any uncouth sage saying accusing words against my husband!' Saying so, I walked out.

I avoided the feast that evening. I stayed in my palace as I didn't want anyone to gauge my disapproval of Dashaanan's actions. If an outsider like Gritsamada could create so much unrest in my mind, I feared the other ladies would start gossiping about me too.

Since almost everyone was at the feast, I decided to spend some time with the dasis who served me. I heard their grievances with their mothers-in-law, heard amusing tales about their children, different rumours about the ladies at the antapura and their problems related to their husbands.

In the middle of one such session, the guard stationed outside announced Dashaanan's arrival. My dasis dispersed and I waited to welcome him inside. I kept a polite face; avoiding any topics that had annoyed Dashaanan the last time he had come to see me.

'Welcome, my lord. I am surprised to see you here. Isn't the feast still in progress?'

'And I expected to see you there and not here.'

'Pardon my absence, Lankeshwar. I thought it was your wedding night with your new wife and the celebration was in her honour. I didn't want to outshine her, or to make her feel uncomfortable in any way,' I explained.

Dashaanan grinned and I knew he wasn't buying my excuse. 'You are well aware that the feast is a celebration of Lanka's new peace treaty with its new ally. And yes, the princess from that alliance is a part of it. Why would you outshine her? You are the queen of this kingdom and it's imperative that you understand your duties. An alliance with this kingdom is an alliance with you. No matter if you have to see that ally as a woman wedded to your husband.'

'You know I can't do that. It's not easy for me to see any other woman standing beside you.'

'Very well, then, I am asking you to stand strong beside me. Other women may come and go, I want you to believe that your place is secure in my heart as well as in my kingdom.'

'It is still difficult to share you, Lankesh. No matter how hard I try, I still fail.'

'You know I have more than a hundred other women in the antapura to share my bed with. Nayanadini is just another one among them. What makes you sulk like this over another woman?'

'Because she is your wife, Lankesh! You are married to her and that's a sacred bond to me. You made that bond with me first and I am not ready to share it again. I have unwillingly accepted it so far and I am not sure if my self-esteem can take it any more.'

'Of course, I cannot stop, Mandodari. I have to do whatever is in the best interest of Lanka. Think like a queen and not just a wife. Because if you don't, I might fail. I want you to stand with me.'

'I will try again, my lord. My love for you is more than anything else. I will not let you fail.'

We spent the entire night together. I slept in the arms of the man I loved so much, hoping to rid myself of all the repulsive thoughts of losing him to someone else.

When I woke up in the morning, I saw Dashaanan lying next to me on my bed, staring at me affectionately. I soon became aware of the events of the previous night; it would have been unfair to the newly married princess that Dashaanan remained absent on their first night together. She would have waited for him at the feast and later in their room.

'This doesn't feel like you, my lord. Waking up early in the morning, before me, and making me feel like I have kept you waiting,' I teased him.

'You sure did keep me waiting and I need to be duly compensated.' Saying so, he pulled me into his arms. It felt like old times again.

'My lord, the princess would be waiting for you since last night. I hope we haven't infuriated anyone with our actions.'

'And why do you care so much about her now?' asked Dashaanan playfully.

'I don't intend to take away her post-marital rights, or she'll turn into a rival.'

'Anyone from the antapura you consider as your rival?'

'Not that I recall, my lord. Dhanyamalini is younger but a lot more mature when it comes to these matters. This one, my lord, there's something not right about her. She doesn't look very friendly.'

Dashaanan laughed out loud. 'That is the most amusing thing I have heard in my entire life.'

'If you wish, my lord, I can narrate more amusing incidents about other women staying at the antapura,' I tried to tease him.

'I don't wish to talk about anyone else, Mandodari. Do you know what I really wish for? I wish to have children with you. First, I want a girl—as beautiful as you, as considerate as you, as poised as you.'

'I did not know you longed for a daughter, my lord.'

'I want a daughter with you, Mandodari. I am known to be a rakshasa who didn't hesitate for a minute before killing the Brahmins. I am known to be egoistic, selfish and proud. I am known as a womanizer, full of lust and greed. But my daughter, she will be my pride. I will win the world for her. I will fulfil all her dreams. I will care for her, protect her from every evil.'

I was overjoyed to see how Dashaanan talked about having a daughter. No one could have imagined this side of him, not even I. The thought of having children delighted me. We'd been married for over a year now and it was probably the right time to think of having children of our own.

Breaking my chain of thoughts, Dashaanan intruded, 'Mandodari, what are you thinking about? What do you suggest we name our children?'

'But, my lord, I should excuse myself as I need to see Mata Kaikesi today.'

'You can meet her later. Be here with me today.'

'If it weren't necessary, I would have delayed meeting her. But it is concerning a guest staying with us and Mata Kaikesi wants us to treat him with great respect.'

'Who is this guest? Mata Kaikesi didn't mention him to me.'

'It's been a few days since Rishi Gritsamada has been housed as a guest in the silent chambers of your palace. I am surprised that you haven't been informed about it yet.'

'You know I am not very fond of such guests. And why will my kingdom serve Brahmins when they have always treated me like a half-caste bastard? They ill-treated my mother too. How can she allow him to stay with us without my permission?'

'The rishi belongs to the saptarishi clan and Mother wants to be a good host since he is travelling through our kingdom,' I clarified. But Dashaanan seemed annoyed by the news.

'If mother wishes to be a host to him, she may do that on her own account. Why has he been staying in the palaces of Lanka? And you being the queen of this empire, why do you attend to him personally?' he sounded angry and got up to leave.

'No, my lord, I wasn't attending to him personally. I was simply following Mata Kaikesi's orders.'

'You can't take orders from Mata Kaikesi!' Dashaanan yelled. 'Should I remind you again, Mandodari, that you are a queen? Unless you have some personal attachment with that sage . . .'

'My lord, please do not say such things! I was simply following her directions,' I interrupted.

'In that case, you will follow my directions from now on and I command you to ask him to leave.'

'But it would look very inhospitable if we ask him to leave so suddenly. He is on a tapasya and we cannot ask him to abandon everything.'

'I want him out. Now! I cannot bear any sage living on my land,' he declared and left my chambers. I was astonished to see so much rage in Dashaanan for Rishi Gritsamada.

Following Dashaanan's orders, I went to meet rishi Gritsamada to tell him that we could no longer accommodate him and that we would help him set off on a voyage to his next destination where he could continue his tapasya.

Gritsamada was meditating when I entered. He was seated in the centre of the veranda, facing the huge identical pot that he had demanded from us. He was chanting a mantra with his eyes closed. Sensing another presence in the room, he opened his eyes.

'I regret to disturb you, rishi muni, but there is something I need to talk to you about.'

'The reason I requested a quiet place is because I wanted to avoid any hindrance in my tapasya. It is not easy to attain silence here, I guess. The guards keep doing rounds; the maids keep coming in.'

'I expect you to understand that this is the king's palace, which is why it's so busy throughout the day, but we didn't intend to disturb you. Now you won't have anything more to complain about as I have come to arrange for your voyage to your next destination. You can continue with your tapasya there,' I declared.

'So, do you want me to leave . . . or . . . does Lankesh want me to leave?'

I chose not to respond to his question, further insisting, 'I will ensure that you are being served well on your way and that you do not face any discomfort.'

The sage smiled, 'Rani Mandodari, I am a hermit, a sage, and I don't require any luxurious service that you offer. I understand my ways and words have not been pleasing because what's in my heart is on my tongue. However, I want to complete my tapasya before I leave this place and head anywhere else. The siddhi I wish to attain cannot be achieved if I switch places. I ask your permission to let me stay here for just a few more days.'

'Pardon me, but that is not possible. And what kind of siddhi is restricted to a particular place?'

'I am practising penance to invoke Goddess Lakshmi.' He pointed towards the large pot and explained: 'This large pot here contains my experiment. Filled with milk and grass, purified with mantras, Goddess Lakshmi will dwell in it. I will implant a living cell from this pot into a woman's womb. I will bring her up as my daughter and she will restore balance on earth. I cannot uncover the contents of this pot as any exposure will turn it into poison. Thus, I request you to extend my stay for a few more weeks, allow me to complete this experiment and attain my siddhi.'

I was unable to object further. Gritsamada looked into my eyes with a lot of expectation. He was discourteous but he was honest and sincere towards his penance.

'I cannot promise anything to you now, but I will try to speak to Lankeshwar regarding the extension.'

※

Having failed to complete the task assigned to me by Dashaanan, I feared it would upset him once he found out that Gritsamada was still lodged at the palace. After sunset, when Dashaanan was back from court, I met him privately. I wanted him to allow Gritsamada to stay with us for a few more weeks. Holding a wine goblet in his hand, Dashaanan was deeply preoccupied with his own thoughts.

'My lord, I don't intend to disturb you but may I take a moment to talk to you regarding some matter?' I asked, interrupting his thoughts.

'You are not disturbing me. Tell me what is the matter?'

'Upon your command, I asked rishi Gritsamada to evacuate the palace premises and leave for his next destination. But . . .'

'But what? Has he left or not?'

'No, my lord. He is requesting an extension for a few more weeks. He says he has still not achieved siddhi and he refuses to leave Lanka before he does.'

'He dared to refuse my command!' Dashaanan was furious.

'He didn't refuse—he is only requesting for an extension for a couple more days.'

Dashaanan was screaming now: 'If the sage wanted an extension, he should have been here to request me in person! But I know he will not ask me because he is full of ego and arrogance.'

'My lord, he is a *tapasvi*. There is no harm in allowing him a few weeks of extension.'

'A few weeks? I cannot tolerate that sage on my land for another day. Send him back. Send him back, Mandodari, before I kill him for refusing my orders.'

'Why do you speak about killing him? He has merely requested for an extension.'

'Are you afraid of asking him to go? Why do you favour his stay so much?' he asked, looking at me suspiciously. 'Are you hiding something from me? Answer me . . . why are you trying to defend him?'

I was shocked at Dashaanan's accusation. I didn't expect the conversation to turn against me.

Fearing for Gritsamada's life, in the most subtle way I replied, 'My lord, he is practising penance to have Goddess Lakshmi as his daughter. He is conducting an experiment to develop life in that palace by achieving siddhi and I feel that we should allow him to complete it before he leaves. He has preserved some contents in a large pot and says he doesn't want to disturb it with movement or travel. I have no personal purpose, but I do request you to grant him an extension on humanitarian grounds.'

'He is fooling us! There are no contents in any large pot. He is merely a spy who has come to inspect our power so he can provide our secrets to our enemies. And I will prove it to you. I will prove to you that there is no life or holy content in that bloody pot.' He became enraged and started walking towards shanti bhavan.

I was scared that he might humiliate Gritsamada and end up taking a curse on himself. I ran after him, instructing the guards to quickly call for Vibhishana and Nanashri.

Dashaanan entered the room where Gritsamada was meditating. He pulled out his Chandrahas sword and aligned it on Gritsamada's neckline.

'How dare you disobey my orders? Don't forget you stand on my land.'

The rishi did not bat an eyelid at the threat. 'Your majesty, I am a sage who obeys only the supreme power and I am free to wander the earth as and how I please. As for the land I stand on, I requested your permission to extend my stay for a few more weeks.'

'You are nothing but a selfish and arrogant specimen of the sect you belong to. I hate the blood that runs in your veins. I want you out of my land—you decide if you wish to leave this land dead or alive!' There was blood in Dashaanan's eyes. I saw him clenching his fists as if he had no control over his anger.

Gritsamada answered, 'You call us arrogant? Don't forget that the same blood runs in your veins since you're a Brahmin as well. And don't forget that the sect you call selfish has taught you all that you have mastered today. We have given you all that you know and all that you've earned, even though most of what you have earned is not even rightfully yours!'

Dashaanan roared in anger and raised his sword. Without any hesitation, he cut off Gritsamada's head from his shoulders! The body fell on the ground with blood splattering everywhere—on the pot that was part of Gritsamada's penance, on my clothes, on the walls. Before I could make sense of what I had just witnessed, Nanashri and Vibhishana entered the room. It was horrifying; they were shocked at what they saw.

Dashaanan tried to leave; I stopped him.

'Why, my lord? You promised me. You promised me, and yet you have taken another innocent life.'

'He was not innocent. He disobeyed me and accused me! And why are you so hurt? Were you fond of him?'

'Enough, my lord. You have taken a Brahmin's life and now you question my virtue!'

'You should be thankful that I spared your life!'

'Really, my lord? Is this what I mean to you? In that case, I spare you from taking my life. I will end this life on my own!'

I reached for the contents of the pot, scooping out the greenish potion and drank it. Dashaanan rushed towards me, but by then my vision was blurring and I collapsed on the ground soon after.

NINE

I felt no pain but peace. I saw myself walking on grass. There were green, crop-yielding fields around me. Then I heard someone giggle. I turned around to see who it was and saw a young girl running towards me. She was beautiful. For a moment I thought it was me at a younger age. She was smiling and playing. I wanted to ask her who she was. I stretched my hand to hold her but she ran away.

I got up with a sudden jolt. My head felt heavy and there was a weird pain around the nape of my neck. My dasis rushed to attend to me.

'Your majesty, you should lie down—you still need to rest. Your majesty, I will call the physician now. Please lie down,' said one dasi.

'She is awake . . .'

'The queen just opened her eyes, let's inform Lankeshwar.'

'She has a long life . . . The queen is awake.'

'Call the physician . . . We should ask her to rest.'

A physician came in and while he examined my pulse, I learnt that I had been unconscious for the past two days from the effects of the poisonous potion I had consumed. The potion lying in that pot at shanti bhavan was contaminated and became highly poisonous when the ingredients reacted with Gritsamada's blood. I fell sick again on remembering that scene as if I could still taste blood in my mouth. I was nauseated, and the physician advised that it could be because of the antidote given to me.

Dashaanan's entrance was announced. I wasn't ready to face him again. The physician explained the state of my health to him and took leave. I closed my eyes and remained still. I felt immense shame for my act of attempting suicide. I was a queen and I had let my subjects down. I had let my husband down. On the other hand, I felt miserable that I was alive. I was back to the same life where my husband would regret his actions for a few days and then go back to his old ways. I was a dejected wife, who had to unwillingly share her husband with other women; a struggling queen, who failed to match the king's ambitions.

Dashaanan sat near my bed, taking my hand in his. 'Mandodari, can you hear me, my love? Please open your eyes. I am deeply sorry for whatever happened. It is entirely my fault. Talk to me. Are you listening?'

I opened my eyes and looked at my concerned husband. 'My lord, I regret what happened. I don't know what to say. I don't know what I can say to explain my actions.'

'You don't need to explain anything. It was my fault yet again. I provoked you to take such an action! I never imagined that my anger could take your life! I almost lost you!'

'Both of us are guilty, my lord. You are guilty for your anger, your violence, whereas I am guilty for giving up my tolerance, my rationality. However, I didn't expect to live, my lord. It would have been better if my soul . . . '

'Let us forget about the entire incident! I have been assured by physicians that they will make you healthy in a month's time. By then, I hope you forget the entire episode. And I hope you forgive me by then too.'

'I will try, my lord. Even though my heart wishes for something else, I will still try.'

'I will let you take some rest now. Nanashri and Mata Kaikesi will visit you later today. And I want to see you better next time.' He kissed me and left.

※

I gained my health back gradually but my nausea couldn't be cured completely. I felt my strength being taken away from me. I could barely walk; I felt like resting the entire day. I wasn't sure if it were the medicines that were making me drowsy. I was regularly visited by members of the royal family. Dhanyamalini, Bajrajala and Sarama came twice a day to check on my progress. Nayanadini came too, but more as a formality and less out of concern. Trijata, who recently had a miscarriage, supervised all the services of my chambers sincerely. Dashaanan sent for my Mai at Mayarastra, hoping I would recover faster if someone from my maternal house was taking care of me.

After a month, Trijata called for a physician discreetly. She had noticed a change in my meal preferences. I preferred tangy curries and couldn't even look at sweets. She had also noticed that my face looked pale and she suspected that there could be something about my condition that the physician was missing. Hence, without raising unwanted alarm, she arranged for my health examination.

A physician sat beside my bed and examined me, 'Your majesty, are you taking your medicinal potions on time as prescribed?'

'Yes, but the nausea doesn't stop. And why do I feel so lethargic with these medicines?' I enquired.

'That's surprising, your majesty, because the potions given to you will purely cleanse the remaining effects of the poison from your blood stream. There is no drug to make you feel lethargic or sleepy in your prescription.'

'But she is sleepy most of the time,' intervened Trijata.

'In that case, I shall check the contents of the medicinal potions again. However, your majesty, I still wish to ask you if your monthly menstrual cycles are regular or did you happen to miss any . . . '

'Well, I kind of lost track of it after the incident,' I answered.

'It's okay, your majesty. I shall come back later.'

'But what do you think is causing the delay in her majesty's recovery?' intervened Trijata again.

'On the contrary, her majesty seems to have recovered quite a lot. I have examined her pulse, *pitta* and *vata*. It seems like she is recovering faster than we realized. However, the kind of symptoms you highlight and on the basis of my basic examination, I can surmise one thing . . . '

'What is it? Tell me now . . . '

'Your majesty, I think you are with child!'

My heart started beating faster. I felt a sudden rush of emotions. I could feel tears of joy rolling down my face.

Trijata looked even more excited than I. But the physician remained silent. Then I saw the look on his face and realized that his tone of delivering that news to me was not joyful. He sat still and lowered his eyes.

'What is it? Is something wrong?' I asked him.

'Your majesty, I cannot confirm anything right now. I will need to perform a few more tests to confirm the pregnancy. Also, we are not sure of your menstrual cycle for this month.'

'Well then, do it . . . do whatever you want but why do you still sound so doubtful?'

'Forgive me, but even if I confirm this pregnancy, I would suggest you get yourself examined by a midwife first and then break the news to everyone.'

'Why? It is such a blessing . . . such wonderful news . . .' interrupted Trijata.

'Your majesty, the effects of the poison and the medicines consumed so far must have impacted the development of the foetus. In such cases, forgive me, but we suggest timely termination of the pregnancy.'

'That is impossible,' I objected.

'Forgive me, your majesty, but it is yet to be confirmed and this is quite an early stage for me to comment on further. I can also say that this may be a complicated stage of your recovery and the symptoms are a mere coincidence. I can confirm with a few tests, if you wish.'

'No, there is no such need. And I command you to keep all this to yourself. If I need your services again, I shall send for you. But remember not to disclose our conversation to anyone outside this room.'

'Certainly, your privacy will be maintained.'

I signaled Trijata to escort him outside. I remained in my bed, thinking about the life growing inside me and went to sleep.

※

The next morning, I woke up to a familiar voice. I opened my eyes and saw Mai sitting at my bedside. I embraced her at once and she sobbed with the happiness of meeting me again.

'How are you, my princess? Oh, I have missed you so much. Ah, I am sorry! My little princess is a queen now. How wonderful is your palace! Ah, and the building, everything is really golden! The walls are plated with gold and the pillars are coated with liquid gold!'

'Mai, how is everyone back home? How is my mother? And Pitashri? How is Pitashri? I miss everyone . . .'

'We are very well, my princess. We were so worried about your health. Lankeshwar had sent a messenger informing us about your health and that you accidently consumed something! He said that you were recovering well but your parents were anxious about you. They might come visit you in a few days. However, Lankeshwar specially asked me to sail along with the messenger and I hurried with him to be with you. You look very pale, Mandodari. Is everything all right? Is Lankeshwar treating you well?'

'I am treated well, Mai, don't worry. However, I want to ask you something. I haven't told anyone yet because I am waiting to confirm it myself first and you must make sure you don't tell anyone either.'

'What is it, my princess?' asked Mai. I gestured to Trijata to dismiss the maids for privacy.

'Mai, please make sure you don't overreact. I am hoping that you can help me. One of our physicians told me that I could be pregnant, but he can't say for sure without performing certain tests. But I know for certain that I am with child—I can feel it.'

As expected, Mai was overjoyed with the news. Her eyes immediately lit up. 'That is wonderful news, princess!'

'No, there is more. He has suggested that in case the pregnancy is confirmed, I should terminate it because the poison and medicines may have infected my foetus. As a result my child's development can be impacted.'

'And which poison are you referring to? Was it the poison you accidentally consumed?' Mai looked worried. I couldn't provide more explanation. Then, without expecting an answer she replied, 'Yes, there is a possibility that the medicines may have caused some harm but we can still take precautions to protect the child.'

I was relieved on hearing that. And then I was clear about what to do next.

Trijata, who had been standing in a corner listening to our conversation, said: 'So, your majesty, if you can keep the child, should we inform the king about your pregnancy?'

'No, tell no one. I want you two to promise me that you will not disclose the news of my pregnancy to anyone.'

'Why, Mandodari? What do you have in mind?'

'My child is in danger. I am not feeling too well and if we tell everyone, then the physicians will warn Dashaanan about the effects of the poison on the child. They will ask me to abort it as I am sure that Dashaanan will never risk the birth of an unfit child. They will force me to terminate my pregnancy. I want to keep my child!'

'But that is an ideal thing to do. If there is risk to the well-being of the child in your womb, then you should terminate it at this stage! Why do you want to go through the pain of bringing an unwell child into this world? Also, it is not just your pain . . . but your child will suffer throughout its life,' Mai explained.

'Mai, I want to wait and see how I feel about this child in my womb. But if we tell them now, they will not wait. If I sense any danger, I will take a decision. But for now, I want to wait and see how this child develops inside me. And now, you are here to help me.'

'I am always there for you, my princess, but how will you hide your pregnancy? You will start to show in a few months and your health is closely reported by your physicians. It is impossible to hide this news.'

'It is not. I will tell Dashaanan that I wish to see my parents. I will stay away from everyone for a few days. Let my baby grow stronger inside me. If everything seems normal, I will inform everyone.'

They were tense about my decision. However, I had decided what I had to do. I feared for my baby's life. I also wasn't sure if my pregnancy would shape up the way I was imagining. I closed my eyes and thought about Shiva. I asked him to bless my baby's health and to provide me with strength.

In a few days' time, my nausea subsided and I gained enough strength to walk around. Mai attended to me very well and I stopped taking any medication altogether. I got out of my room after a long time to meet the women of the family. Everybody wished me a warm welcome. I saw some women from the antapura too. I couldn't recollect their names but they smiled at me concernedly. All our women servants and dasis were also present.

'It is so good to see you here, Mandodari. I wish you good health and happiness,' said Mata Kaikesi.

'Thank you, Mata. It feels good to be back amongst everyone here. I was getting tired of being inside my chambers all day long. But I am better now.'

'That's good to hear. But I insist you still take proper rest. Dashaanan needs you, Mandodari. He needs your counsel. Try to spend some time at court too. Your people need to see you.'

'I understand, Mata, I shall resume my duties from tomorrow.'

She leaned into whisper, 'Dashaanan will be happy to see you. I wish you all the best and may god bless you with the fruits of motherhood soon.'

Had Mata Kaikesi got a hint of my pregnancy? I knew I was responsible for producing an heir but I was surprised by Mata Kaikesi's sudden mention of it. I said nothing but simply smiled at her. All of us dined together that evening and I caught up on all that had been happening in my absence. I was back to my routine but I still had the major task of telling Dashaanan about my wish to go on a pilgrimage.

The next morning, I had to fake my menstruation. I asked Trijata to dampen some red dye on my bed sheets to make it look like blood. This was further reported to the physicians by my dasis and everyone consented that I had got my period.

Dashaanan was most happy to receive me back at court. 'I welcome you back, Mandodari. I can't express how happy I am to see you back in good health.'

'Lankeshwar has missed your company, Rani Mandodari. We welcome you back,' said Nanashri.

'Tell me, how should we celebrate your health? Should I order a feast in your honour?' asked Dashaanan.

'It feels good to be back, my lord. And as far as the celebration is concerned, I would like to celebrate in a different way, if you allow it.' I took the opportunity to mention the tour.

'Of course, whatever you suggest.'

'My lord, in the past few weeks I have sensed the need to purify myself with penance and prayers. I want to pray for your safety, success and prosperity. I want to pray for our future. Hence, I wish to go on a pilgrimage,' I proposed.

'A pilgrimage? Why, Mandodari, you can perform penance here. You will have whatever you wish here.'

'No, my lord, I wish to go on a pilgrimage to all the holy tirthas of Bharatvarsh. I want to purify myself at these places. I want to collect the holy waters and bring them for you.'

'But that will take months! I cannot send you off for so many months! And with whom will you travel?'

'I want to go north near the Himalayas, bathe and cleanse in the waters of the holy Ganga. I want to go to

Badarikasrama. I will stop over at my father's house too. It has been a long time since I saw them. I feel like going to Mayarastra for a few weeks. If you allow me, my lord, I shall visit the holy tirthas and meet my parents too.'

Dashaanan was still not convinced. 'My lord, I insist. It is only a matter of a few months, for I shall return with a content mind and soul.'

Dashaanan stayed quiet for some time. Concerned about my health and happiness, he took it as a humble plea.

'All right, as you wish. You have my permission for your pilgrimage. But you should report your timely whereabouts to us.'

He turned to Vibhishana, 'Vibhishana, you will ensure Rani Mandodari has everything she needs for her travel. Also, send a group of trusted escorts and guards along with her. She can choose the dasis she wants to take with her.'

Vibhishana gave an affirmative nod and I was relieved that the most difficult task of asking for Dashaanan's permission was over.

TEN

I made arrangements for the tour. I selected two of my most trusted dasis to travel with me, along with Mai. I asked Trijata to report on all important matters to me through messengers. I had also assigned Sarama for all antapura-related affairs. I had to keep my pregnancy safe and nurture the child in my womb. I felt strong from within, believing that it was no ordinary child inside me. And I was somehow certain that it was a girl. Dashaanan had once expressed how he longed for a daughter. I felt sorry that I had to keep it a secret.

Soon, I commenced on my journey. Considering the number of months I would have to travel for, our luggage was elaborate. Not only did we carry plenty of clothes, food and tents, but also four-equipped chariots with horses and a palanquin for the road journey. Along with eight martial guards, two messengers, four maidservants, two trusted dasis and Mai, I set the course through waters on a huge ship.

We sailed to the southernmost shore of Bharatvarsh after three days. Travelling by sea made me sick. We took a day's rest near the shore and then started our road journey towards the north to reach Mayarastra first. I longed to meet my parents and spend time at my father's house, which would allow me more time to think about my pregnancy. I wanted my mother's counsel. No matter how supreme my position was, I still felt the need to find comfort in my mother's presence.

We halted multiple times during our road journey. We visited some of the most renowned temples of Bharatvarsh. I prayed for my family and unborn child. I bathed in the holy waters, donated alms to the needy and read the Vedas to strengthen my child. After almost a month's travel, we reached Mayarastra. My parents rushed to welcome our troop. The people of Mayarastra gave us a warm welcome. I exchanged quick pleasantries with everyone and went straight to my mother's private chambers to talk to her.

'How are you, Putri? We heard about your health and it scared us. Is everything well now?' asked my concerned mother.

'Yes, Mother. However, there is something you need to know. And promise me that you will not react and patiently listen to everything I have to say.'

'What is it, Putri?'

I told mother everything about my discreet pregnancy and my decision to deliver the baby away from Lanka. As expected, mother was anxious. She feared for my father's reaction but I believed she would support my decision.

'Putri Mandodari, do you realize you are putting your and your unborn child's lives at great risk? Also, can you imagine how Dashaanan will react when he learns about your pregnancy and the fact that you lied to him about all this?'

'I know there is great risk involved, Mata. But this is what I choose to do. I don't want to terminate this pregnancy. And had I stayed there, I wouldn't have had the privilege to take my own decision. Hence, I sent a message across to Pitashri, asking him to cancel his visit to Lanka so I could come here instead.'

'And you think your father will allow you to keep such secrets from Dashaanan? For all we know Dashaanan will be enraged and might take strict action against you and perhaps against us and our kingdom as well. Why are you doing this, Putri? There is still time. I think you should inform Dashaanan immediately.' Mother declared and began to leave the room as if wanting to avoid further conversation.

'Mata, aren't you going to help me? I have come all the way here hoping that my parents will support my decision.' I appealed, expecting an affirmative response. However, mother was very clear and firm.

'You are the queen of Lanka; you have certain responsibilities towards your husband, your people and your family. We are your parents, but we expect you to fulfil your duties towards your title. We have taught you well. You have seen me fulfil my responsibilities as a queen. And what you ask today is against our principles. Moreover, it will invite terror to our kingdom.'

'Please let me explain myself to Pitashri once . . . he will listen to me.'

'He will undoubtedly listen to you, Putri. But let me assure you that his response will be no different than mine.

He will send you back with his guards or inform Dashaanan immediately. In no way will he let you keep this matter discreet!'

I felt disowned. My only hope for bringing my child safely into this world was being crushed. I cried with helplessness. Mother rushed to comfort me. 'Putri, I am sorry that we can't help you. Mayarastra is a small kingdom. Everyone knows how powerful and equipped Dashaanan is. If he comes to know about all this, he will destroy us. He might even kill your father.'

'No, Mata, I don't want to be the reason for any destruction. But what will I do, where will I go? I can't go back with this complicated pregnancy. I can't tell father and I can't stay here. I have no options.'

'You have come home to your parents. Eat well, take rest and sleep. I suggest that you don't tell your father or anyone else about this pregnancy. And if you have decided to bring this child into this world, I will guide you further.'

'Tell me, Mata, what should I do?'

'Not now, let me think about it. You will not start to show for two full moons at least. Till then I suggest you take proper nutrition, medication and precautions that my personal physician can recommend. You have Mai and your dasis to help you. My physician will train your dasis too and Mai is already an expert. Be ready to leave with your troops after two full moon cycles, and I shall tell you where you can deliver your child. I will ensure that everyone thinks you are continuing on your tirtha yatra.'

Two months passed and I instructed my dasis to organize my travel. The guards and the dasis were waiting to know the details of our next destination and I waited for my mother's guidance. I was about to show and had to leave before anyone grew suspicions about my physical appearance. I felt my child growing strong inside me.

'Mata, I plan to leave now. I haven't instructed the guards about my next destination yet. Tell me, Mata, where should I go?'

'Putri, keep your plans with regards to the pilgrimage. Go north to the tirthas of Badarikasrama. And then you shall return to the plains and deliver your child at an ashram. Mai knows the place, I have told her. We know a sage who keeps the ashram well maintained and will keep it equipped with all that you need for your comfort. Also, take only four of your guards. Instruct the other four to proceed towards the south and meet you on your way back to Lanka. That way you will have fewer eyes on you. Go now, Putri, be blessed and be safe.' Mata kissed my forehead and I took leave from her. I met Pitashri before leaving.

Pitashri sensed my troubles. He knew I had a distressed marriage, but couldn't interfere due to Dashaanan's status and power. He also knew I had huge responsibilities as a queen. But he never asked anything directly. I went into his chambers; for a change he was not at court that morning. He kept staring outside his balcony when I stepped inside to avoid eye contact. There were tears in his eyes. Without saying much, I embraced him and he gave me his blessings. This was the longest I had stayed with my parents after getting married. I said goodbye to my brothers and their wives, my nieces and nephews. And then I stepped into a chariot to proceed towards the north of Bharatvarsh.

We reached Badarikasrama after twenty-five days. Badarikasrama was considered the most sacred holy shrine, the abode of Narayana. It was believed that two saints named Nara and Narayana performed tough penance in these mountains. Our chariots couldn't climb the mountainous landscape so they were left behind in the valleys. I was shifted to a palanquin while others went on foot. I made fewer halts this time to ensure a timely return from the mountains to the plains. My belly had started to show. It was the sixth month of carrying my child in my womb and after this it would get difficult for me to travel to higher altitudes. I bathed in the holy waters of Alaknanda. I felt my soul and my mind cleansed. I felt my child protected by the positive energies I had gained.

I wished to travel more. The Himalayas housed more holy shrines, also considered to be the abode of Shiva. But Mai indicated that we had little time. The mountains were rough, cold and windy. Even though I sat free from harm inside a palanquin, it was not safe for me to travel further into the mountains. Hence, we started to descend. We proceeded towards the plains of Bharatvarsh. Descending from the mountains took less time. Mai took us to the secluded ashram hidden inside a forest in the plains. We settled there with the help of the sage my mother knew and had informed about my arrival. My clothes were arranged, my kitchen was set up and the guards were stationed outside to keep watch.

The seventh month was the most difficult time I had throughout my pregnancy. Mai felt that it was the result of too much travel and thinking. I suffered pains and restlessness.

'Mandodari, the way your child is making you restless, I feel you will deliver before time,' said Mai.

'Isn't that dangerous, Mai? Isn't it very soon? Do you think my child is healthy enough?' I was worried at the early indication.

'Listen, my princess, stop worrying so much. Yes, it is rare to deliver a child in the seventh month but not an impossibility. Your child is completely formed inside you by now.'

'How can you be so sure, Mai? What if this is a result of that poison I consumed? What if my body has started to give up?'

'Shhh . . . don't panic, my princess. Again, you are overthinking. I know you can't stop thinking but this could harm your child.'

'Mai, what do you feel? Will I have a daughter or a son?'

'Well, looking at you appearance, I think it's a girl.' I smiled at that reply because I had sensed it from the beginning.

'Mai, am I doing anything wrong? You know Dashaanan once told me that he wants a daughter to pamper and play with.'

'Putri, you are bringing your child into this world. There is nothing wrong in that. And you have decided well; once you deliver a healthy child, we shall inform Lankeshwar. He will be overjoyed and he will forget that you kept the news of your pregnancy from him.'

'But Mai, what if my child is not healthy?' This was the question that all of us had been avoiding so far. All of us who knew about my pregnancy were frightened to think about it. We kept it a secret for so long, made numerous excuses, made various arrangements because we all knew it was a great risk to bring this child healthy into this world.

'Well, we all know that you will have healthy children in the future. And as far as this child is concerned, let us leave it in the hands of god.'

※

The weather was hot and humid due to the drought-like condition in the area. I couldn't sleep peacefully. It was past midnight and my labour pains had begun. Mai was right. My child wanted to be born earlier than we expected. I felt a sudden thump inside my stomach and then a greasy liquid flowed down my legs. My water had broken! I stood up gathering all my might and roused a dasi. She in turn alerted Mai and the other dasis who were fast asleep. They forced me to lie down for some time, but I couldn't. I couldn't rest my back on the ground. We quietly stepped outside the ashram, walking past the guards who were fast asleep. I hurried towards the fields facing the ashram for some air. I wanted to scream. But I kept walking and the women followed me. I was conscious of making any noise. I was afraid that my shouts would alert the guards about my labour and they would want to know about my child's health.

I walked across the narrow fields with my remaining strength and at some distance saw a city. It was the city of

Mithila. I couldn't manage to take another step. Mai held my hand and I heard them talk. My body could no longer hold the child, I stood with my legs apart, my knees bearing the weight of my body.

'Your majesty, push . . . take a deep breath and push!', 'Putri Mandodari, you are doing well just push harder.'

And momentarily, right at dawn, I gave birth to a beautiful girl. I lay down to rest; the dasis cut the umbilical cord, cleaned the child and wrapped her in soft linen. Mai brought her to me and I held her in my arms. She was delicate; her face was golden like the rising sun. I touched her skin, felt her soft body. I touched her tiny fingers with mine; a black birthmark on her right hand above the elbow caught my attention. I smiled because I had something similar on my right hand too. My daughter, certainly she would be my replica.

'Putri Mandodari, she isn't crying. I can barely feel her heartbeats. Can you feel it?'

Suddenly I was taken aback. I panicked and held her closer to my chest, rubbed her feet and back. But I couldn't feel her heartbeat. The dasis tried too, but in vain. I kept her close to my chest hoping that she would live, but in vain. I cried, prayed to the gods to give her life. Nothing worked.

'Putri Mandodari, it is sunrise. Give me the child now. It is god's will.'

'Mai, what are you saying? She will live, I am not giving up on her!'

'I know how you feel. But we knew this from the beginning. Very soon, the people of the city will discover us. We have to leave.'

'I will not leave my child!'

'She is not with us, Putri. Give me the child; I will render her in Bhoomi Mata's womb. She will be amongst the gods.'

Mai took her away from me. She placed her in a wide earthen pot and covered it will linen. Then she dug some soil and buried the pot. I cried like I had never cried in my life. I prayed for my child's soul and left the spot.

We returned to the ashram and prepared to leave. I had turned to stone after the incident. I could only see my newborn's face in front of my eyes. I could still feel her delicate body in my arms. I wanted to rush back to the place where we had left her, to see if any miracle had brought her back to life. But Mai convinced me to gather myself. The next day, we began our journey back to Lanka.

ELEVEN

The days and nights meant nothing to me. I was still mourning for my child. It was a loss I could never be overcome. At first I had thought I could handle everything and had, therefore, planned to stay away from Lanka. I was aware of the circumstances; still, the grief was inconsolable.

It took us a month and more to reach the southern tip of Bharatvarsh. The guards whom we had asked to travel south were waiting for us there. But we had to deal with the ones who knew our secret. Although had instructed them to be discreet, we knew we would not have any control over them when they met the others. Hence, one of my dasis came up with a plan. She prepared a delicious meal for the guards and added poison to it. They were served their last meal and they slept, never to wake up again. Their bodies were buried in the same place.

We prayed for the murdered souls and proceeded in the direction where the other guards were waiting. We knew there was no other way to keep our secret safe. We had decided to announce that they had died as a result of consuming contaminated food and due to the unavailability of medication. With a stone-cold heart, I instructed my dasi to provide alms to the deceased guards' families.

At a distance we spotted a vimana, waiting for us with the remaining guards. Dashaanan had been informed about my return and he had sent a vimana to fly us back sooner. I took a final day's halt before boarding the vimana. Tents were erected and I decided to let go of my sad feelings. I took a long bath, sat in meditation and gathered myself before seeing Dashaanan again. Any change in my behaviour or appearance would make him suspicious. Hence, I ate a healthy meal and slept well before leaving the next day.

I was dressed and adorned in finery. I wore fine silk and draped exquisite stoles, and concealed my sorrows behind a smiling face. I stepped out of my pavilion and headed to Mai's. She wasn't going to fly with us. She said she was like a mother to me, a pillar of strength but it was not customary for a mother to stay with her married daughter for a long time. Also, she was required back at Mayarastra.

'You look beautiful. I am happy to see my princess like this!'

'Mai, should I tell Dashaanan about what happened? He is my husband, the father of my child . . . '

'For god's sake, Mandodari, if you wish for your married life to remain peaceful, then never mention anything to Lankeshwar.'

'But I am feeling guilty. I can hide my grief but how will I cover my guilt?'

'What is there to be guilty about?'

'The guilt that I kept a secret from my husband, the guilt that I gave birth to a daughter he longed for but he couldn't even see her or hold her!'

'You don't have a daughter. It's not like you have hidden her from him'

'But what if he had known? What if I had told Dashaanan and he had allowed me to deliver the baby? He might have discovered some remedy to keep my child safe . . . what if he could have kept her alive?'

'Stop feeling guilty. Rather make yourself strong. You cannot face Dashaanan with such a guilty state of mind!'

'How else should I face him then?'

'Consider it revenge! You have hidden this unfortunate phase of your life from him but he has hidden a lot from you. Remember his weakness for women. Remember his ego; he considers no one as great as him. Remember that he crushed your dream of a happy married life!'

'And avenge myself?'

'Yes, you have avenged yourself. He has touched several women with his lustful hands and so he wasn't fortunate enough to hold his own daughter with those hands!'

No matter how harsh her words were, she had released me of my guilt.

I stepped on to the vimana and flew towards Lanka.

*

As soon as the vimana landed, Dashaanan hurried towards me. He had a sparkle in his eyes.

'Welcome back, Mandodari. You look beautiful. I hope your tirtha yatra was fruitful,' he said, smiling.

'It was, my lord. Thank you for allowing me this privilege.'

'Well, you should rest now. I will visit you in your chambers tonight.'

I was greeted and welcomed like a warrior returning home from war. The women at the queen's palace lined up to offer their greetings. I had been away for almost nine months and the antapura was filled with new faces. This meant that Dashaanan had stocked new women for his bed in my absence. But sadly and as usual I didn't have a say.

Bajrajala, Sarama and Dhanyamalini waited outside my chambers to greet me, ready with their hysterical chatter. After the rough nine months of travel, medication, labour and loss, it was good to be back home finally.

Dashaanan visited my chambers that night. We talked for a very long time. Sadly, I had to alter all my stories about my travel. I avoided looking into his eyes for he was good at figuring out when I was lying to him.

'It feels as if you were gone for a decade!'

'I was gone for merely a few months, my lord.'

'Ah . . . then the days of the months must have increased.'

I smiled at his flattery. I asked him about the matters of court and progress of Lanka's projects.

'Well, about the matters of court, there is a lot that I need to tell you about.'

'What is it, my lord?'

'Our long time enemy Kartivya Arjuna, from the kingdom of Haihayas, tried to form an alliance with Indra. Kubera of all devas cautiously convinced Indra to decline the offer.'

'Their alliance would have been ominous for us.'

'Indeed; Kartivya Arjuna is a powerful king. Indra could have used him against me; however, Kubera didn't risk a new friendship against an old rival.'

'So we still have to be vigilant?'

'Yes, but we have to be more vigilant about the enemy hidden inside our kingdom. My ministers and I have a feeling that Dushtabuddhi is plotting something against me along with Kartivya Arjuna. Our sources have confirmed that Dushtabuddhi has travelled to Haihayas twice in the past few months. I have a feeling that Meenakshi knows about it too. I need you to ask Meenakshi about her husband's intentions.'

'Dushtabuddhi's intentions . . . but, my lord, sister Meenakshi wouldn't like it if I asked her directly about it. She might find it offensive.'

'That is why it's a personal matter more than a matter of court. I want you to gain her confidence so she confides in you.'

'What do you think he is up to, my lord?'

'It could be anything—to cause harm, destroy me or make me angry.'

'Now that I am back, my lord, nothing can cause you harm' I assured him.

I invited a few ladies from the antapura and the queen's palace for a gathering in my palace gardens. I wanted to meet everyone after my arrival. The gathering was also a way to invite Meenakshi into the common area so I could casually bring up Dushtabuddhi. All those invited soon started showing up and slowly the palace gardens were resounding with their chatter and giggles.

I met Trijata for the first time since my arrival.

'My greetings to you, your majesty,' she bowed.

'Why, Trijata, I was looking for you everywhere. Where had you disappeared? I sent my dasi to call you but there was no one at your house, she said.'

'I heard about your arrival. Sadly, I couldn't make it yesterday.' She looked weak; her eyes were swollen.

'Is everything all right, Trijata? You look . . .'

'I lost my child, your majesty,' she interrupted and tears ran down her face.

I was stunned. Suddenly my past flashed before my eyes. Fifty days had passed since I had lost my child on that unfortunate day. My wounds were still fresh.

'What? I am sorry for your loss, Trijata . . . How did it happen?'

'She was my first child, my only daughter, she was only four years old, your majesty. She had been ill for the past two months, and then a few days ago, her fever just wouldn't go down. I tried everything; Lankeshwar sent his own physician to help me. But we couldn't save her!'

I could relate to her sorrow. Deep down in my conscience, I was still mourning for my stillborn child. And poor Trijata, who had been through several miscarriages in the last year, had lost her only surviving child. Gods were cruel to her. While she longed for another child, she was deprived of her first child too.

'There is nothing I can do to lessen your grief, all I can say is . . . we are sailing in the same boat. I have lost my child too. Let us pray for their souls.'

I relieved Trijata of her duties for a few days so she could cope with her loss. I glanced around to see those who were present; I did not see Nayanadini, my husband's new wife, whom I hadn't met since my return. I turned towards the noisy group of women seated beside me and spotted Meenakshi. She had a certain innocence about her. I was sure that she knew nothing about Dushtabuddhi's plot against Dashaanan because she loved and respected her brother. I managed to get a private moment with her.

'Bhabhi Mandodari, I am so glad you arranged this gathering to meet us . . . tell us about your journey. Any interesting places that you visited?' asked Meenakshi.

'I did . . . I have a lot to tell you, sister Meenakshi. After visiting my parents at Mayarastra, I took a journey towards Badarikasrama to perform my pilgrimage duties. It was beautiful! The mountains, flora, birds and the waters . . . everything was heavenly. You know . . . I feel you should visit the north of Bharatvarsh sometime.'

'Maybe sometime, Bhabhi Mandodari,' replied Meenakshi with a less cheerful face now.

'Is everything all right, sister Meenakshi? Are you happy in your marriage?'

'Oh, certainly, it is only that sometimes he gets very secretive. Vidyutjihva tries his best to keep me happy, but some ministers from the Kalkeya clan are trying to influence him, I feel.'

'Influence him? In what way? Have you spoken to him about this?'

'No, I haven't. But everyone knows that our marriage didn't please the king. My husband wasn't happy with the new name given to him. His community also didn't take it well. Things were not pleasant between Lankeshwar and the Kalkeya clan and now this insult of their prince has enraged them.'

'But Lankeshwar has been kind enough to appoint Vidyutjihva as one of his ministers. I hope he appreciates this and forgets the past.'

'Is that enough, bhabhi? Vidyutjihva is a fearsome warrior; he can guide an army but is limited to serve as a minister in my brother's court.'

'I don't mean to be impolite but if your husband is not happy with the position given to him, shouldn't he say something to Dashaanan?'

'I am afraid that bhrata Dashaanan will not consider his request. And hence, my husband gets concerned and secretive about his feelings.'

I concluded that Meenakshi was a naïve person and knew nothing about Dushtabuddhi's true intentions. I showed her some empathy but was certain that Dushtabuddhi was hiding something from her, and it wasn't just about his position.

The next morning I entered the court when Dashaanan was busy planning something with his ministers and advisers.

He was seated in the centre, writing something on a scroll with a feather. I wanted to tell him about the conversation I had had with Meenakshi.

'Ah . . . Rani Mandodari! There is something I need to show you!'

'My lord, I wanted to speak to you in private.'

'All right, but first, why don't you come here and have a look at this chart I prepared? This is a horoscope and the details below indicate the auspicious time, the auspicious day and a few other details of birth.'

'A birth chart and a horoscope . . . whose is it my lord?'

'It will be our son's horoscope,' he said proudly.

I gulped nervously. 'Our son?'

'Yes, our son . . . this is probably the first time in history that someone has planned a child's birth. And why not? We have knowledge, calculations and the skill to do so.'

'My lord, you are aware that I have not studied astrology and I am not very sure how you can create the horoscope of an unborn child.'

'Let me explain, Mandodari. When a child is born, it is possible to sketch a horoscope and birth chart according to the day, time and place with the help of planetary positions. I have reversed that process and created a horoscope so our son is a born maharathi. He will be knowledgeable; he will be a master of all weapons and strategies. He will be the perfect son to a perfect father.'

'My lord, I don't distrust your calculations but how can you be sure that a son will be born?'

Dashaanan smiled at my question. 'Dearest Mandodari, it is simply a calculation derived from our horoscopes. And also, as per your horoscope, it shows a period of one year where you may suffer a fatal pregnancy; however, that period has passed and now we can predict that the child born will be a son.'

I sighed with relief. Dashaanan didn't point out anything unusual regarding my past year.

'What can I say, my lord . . . I am eager to see if all these predictions can actually come true.'

'Well, why do you doubt?' asked Dashaanan and smiled at Nanashri. 'In order to ensure that these calculations work, we already have the planetary positions in our control. The mentors who read planets are under my direction. The navagraha gurus—they are my captive guests till I have achieved what I want to.'

'I regret to say this . . . but Lankeshwar, is it fair to use their siddhi for personal benefit?' I couldn't help but point out his mistakes.

Dashaanan turned angrily and it was clear that he wouldn't entertain any objections from me in this matter. 'We have discussed this before, Mandodari. And whatever it is that you wish to talk about, I shall meet you in the queen's court privately.'

I quietly made an exit and waited to meet him. He was foul-tempered when he entered and I was careful not to aggravate it further. I told him how sister Meenakshi wasn't aware of Dushtabuddhi's intentions and warned him that he may be up to something because he operated discreetly.

'What can Dushtabuddhi possibly plan?'

'I will find out soon, Mandodari. I will ask Khara to monitor his actions. For now, I am glad that he hasn't incited Meenakshi against me.'

'Also, I want to apologize for my sudden reaction at the court. I don't mean to interfere much but I just feel it's unfair to keep the gurus captive like that. Their wrath can cause destruction.'

'They are kept as guests and not prisoners. You should not worry about them. Also, not all of them are captive. It angers me when you fail to understand my motives, Mandodari. I am planning the birth of my son and I want the planetary positions to be perfect. I don't want my son to struggle like I did. My childhood and youth were ravaged by a constant struggle to uplift my people. I fought for my rights, my education, my caste, my clan and my family. Hence, I want my son to have all advantages. Do you still think I am wrong?'

'My lord, my perception may be limited; you have justified your actions and I don't think you are wrong as a father.'

No matter how wrong his actions were, his motive did convince me that he was a father wishing a perfect life for his son.

TWELVE

The flowers on the trees outside my veranda had blossomed. I stood at my bedroom window that gave me a good view of the trees, admiring the colours of the freshly opened buds. My dasi rushed into my room to convey the confirmation given by my physician. She looked happier than I. This time we didn't have to hide it. This time there were no secrets and the news delighted everyone.

I rested my palm on my stomach. A child had been budding in my womb for the past two months but I couldn't feel it communicating with me yet. Mata Kaikesi said it was too early to expect any connection or feel any movement. But I couldn't tell her that a child inside my womb previously did connect with her mother at such an early stage too. The word spread and everyone celebrated. The women at the queen's palace were joyful; streets were decked up and the skies at night were set ablaze with fireworks.

Dashaanan ensured that I had every comfort and luxury in my chambers. I was relieved from my duties as court regent for a few months. The women in the queen's palace were advised not to discuss anything terrifying when I was around. I was happy to get Dashaanan's attention. He cared for me like never before. In my thoughts I always wondered how different it would have been if I had told him about my first pregnancy. Some physicians had ways to determine the gender of child; however, I was sure it would be a boy because I was feeling the opposite of how I had felt before.

Soon, with a growing belly, my distance from my husband grew as well. Bedding a wife with child was forbidden by physicians. As a result, Dashaanan started spending his nights with the other women in the antapura. But he was careful not to distress me. He visited me every day and kept his whereabouts discreet during the evenings. He was trying to respect me by not openly announcing his infidelity with other women. And in return, I never asked him details of his whereabouts in the evenings.

Time flew by and I was three weeks away from my due delivery. Sarama and Bajrajala arranged a small ceremonial gathering wherein royal women would present me with gifts and bless the expected child. Mata Kaikesi brought a bow and arrow made of gold to bless the heir with immense valour and warrior skills. Meenakshi brought a decorated cradle. Anaala brought fine clothes, whereas Sarama and Bajrajala brought various toys for the expected one. Dhanyamalini presented me with a necklace made of ivory charms. She said people in her tribe believed it would provide strength to the woman wearing it during childbirth. Then there were a few royal women from other kingdoms who gave me gifts as well. At last came Nayanadini, who always kept herself at a distance from me.

She somehow ensured that in spite of living in the same palace, we wouldn't cross each other's path or share the same roof at any point of time.

'I congratulate you and present you with a few gifts from my native land,' said Nayanadini and bowed slightly as if she didn't mean to bow at all.

'I will be obliged to receive them,' I replied cordially.

She gestured towards four pretty women standing at a distance. 'These are Naga women who live near my native land. They can dance, sing and entertain you. Accept them as your dasis or women in waiting.'

'Well, Nayanadini, that's a rare gift. However, these women don't seem like dasis. Why don't you ask them to join the courtesans if they can dance well?'

She smiled wryly, 'Well, my queen, they are willing to serve you as dasis and do not wish anything more. Accept them, for they have been trained to serve you well.'

I already had plenty of dasis and chambermaids attending to me. Adding four more seemed crowded and needless. However, this was the first gift from the far-east princess and I decided to accept whatever would bring harmony to our relationship.

'All right, princess, I accept your gift. I am thankful to you,' I replied and thanked everyone who attended the ceremony.

I tried to kill time with various activities. Since my due date was very close, the physicians advised me to observe complete rest and avoid going outdoors. I lay in my room passing most of my time writing letters to my mother, father and Mai at Mayarastra. I asked them to visit us and bless their grandchild in person. Some of my dasis brought games of dice in my room to engage me. Others brought palace gossip for my entertainment.

Monsoon was expected any time and so was our child. One morning while bathing, I felt a huge thump inside my belly and the impact forced me to stand. The attendants rushed me inside a room and the physicians were alerted. No sooner had my child tried to force himself out than the clouds started thundering. A midwife was called and Dashaanan was informed. The heir of Lanka was ready to be born.

I was in labour till evening. The pain was much more than I had experienced earlier. I clenched my teeth and tried to breathe deeply to release the pain. My daughter's face was still clear in my mind. I began to wonder if it was really that painful the first time and I knew it was not. I blinked again and saw the little girl I had once seen in my dreams. She was smiling at me and pointed towards something. But I blinked again and she disappeared. I was in the midst of excruciating cramps and hallucinations.

'Your majesty, you are doing fine. Just push harder once again!' yelled the midwife.

'Your majesty, keep breathing,' said the physician.

Each time I pushed harder thinking that it was the end of it. But this child gave me a tough time. The clouds were thundering throughout and then we heard a loud bang indicating that lightning had struck somewhere.

I closed my eyes for some time and then saw a woman dressed in black antelope skin. It was the same woman who had appeared in my dreams earlier; her hair was open this time and she was angry. She turned towards me and I heard her saying, 'A woman will be the reason for your death and that woman will be me!'

I opened my eyes in terror and heard noises in the room again. The sky was terrorized by lightning too. The thundering was as bad as my labour.

'Once again, your majesty, push harder . . . this is it!'

I pushed with all my might and heard the wailing of a baby a few seconds later.

I saw the midwife take the baby in her arms and my dasi hurriedly announced, 'Your majesty, it's a boy! You have a son!'

The midwife declared his birth outside the room. 'Rani Mandodari has given birth to a boy.'

I heard Dashaanan asking her, 'My son! How is he?'

'My lord, he is beautiful. He is healthy and strong. Even the thundering clouds couldn't drown out the sound of his cries!'

Dashaanan sounded overjoyed, 'How is my queen?'

'She is tired at the moment. Your son gave her a rough time but she is a strong-willed woman,' replied the midwife.

'You have brought me the news I was waiting to hear. I will bestow you with gifts that you cannot count! I want to see my son now . . . '

Dashaanan entered the room to see us. Instead of our son, he walked towards me first.

'How are you feeling, my queen?'

'I am delighted, my lord. You wanted a son and you have him now!'

'I have him because of you!'

'I thought you couldn't wait to see your son . . .'

'I can't! But I wanted to thank you first.'

'My lord, I can't express how honoured I feel right now!'

He took our son in his arms and I saw a glimmer in his eyes. He was proud.

'My son and the supreme heir of Lanka! A boy whose cry is the sound of thunder . . . I name him Meghanath!'

I observed a small period of confinement after Meghanath's birth. I breastfed him twice a day and the remaining time he was fed by a wet nurse. Queens were restricted to feeding their babies so they were free to resume their duties soon after the confinement period. During this period, Dashaanan was not allowed to visit my chambers. We had to observe distance with regards to physical intimacy until the confinement was over.

Our little son soon became a favourite pastime for the ladies at the palace. Everyone sought new tricks to make the baby smile and giggle. This new phase of motherhood in my life had diminished the unpleasant memories of the past. In between the smiles and giggles of my baby, I discovered a new side of my personality. I became more alert, much more caring and gentle. I was amazed at my ability to sense different feelings. I knew when he was about to cry and I sensed when he wanted me around.

Dashaanan visited Meghanath every evening after court, and I was happy to see a different side of him. He spoke to him as if the little one could actually understand what he was saying and little Meghanath would look straight into his father's eyes as if he followed everything.

One such evening, my little son and I waited for Dashaanan in the garden. But that evening he skipped our meeting. When I asked my dasi to enquire about his whereabouts, she returned with a hesitant look on her face. Dashaanan was on his way to meet us when he was distracted by some scantily clad women playing in a pond. Those women were none other than the maids brought by Nayanadini. They wanted to draw his attention by luring him.

I was furious. Clearly they were working on the instructions of someone else. I went straight towards Nayanadini's chambers to confront her.

Nayanadini was playing a game of dice with her dasis when I stormed into her chambers. She stood up slowly, bowed slightly like she usually did—with condescension.

'What a pleasant surprise! Would you like to join us for a game of dice, your highness?'

'No, thank you! That's not what I am here for . . . '

'Well then, how I can help you, Rani Mandodari?' she asked loftily—something I had never liked about her.

'Those dasis that you presented as gifts to me . . . what kind of girls have you brought to serve us?'

'Well, I hear they are serving the king quite well . . .' said Nayanadini with the most vicious smile I had ever seen on a woman.

'How dare you! You seem to have planned all this! What kind of tricks are you playing with him?'

'The same kind of tricks that you always play with me . . . '

'You must be insane. Which tricks have I ever played with you?'

'You don't remember? You have always tried to lure my husband away from me. You have played your tricks from the very first night of my marriage when you kept him engaged for the whole night and I kept waiting for him!'

'I didn't keep him away from you! He came to me on his own. On the contrary, I told him that he should be with you! And don't forget . . . he is my husband too.'

'You don't need to play innocent with me. I understand you envy me and that's the reason you always try to draw his attention towards yourself. You must be so insecure. However, you need to understand that our husband needs a change in his appetite. And most importantly, he needs a change from you! Also, what better timing than when he cannot sleep with you; consider us even now.'

'It is a pity that you think this way. I thought you are arrogant but graceful enough to understand how things work when you got married to a king. But I was wrong!'

'You call me arrogant? Certainly you are not aware of the immense dowry that came along with me! A lot more than you, I hear . . . '

'Choose your words carefully, Nayanadini! Your union with the king may have got him wealth but certainly you can't love him the way I do. It's a shame that you planned such a deceitful act to make your own husband bed some petty whores. And all that because you wanted to avenge yourself for that first night and consider yourself even with me.'

I wanted to say much more but I knew there was no point in engaging with a woman so envious and arrogant.

'Think about what you have done, Nayanadini. You envy other wives of your husband but you are ready to share him with women below your status,' I said and walked out.

Dhanyamalini was furious when she heard about Nayanadini's misbehaviour. 'You shouldn't have been so lenient with her. Dismiss her dasis; ban her from the queen's palace and even the court for that matter,' she suggested. She was pacing furiously in front of me.

'I cannot do that. Other women at the antapura will make up stories about how I tried to oppress my husband's new wife. Also, I hardly feel bad about what she has done. I am concerned about his reputation; about the gossip that the king is sleeping with the queen's dasis!'

'I hope she learns the difference between sharing a husband with other wives and sharing a husband with whores. First, we had women from the antapura and now our own dasis are available to him. But don't you worry . . . we will figure out a way to keep Lankeshwar away from those girls,' said Dhanyamalini.

I was relieved after my discussion with her. She was genuine in her concern.

'I don't know how to say this but I am thankful to you, Dhanyamalini. When you came into our lives, I never expected to share such a bond with you.'

She smiled, 'I told you . . . I will be like a sister to you. But now we need to be careful of our new sister! First, let me make arrangements to send her so-called 'serving gifts' back to where they came from.' We smiled at each other like two friends and I went back to my chambers to tend to my little one.

My confinement period was about to end in a week's time. Dashaanan had announced that he would perform a yagna to purify us after the confinement and called astrologers to interpret Meghanath's horoscope. The yagna was to be followed by a formal announcement about the newborn heir. A royal feast was being arranged for the masses to celebrate his birth.

After the incident with Nayanadini's dasis, I met Dashaanan directly at the yagna. He visited Meghanath in between those days during my absence. He obviously wanted to avoid my reaction at his indecent actions. Without looking at him directly, I walked with my son in my arms and sat next to Dashaanan for the rituals.

Guru Shukracharya performed the rituals for us and made a formal announcement in the kingdom to declare Meghanath the prince. Everyone from the family showered their blessings on our son. Next, we gathered at court to hear predictions about Meghanath's horoscope. Numerous claims were made by all the astrologers present to impress Dashaanan.

'Impeccable timing of birth . . . his *kundli* shows that he will be an invincible warrior!' said a voice from one corner.

'Atimaharathi yoga in his horoscope . . . just like you wished for, your highness,' said another.

'He will defeat your enemies . . . will always obey his father.'

The claims were getting too ambitious till Guru Shukracharya pointed out something from the horoscope, 'Only one thing may need caution at a certain time . . . no doubt he will excel and conquer his enemies, but the way Shani is positioned during his birth, it may bring him some misfortune.'

There was silence in the court. Dashaanan's proud smile, which hadn't left his face since morning, suddenly faded.

'I regret but . . . Shani during his birth was positioned in his twelfth house. As a result, he may lose his life while facing an enemy at a certain point,' explained Shukracharya.

Dashaanan became furious and ordered his prime minister, 'Mahamantri, release the lords of navagraha from the tower except for Shanidev! Keep him captive till he repents what he has done . . .'

I objected, 'My lord, I request you to withdraw your command.'

'Mandodari, stay out of this!' shouted Dashaanan.

'No, my lord, I will not stay out of this matter any more. You told me the purpose of holding the navagraha mentors captive is to gain their influence for your benefit. You tried to force your will on them but it seems it hasn't worked. You wanted a son with impressive supremacy and you have one. But you can't control every event of his life. Let him design his own fate.'

'I trust my son, but I will not let anyone play with his destiny. If Shanidev has been too rebellious to support me, then I will show him how rebellious I am . . . '

'I request you one last time, my lord. I have never opposed any decision of yours expect in case of the navagraha gurus. I beseech you . . . withdraw your command given in anger. Do not invite the wrath of those deities. They may have supreme powers to influence ones destiny but they cannot change what's written. As a mark of respect, release them all now!' I appealed stronger than ever to convince him.

'It is for your concern for them that I am going to release them. And remember that this is the first and the last time that I have let someone go because of your appeal.' And so the navagraha gurus were set free.

THIRTEEN

Seasons changed and the months passed by swiftly. Meghanath turned three years old in no time. Nayanadini became a mother too. Her son was named Prahasta and had just begun walking. Dhanyamalini, sadly, couldn't conceive yet and there were rumours that her womb was barren. Dashaanan discovered a solution to that as well. He prescribed medicines and treatment to boost her fertility and she followed it with utmost discipline. In a few months, her obedient efforts bore results. She got pregnant and delivered a son to Dashaanan too. He was named Atikaya.

Our differences as co-wives never influenced the affection amongst our children. Meghanath was the eldest and never differentiated between any of his brothers. They ate meals together, played together and sometimes even slept together. Meghanath was four years old when Nayanadini and Dhanyamalini were expecting their second children. Dashaanan wished to see a daughter this time since he had sons from all three of us. But both gave birth to sons again. Dhanyamalini's second son was named Trishir and Nayanadini gave birth to twin brothers Narantaka and Devantaka.

Once Meghanath turned five, he was introduced to the scriptures and texts. He started learning different languages too. Guru Shukracharya started teaching him the secrets of warfare. When he turned six, I gave birth to another son—Akshayakumara. Akshayakumara was the prettiest of all our sons. He was the youngest prince. In addition to seven sons from his three wives, Dashaanan also had a few illegitimate children from the other women of the antapura. Surprisingly, none gave birth to a girl and Dashaanan's longing remained unfulfilled.

With seven children growing up together in the queen's palace, we never had a dull day. Nothing much changed over the years. My duties as a regent and queen remained unchanged, my association with the family members remained stable, and so did my relationship with my husband. We had our differences over the years, especially when Dashaanan talked about his illegitimate children from other women.

Nayanadini had become much calmer than before. In between responsibilities of her three children and the constant pursuit of Dashaanan's favours, she had lost her ability to create troubles. We still spoke to each other only on occasions, and if required. Also, we only spoke to each other publicly in order to avoid any unwanted gossip from other women in the palace.

As co-wives, Dhanyamalini, Nayanadini and I spent most of the time parenting our children together. We took a planned approach to our responsibilities of supervising their studies and learning. I took care of their studies related to literature, the Vedas and the shastras. Nayanadini and Dhanyamalini supervised their lessons in the arts, music and statesmanship.

Our children were as brilliant as Dashaanan. At the age of eleven, Meghanath had not only learnt but mastered all the weapons and warfare strategies from Guru Shukracharya. He was also knowledgeable about politics. He took a keen interest in occult science. He also mastered the art of sorcery and magic. Meghanath was indisputably his father's favourite.

The other children too developed different talents. Prahasta, along with Dhanyamalini's son Trishir, learnt unique combat skills. Atikaya mastered archery and could shoot five arrows at a time. He learnt secret mantras to invoke divine weapons. At the age of ten, Dashaanan gave him an invincible armour, which was won by him and Kumbakarna when they had performed penance for Prajapati Brahma's favours. Dashaanan was a proud father seeing his children developing talents at such an early age.

※

One day, we received an invitation for a *swayamwar* at our court. Nanashri read the correspondence written on a scroll. A swayamwar was the practice of choosing a husband for one's daughter by inviting prospective suitors from neighbouring or overseas kingdoms. Mainly, the suitors were asked to participate in some kind of contest to win the bride. A father who wished to wed his daughter to the most suitable man would host a swayamwar and send invites to all possible suitors. The bride would then choose her husband from among those participants.

Along with the scroll, came a long and heavy arrow wrapped in a blue velvet case. There were other pleasantries that accompanied the invite too—dried fruits of various kinds, essential oils and an embroidered silk stole for the king or prince who would participate in the swayamwar. We were anxious to know the host as a swayamwar was an expensive event. I sat next to Dashaanan observing the details. Nanashri pulled the arrow out of its fancy cover and presented it.

'At first I thought it is polished, but this arrow is made of *panchdhatu*—an alloy of five metals,' said Nanashri and handed it over to Dashaanan.

'Indeed, and it is heavier than it usually is. Who brought the invite?' asked Dashaanan.

'Two guards along with their minister. The invite comes from the king of Mithila—popularly known as Raja Janaka of the Videha region,' answered Nanashri.

'Raja Janaka from Mithila . . . Well, I am impressed with the invitation. But why would someone only send an arrow without a bow? Does it symbolize something?' asked Dashaanan.

'It sure does, my lord!'

'Hmm . . . so what does the invite say, Nanashri?'

'Raja Janaka has sent his humble invitation to Lankeshwar Ravana. He is hosting a swayamwar for his daughter and is requesting your honourable presence. His beloved eldest daughter Sita turns thirteen this year. He says his beautiful daughter possesses the greatest of womanly virtues and is now of marriageable age. The swayamwar will be held for three consecutive days and includes a contest. The winner of this contest will be considered eligible to marry his daughter,' said Nanashri.

'Considered eligible? So the contest does not guarantee a wedding?' asked Vibhishana.

The minister from Mithila stepped forward and bowed. 'I am honoured to present this invite to the mighty emperor Ravana on behalf of my king—Janaka of Mithila. Kindly accept the invitation.'

Dashaanan nodded in appreciation.

'My lord, are you considering it?' I asked Dashaanan in a hushed tone. I was certain that Dashaanan wouldn't take another wife and that an alliance with the kingdom of Mithila did not interest him much.

'I am not sure. Let us hear about it anyway,' said Dashaanan in the same tone.

'Is it true? Winning this contest does not guarantee a wedding and the winner will merely be considered eligible. Isn't that against the rules of a swayamwar?' Vibhishana asked again.

The minister added, 'My lords, my king has a condition in this contest. Whoever wins the contest first will be considered most eligible. However, his daughter will have a final decision to choose her husband. Hence . . .'

'That means she can reject the first winner and so on until she wishes to!' said Nanashri.

'No, my lord, my king believes that the contest is not so easy. He invites the most valorous kings and princes for the competition, but he is certain that there will only be a couple of victorious participants among the suitors,' said the minister.

'What is the contest?' asked Dashaanan.

'In order to win princess Sita's hand in marriage, the contestant must overcome the task of stringing a bow,' said the minister; there were titters in the court.

Nanashri lifted his palm indicating silence. 'String a bow! Is that what this competition is all about?' he asked, amused.

The minister from Mithila answered, 'It is not an ordinary bow, my lord! It was gifted to Raja Janaka by the great warrior sage Parasurama. It was perfectly crafted by none other than the celestial architect and craftsman, Vishwakarma. And my lord, the bow belongs to none other than the supreme lord, Mahadeva Shiva!'

Dashaanan was stunned to hear about Shiva's bow. His eyes narrowed in a semi-conscious state as if he was imagining the bow in front of him. The other gentry in the court, who were critical of the contest, lowered their voices.

I knew that the swayamwar fascinated my husband very much. I asked him once again, 'My lord, what are you thinking about? You aren't participating, are you?' But he ignored my question.

The minister further added, 'My king believes that only a true Shiva bhakta can lift this great bow and string its enormous ends. Hence, instead of a mere announcement and propaganda, he sent me to personally invite the great Lankesh who is not only Shiva's parambhakt but also a conqueror of the three worlds. Disciple of Shiva, defeater of Indra, Lankapati Ravana!'

Dashaanan was impressed by the grandeur of the words used for him. I knew there was no way I could stop him now.

'Who are the other suitors invited by your king?' asked Vibhishana.

'Nearby as well as faraway, all the greatest kings and princes from various Brahmin, deva, rakshasa and Kshatriya clans have been invited.'

'Well, tell your king that I have accepted his invitation! And that I will be arriving on the last day of the swayamwar. Also, I will send a representative to express my gratitude towards him,' announced Dashaanan.

I couldn't wait to state my disapproval. I found a private moment with him to talk, 'My lord, Mithila is not even an equal to consider alliance, then what reason would you have this time to marry another woman?

'Haven't you heard, Mandodari? They have a bow that belongs to Mahadeva!'

'No, it is not about the bow! You possess so many weapons yourself and it is certainly not the bow that lures you to the swayamwar. You want another woman, don't you?'

'All I am concerned about is Shiva's bow. I have to bring it to Lanka. If any king can possess that celestial bow of Shiva, then it has to be me! Vibhishana, I want you to represent Lanka at the swayamwar before I arrive there. Take our guards along with you and ensure that the celestial bow they talk about is indeed worth winning.'

'But bhrata Dashaanan, why do you want to attend it on the last day? What if someone wins the contest already?' asked Vibhishana.

'If the bow they talk about is indeed that grand, then I am sure it will not be easy to win that contest. And also, I want to see who all are contesting as suitors. It is not appropriate for an emperor like me to line up in a petty contest. However, I am sure I will bring that bow with me. Mahadeva will never let me fail at this,' said Dashaanan arrogantly.

Vibhishana lowered his face against Dashaanan's egoistic claims, 'Very well then, my lord. I shall leave for the swayamwar accordingly with your favours and will ensure that all the arrangements are satisfactory.'

None of the wives took Dashaanan's decision well. Dhanyamalini rushed to his chambers to express her disapproval but Dashaanan didn't heed any of her arguments. Nayanadini was distressed too. My dasis overheard palace gossip that she was so offended by Dashaanan's decision that she threw at him whatever object she could get hold of in her room. I wondered why Nayanadini was so offended by the news. Dashaanan had other wives she knew, but she may have expected to be the last one. She took pleasure in being the newest; the king's last wife who contented him the most and after her, he needed no more. But sadly, Dashaanan wasn't a man whose desires could ever be fulfilled.

He met me the night before he left. 'Are you still angry with me, Mandodari? I wanted to talk to you before leaving.'

'I used to be . . . I don't get angry any more,' I replied.

'You understand why I am doing this, don't you?'

'I don't think I do, my lord . . . but let us leave it there. Lanka is prosperous, we have children and our family is progressing. This time we don't need any allies, and if we do, then certainly not Mithila. You have two other wives, and a variety of woman in the antapura to satisfy your desires. And you still want to marry another woman? I fail to understand you, Lankeshwar.'

'Do you really think I want to marry that woman? I just want to win the contest for that bow, which belongs to my Shiva.'

'And after you win the contest, the prize is that woman Sita . . . the bow is not the prize, my lord!'

'I haven't thought about that yet!'

'So what have you decided, Lankeshwar? You will win that contest and king Janaka will let you walk out of his kingdom without marrying his daughter? I know you, my lord, you wouldn't mind getting her along with you.'

'I don't understand; you envy a woman that I have never seen!'

'So you think I envy her! I don't envy any woman any more, my lord. I have never objected to your visits to the antapura. I don't care that you have illegitimate children with other women. All I care about is our family, our position and your reputation.'

'I am leaving tomorrow, Mandodari. I shall be back in two or three days. If you care about me and my aspirations, then wish me luck. I will bring Mahadeva's bow with me,' said Dashaanan and walked out.

Palace women and dasis discussed the outcome of the swayamwar. When Dashaanan left, they were prepared to receive the king's latest wife into the queen's palace. For me, somehow, it made no difference. I just wished that Dashaanan would come back soon without any accusations or allegations against him.

Dashaanan and Vibhishana returned after three days. Except Nayanadini and I, all the women from the palace went to receive them. I waited in my chambers to receive the news. Wondering if he actually married once more, I kept pacing my chambers but heard nothing. After sometime, my dasi reported back to me and she finally said what I was waiting to hear.

'There was no woman on that vimana. Only Lankeshwar, a few ministers and guards stepped out. Also, Lankeshwar headed straight to his palace. He was not looking pleased.' she said.

What must have happened? It certainly meant Dashaanan didn't win the contest. I asked my dasi if she saw a bow or anything else that was treated with extra care, but she had seen nothing. I wanted to rush to Dashaanan and ask him everything, but I knew it would enrage him. Instead, I summoned Vibhishana to ask him the details.

※

Vibhishana narrated the events of the swayamwar to Dhanyamalini, Mata Kaikesi and me. He explained the luxurious arrangements for accommodation made by king Janaka. He mentioned that it did not please king Janaka that

Lankapati Ravana had decided to attend the swayamwar only on the last day. The others present found Lankeshwar very arrogant and neglectful. Although they didn't get to see Sita, everyone had a high opinion of her beauty and virtue. The bow that belonged to Shiva was the most valued possession of her father.

'It came as a surprise that Sita was an adopted daughter. King Janaka avoided the subject throughout the swayamwar but when matters started getting out of control, someone from the crowd brought it up,' said Vibhishana.

'So she is an adopted child? Who are her real parents then?' I asked.

'No one knows. The locals say the king found Sita while performing a yagna. The Videha region once went through a severe drought for three consecutive years but the day Janaka found Sita, it rained like the gods were pleased.'

'Tell us what happened when Lankesh arrived there. Did he participate in that contest?' asked Dhanyamalini. And Vibhishana narrated further.

'Yes, he participated. By the time Lankesh arrived at the swayamwar, close to a hundred suitors had already tried stringing the bow. Shiva's bow was more magnificent than what we had imagined. One by one the suitors lined up to win the princess, however, no one succeeded. They could not even lift the bow, leave alone stringing it. Some participants accused Janaka of deceit, whereas some others took it as an offence. When Lankesh stepped into that courtyard, needless to say, he needed no introduction. He walked towards the chariot where the bow was placed, mocking the other suitors for their failure. He went for the weapon at once and held it firmly with his right hand; he took a deep breath and closed his eyes in devotion. I admired his potency; he lifted the bow above his shoulder. Everyone present watched without blinking their eyes—some feared his might and some applauded. But shortly, after Lankesh couldn't control the bow any more and dropped it back to its place.'

We took time to respond, 'So, Lankesh didn't try it the second time?' I asked.

'He tried, but failed. Just like the other participants, he couldn't move it,' said Vibhishana.

'But he did lift it! No one before him did that,' said Dhanyamalini.

'The terms of the contest were very clear; the bow had to be strung, not just lifted. Hence, Lankesh failed at the task. His failure raised mockery and laughter amongst the spectators. The previous participants momentarily forgot their own failure and joined in mocking him. Lankesh got infuriated by this public humiliation. Without saying a word, he folded his hands in devotion to the bow and decided to walk out of the venue,' said Vibhishana.

We were all speechless, unsure if we should breathe a sigh of relief or feel sorry for Dashaanan.

'How is he taking it now? I mean whatever happened at the swayamwar, did he say anything about it?' I asked.

'No, bhabhi, he didn't say a word to anyone. He was so enraged that I didn't want to infuriate him further by talking about it.'

I knew what Vibhishana feared. He could have easily been the scapegoat for Dashaanan's anger. 'Hmm . . . You are right. Let us make Lankesh forget about what happened. We don't want him to get mad at Janaka or the others and seek any sort of revenge.'

'But tell me one thing: did any one actually win that contest?' asked Dhanyamalini.

'Yes, after we walked out and started on our journey back, we heard from the natives that a Kshatriya prince from Ayodhya successfully tied strings on both ends of that bow. However, later we heard that he even broke it while performing the task,' said Vibhishana.

I decided to talk to Dashaanan about what had happened at Mithila. It was important to know how he felt about it, whether or not he was still smarting from the insult. He was in his room, looking out of the window when I entered.

'Where were you yesterday, Mandodari? Why didn't you come to see me?'

'I thought you needed sometime for yourself. I am sorry about what happened . . . I heard about it from bhrata Vibhishana.'

'You didn't want me to go . . . '

'Yes, my lord, but I didn't wish for you to lose at that contest. I was concerned about the marriage, not the contest!'

'And I went there for the contest, for the bow. I failed, Mandodari. I was nothing but a pompous man that day. I was about to seize his weapon but I didn't even pay respects to Mahadeva. There was a brief moment before I held that bow in my hand, I closed my eyes to visualize my lord, but he did not look pleased. He wasn't pleased at my impudence. I still went ahead and lifted it, but it pulled me back.'

'Forget about it, my lord, don't think about it any more now.'

'I cannot forget the mockery and laughter that followed.'

'It was not meant to belong to you . . .'

'My devotion towards my lord didn't change. Do you think it was my arrogance that failed me? How have I changed, Mandodari?'

I realized that more than the humiliation or the failure, Dashaanan struggled to understand the person he had become. 'Arrogance is now one of your characteristics, Lankeshwar, and it makes you who you are.'

FOURTEEN

Lanka's stability and sovereignty started causing disputes with its enemies. Not only were there enemies outside the kingdom but also inside its boundaries. Dashaanan's ministers were concerned about Dushtabuddhi's behaviour. Dushtabuddhi was one person in the family whose relationship didn't prosper with anyone. Dashaanan disliked him from the beginning and due to Dushtabuddhi's actions over the years, he hated him even more now. All these years his antics were ignored; however, now he took advantage of our feigned ignorance even more. He remained absent from his court appearances, cheated on sister Meenakshi most of the time, seized a lot of wealth from our assets, forged credentials to acquire land in his favour, and recently we heard he was scheming against Dashaanan once again.

At court, Dashaanan's ministers discussed Dushtabuddhi's non-compliance. 'My lord, how far can we consider him family and remain silent about his actions?' complained one of his ministers.

'I am not silent. It's high time now. If you can prove his crime, then action will be taken against him,' said Dashaanan.

'My lord, Dushtabuddhi has influenced a huge group of soldiers from our army. He is conducting secret meetings with his clan and these soldiers to gain victory over you. In the name of mutiny, he wants to use them against you. My sources have confirmed another meeting tomorrow.'

Dashaanan punched the armrest hard; he was furious. 'I tried my best to tame him. A fox would have been tamed by now, but this man! I ignored his actions due to Meenakshi. But not any more . . .'

'My lord, may I suggest talking to sister Meenakshi before taking any step?' I interrupted.

'You have been trying to speak to her for years now, Mandodari. But did she ever tell you anything about him accurately. Let's face it, Meenakshi is too foolish to understand his intentions. She is a mere pawn! That man has used her to reach me . . . he always has!' yelled Dashaanan.

'Lankesh, pardon me, but I suggest we first verify if he really has been planning all this. We have a spy who can do the job,' suggested Vibhishana.

'You think we have the time to do that, Vibhishana? For fourteen years this man has been a traitor to our kingdom and you want to spy on him now! You may not have the nerve to confront him but I do!' said Dashaanan and silenced Vibhishana for his suggestion.

'I think Lankesh is right. We have ignored his actions for years and it can rebound on us now. The Kalkeyas have fed their serpent prince to poison our foundation. It's unbelievable that our soldiers have joined him. I suggest we catch them red-handed tomorrow at their meeting!' said Nanashri, who had aged but was still gallant.

'I agree with you, Nanashri. Send our commanders tomorrow and ask them to detain every single member of that meeting. Also, send Meghanath along with them. He shall observe and report to me,' commanded Dashaanan and looked at me for acknowledgement.

The next day as commanded, our soldiers discreetly surrounded the area where the meeting was supposed to take place. Meghanath accompanied them. They saw that our own soldiers were being instructed by the chief of the Kalkeya clan. No sooner had the meeting started than our commanders broke in and rounded up everyone present. Dushtabuddhi panicked as he had never expected to get caught. Meghanath and a few commanders were sent back to report to Dashaanan. They seized several documents, such as chalked maps, to show us how Dushtabuddhi had been planning an attack on Dashaanan. Dashaanan got furious and took a chariot straight to the location, along with more soldiers.

It was past sunset. I was at the palace lounge when an urgent word was sent by Dashaanan to assemble at court. It sounded like an emergency. Knowing that he was furious when he had left with his soldiers, I was already worried about the consequences. The guards were lined outside the court; their numbers far exceeding the usual count. With an indication of some tragic mishap, I went inside and heard a woman howling. My heart started pounding as I took further steps. I saw a corpse lying on the ground in the middle of the court. Those present had surrounded the body and sister Meenakshi was the one crying. The way she was slapping her chest in grief, it took me no time to understand that it was her husband's corpse.

Dashaanan looked remorseful. Next to him stood young Sambukumara, Dushtabuddhi and Meenakshi's son, with teary eyes. Mata Kaikesi and the other women of the family rushed inside.

'Putri Meenakshi . . . Dushtabuddhi . . . can anyone tell me how this happened?' asked Mata Kaikesi who wasn't aware of the accusation or action against Dushtabuddhi.

Meenakshi screamed, 'Why don't you ask your son? He is the one who killed my husband!' She pointed at Dashaanan.

'What! Lower your voice, Meenakshi! You can't point fingers at your brother like that. Can anyone tell me what happened?' Mata Kaikesi shouted.

'You should ask this murderer!' said Meenakshi.

'Enough, Meenakshi! I didn't intend to kill him, and you should know that well, because if I had to, I would have finished him off much sooner without waiting for fourteen years,' said Dashaanan.

'Yes, of course . . . why not . . . because you can't see me happy. Or I should say that you can't see any of your brothers or sisters happy.'

'Decorum, Meenakshi! That is not the way to speak to your king!' I interrupted.

'No, today I can! Because he is the reason I don't have a husband now! He widowed his own sister and took a father away from his son. He wants to be the favourite son of our mother, controlling all our lives and putting us beneath him. I chose my own husband and this threatened him for years. He couldn't see me happy any more and chose to murder him like this!' cried Meenakshi.

Vibhishana signaled Sarama and softly advised, 'Take her to her chambers; she needs to pull herself together.'

'No, I am not going anywhere! How dare you try to control me, Vibhishana?'

'Meenakshi, I am deeply sorry for your loss. However, before pointing a finger at me you should listen to what your husband was up to . . . ' said Dashaanan.

'That is what you want, isn't it? You want me to obey you. You want to be the emperor who controls everyone. You take decisions and order us to follow! Well, Vibhishana is already your puppet, isn't he? And Kumbakarna is barely present to understand anything.'

'Meenakshi, your brother has always cared for you the most. He has protected you the whole time,' said Mata Kaikesi.

'You are simply blinded by affection, Mother . . . Can't you see, he has trapped one brother into doing petty labour and the other in some ridiculous sleeping boon!' Meenakshi answered back.

'Dushtabuddhi was scheming against us with the Kalkeyas. The Kalkeyas have always eyed our prosperity and your husband was nothing but a traitor to this kingdom by helping them,' said Dashaanan.

'That's a lie!'

'Listen to me, sister . . . he married you not because he fell in love with you, but to destroy me. He aimed for this throne, and what better way than to fool my sister into marriage?'

'Stop talking!'

'No, you should hear the truth about the man you are grieving for. And you know it, sister, you simply don't want to admit it. You were not happy in your marriage at all. He cheated on you and barely valued you.'

'So you did this because I was not happy in my marriage?'

'No, I didn't plan to kill him. I swear on my eldest son. You can ask him if you wish to, he was present there,' said Dashaanan and Meenakshi knew he wasn't lying.

'We all knew that Dushtabuddhi was plotting something for years but had no proof. Everyone was aware of his fraudulent activities. He used my name to conduct trades, acquiring wealth by trickery. He was our enemy from the beginning, trying to cut our roots by using our army against us. Our sources recently confirmed that he had turned a huge number of our soldiers against us. He was conducting secret meetings to plan an attack on us, and one of them was scheduled today. When I reached there, Dushtabuddhi had attacked our commanders with his men. He panicked and started shooting arrows in my direction. He feared that he couldn't escape and charged towards my chariot to finish me off. I warned him but it was too late. He knew he wouldn't be able to defend himself. Hence, before he could kill me, I had to finish him.'

Meenakshi was still. Upon hearing Dashaanan's side of the story, she couldn't blame him further. No one else spoke a word. Sambukumara sat next to his father's corpse and covered it with a cloth.

'Again, I regret it had to end this way . . . I am sorry for your loss. I am aware you both will hold me responsible but I was not the one to start it. I am here for you and I promise you both that I will do anything to protect you,' said Dashaanan.

I saw regret in my husband's eyes. He looked at me for a moment and I knew what he wanted to say. I had never seen him so repentant at anybody's death after any battle. The court was dispersed and Dushtabuddhi's last rites done by his son.

※

Lanka mourned for three days. After that, we barely talked about Dushtabuddhi. Meenakshi and Sambukumara were provided quarters near the queen's palace. Mata Kaikesi was not only concerned about her daughter's future but also about the unvoiced tiff amongst her children. Dashaanan avoided court for a few days and stayed in his palace. I tried to reduce the guilt in him.

'What happened cannot be undone, my lord. After all, it's not your fault . . .'

'Mandodari, remember when I told you about my childhood? My brothers and sister were my pillars then; they still are but weakened with the course that I have chosen. You know once when we were young and Meenakshi was an adolescent, two Brahmin boys laughed at her worn-out clothes and she cried all night with embarrassment. The next morning I cut a lock from the head of one of the boys and made him apologize to her. I strived hard to provide for my family, my people. But I have taken her husband from her . . .'

'It is time we bury this guilt and take good care of Meenakshi.'

'You are right, Mandodari. I will repair the damage now.'

'I trust you will. Also, my lord, tell me about Meghanath. This was the first time you involved him in something like this. Was he brave? How did he perform the task given to him?'

'You surprise me, Mandodari! Do you really need to ask if your son was brave? You underestimate him. He did just as I told him. I kept him away from the battle this time. However, I plan on taking him with me into the next one.'

'The next one? Where are you taking him? He is not prepared.'

'On the contrary, I am sure that he will be prepared after this battle.'

'Which battle, my lord? Your son is still learning.'

'It's a battle against the devas. Indra is greedy for power and has forcefully conquered the neighbouring tribe's territory around his capital Amravati. They have asked me to help eliminate his sovereignty over their territory. I have agreed to help, along with other rakshasa armies. Hence, we will charge against Indra and the other devas who join him.'

'So it's a battle between the rakshasas and the devas? My lord, do you think it is safe to take your son? We all know what tricks they play . . . '

'And you think Meghanath doesn't know any tricks? He is my son; I know this son of mine better than you do. He will accompany me into battle to strike Indra. It is not only a battle, but also an examination for him,' announced Dashaanan. And soon they proceeded towards Indralok.

※

The battle at Indralok was fought for six days. On the seventh day, our army returned. I looked out for Dashaanan's vimana to welcome my son back from his first battle. As soon as they landed, the band started playing the song of victory to commemorate their triumphant return. Meghanath stepped down and beside him, a beaming Dashaanan. 'We must celebrate our son's victory, Mandodari. Flowers and feast will not do justice to his majesty!' said Dashaanan.

I proposed, 'Announce a grand celebration for tomorrow evening and I will make sure it is the grandest you have experienced,' Dashaanan couldn't stop smiling. 'You are all invited to toast the honour Meghanath has brought to Lanka. He has vanquished not only the devas but also their leader Indra.'

I felt a rush of pride for my son. Indeed, this called for the best—fireworks from Malayadweep, dancers from the lands of Misr and Turchia, delicacies meticulously prepared. I barely slept in anticipation of playing the hostess but I did not mind one bit; I wanted Meghanath's name to be known in every corner of Lanka.

The evening was inaugurated with a spectacular fireworks show. I had never seen Dashaanan so happy. Tribal leaders were invited and the people of Lanka cheered Meghanath's name reverently. We waited for Dashaanan to narrate the tale of their victory.

'On the fourth day, Indra caught me unarmed during my evening prayers. He had colluded with the devas to detain me when I could not defend myself. I decided to let them take me without putting up a struggle. It was an opportunity to assess Meghanath's skill. Agnideva conveyed my message to Meghanath; I asked him to retract our army and pleaded with Indra to release me. The message appeared harmless but Meghanath read between the lines. His father prostrated himself to Indra!' Dashaanan laughed, looking at his son. 'The next day when the devas were least expecting it, Meghanath attacked Indra and defeated him.' The crowd burst into applause and cheered Meghanath's name.

There is more,' Dashaanan held up his hand and continued, 'Meghanath would have killed Indra had the devas and Prajapati not begged him otherwise. In return, they offered him a boon. My son asked for immortality. Of course, they could not grant what defied nature so they bequeathed unto him a celestial chariot. He who performs the Nikumbhila yagna and rides it into a war will be invincible.' I hadn't realized I was teary-eyed. I leaned into Meghanath and squeezed his hand. 'I'm proud of you, my son. We all are.'

'Indeed, Meghanath, you have made us very proud,' Nanashri smiled.

Kumbakarna, who happened to be awake from his Nidraasana, too congratulated them. 'First, Lankapati Ravana, and now his son have triumphed over Indra.'

'Most certainly! Prajapati announced that the devas were impressed by Meghanath's courage, and with Brahma's consent, bestowed the title Indrajeet on him.'

The crowd chanted, 'Long live, Indrajeet! Long live our prince!'

Dashaanan bent over and whispered into my ear softly, 'You've been a terrific hostess. I must tell you I am very impressed.'

I caught a glimpse of Meghanath. His victory had humbled him. Dashaanan's test had marked his maturation. He was no longer my little child but a prince. His resemblance to Dashaanan caught me off guard sometimes, the same small tilak, applied from sandalwood paste to mark his devotion to Shiva, the same taste in clothes, his growing moustache. He had always been his father's son.

FIFTEEN

If we were not fighting the devas at Indralok, we were in conflict with the rakshasas of north Bharatvarsh. They were under Dashaanan's stepbrother Kubera's jurisdiction. Meghanath was only sixteen when he and Dashaanan challenged Kubera. Knowing he didn't stand a chance against them, Kubera granted Dashaanan wealth from his treasury and pledged to maintain cordial relations. Their effortless victory was a reminder of just how formidable a team they were. We heard the news with amusement. Dashaanan asked Meghanath to stay back with Guru Shukracharya in the Himalayas and perform penance by praying to Lord Shiva. Meghanath obeyed him to acquire siddhi over various weapons.

He returned to Lanka after ten months, having mastered the art of battle. Nanashri steered our conversation towards Meghanath's marriage.

'I praise Indrajeet—the mighty son of Lankapati Ravana—who has attained such prowess with discipline and talent. At this young age, he can operate weapons like

Brahmanda-*astra*, Pashupatastra and Vaishnavastra,' said Nanashri.

'Bhrata Dashaanan, he has excelled at each one of your tests,' teased Vibhishana.

'He has exceeded my expectations,' said Dashaanan.

'With your permission, I would like to present a marriage proposal for our eldest prince, Meghanath,' ventured Nanashri.

Meghanath beamed.

Dashaanan furrowed his eyebrows good-naturedly. 'Marriage proposal for Meghanath! Isn't it too early?'

Tentatively, I contributed to the discussion. 'My lord, he has turned seventeen. It is certainly the right time to find a suitable companion for him.'

'You mean bind him in matrimony?' laughed Dashaanan. 'All right, then, Rani Mandodari's wish is my command.'

'I have a proposal from Sheshanaga, the king of the Nagas. He wishes to offer his daughter in matrimony to Indrajeet, the legendary prince of Lanka,' announced Nanashri.

'What is she like? Have you met her?' I asked Nanashri eagerly.

'Unfortunately, no. However, I have a portrait of her. I have heard a lot about her beauty,' said Nanashri.

'What is it about her that makes you believe she is suitable for Meghanath?' asked Dashaanan.

I stole a glance at Meghanath to gauge his response. As usual, his face was set in an amiable yet inscrutable expression.

Nanashri addressed Dashaanan's question. 'My lord Lankesh, I have seen many portraits recently. Since the news of Meghanath's victory over Indra surfaced, we have been inundated with proposals. Our beloved prince is the most sought-after suitor. He is talented, brave, knowledgeable, disciplined, and most importantly, very composed. In response to your question, I see a similar composure in the portrait of Sulochana that I received.' He unrolled the scroll and showed it to us.

'She has beautiful eyes,' I said, 'You seem to be right, Nanashri.'

'Mandodari is already impressed! *Putra* Meghanath, I ask your opinion now, are you ready to take a wife? Do you wish to accept this proposal?' asked Dashaanan.

'If you approve of it, Pitashri, I accept the proposal.'

Dashaanan embraced his son. 'Nanashri, inform the tribal king right away. Vibhishana will soon call on them with gifts and favours.

The date of Meghanath's wedding was set a fortnight later. I felt time slipping through my fingers; I had carried him only a little while ago and now he was about to get married. My life was neatly catalogued; first a daughter, then a wife and mother, and now a mother-in-law. We filled trunks with clothes, gold jewellery, precious stones and weapons to be sent to the Nagas. I was thankful Meghanath's marriage was not a political manoeuvre but a choice.

The Nagas upheld a tradition where the bride had to be brought from her maternal home before she was married. Dowry was arranged by the groom's side to respectfully ask for the bride's hand in marriage. The night before the wedding—the ceremony to unite the two families was to be held at dawn—I slipped into Meghanath's room. He was sitting with his brothers and didn't notice me entering. He looked content. All I wanted for him was happiness.

Guests poured in from every part of the world. Kings of different kingdoms, devas from Indralok and Dashaanan's vanara friend Vali from Kiskinda. Dashaanan was sentimental about the occasion. His favourite son was getting married. The city of Trikota was draped with flowers. Gandharvas and gandharvis were called to perform during the nuptials. An apsara named Rambha was sent by Indra to dance before the ceremony. Guru Shukracharya was the priest for this wedding too. Meghanath sat in front of the mandap fire, sincerely performing the yagna as directed by his priest.

Sulochana entranced the guests. She walked in, dressed in a white and golden bridal sari. Her beauty remarkable, but more than that, her composure complemented Meghanath's perfectly. Their names were hailed; everyone addressed Meghanath as Indrajeet.

After the ceremony, Sulochana received a warm welcome in the queen's palace. I gifted her a nine-string necklace studded with precious rubies. Dhanyamalini and Nayanadini gifted her various ornaments too. The women of the antapura teased her but she did not falter. She smiled at their jokes and won everybody's hearts with her charm. In her, I saw the perfect companion for my son.

☙

That year was full of weddings. Prahasta, now the chief commander of Lanka's army, got married after Indrajeet.

Atikaya, Dhanyamalini's eldest son, soon followed. The younger lot of children—Trishir, Narantaka and Devantaka—were promoted to generals in the army under Prahasta.

The younger generation had begun making a life of its own. Some elders were disagreeable to the position they were conferred in the family. Meenakshi sequestered herself in her estate. She held us responsible for Dushtabuddhi's fate, and the loneliness that grew thick around her had repercussions for us too. I met her thrice in her grief. She was full of rage. All my attempts to involve her in Lanka's activities were shot down. Her only remaining connection was with her cousins Khara and Dushana. She was not the only malcontent amid us. Vibhishana's resentment due to his subordinate stature grew. His suggestions were dismissed at court and he was easily sidelined by Nanashri and the other council members. During the battle with Kubera, Vibhishana had suggested we forge an agreement with Kubera as he was influential in the north, but Dashaanan had refused. Dashaanan had wanted to defeat Kubera to diminish his monetary and military wealth and render him harmless. Only before Indrajeet's wedding did Dashaanan and Kubera come to a peaceful agreement. Vibhishana had also proposed a few projects to further develop our infrastructure. He lobbied for a bridge to be built in order to connect Lanka to its overseas territories. Dashaanan was not in favour of this idea, preferring air travel over gratuitous architectural expenditure. Vibhishana's opinions held less and less regard with every dismissal. He dedicated himself to Vishnu as a way of overcoming his bitterness towards Dashaanan.

SIXTEEN

Dashaanan consecrated a shrine in Mata Kaikesi's honour. It took six years to build. He also built a temple near his palace for him and his mother to offer prayers to Shiva. Dashaanan had made her proud; he had served and respected her. All that she had wanted for him, he had achieved. At the shrine's opening ceremony, Meenakshi and Vibhishana's discontent was evident. Soon after, Meenakshi set off for Bharatvarsh with her son. Yet again I tried to persuade her to stay, but to no avail. She was not only lonely but an outsider in her own land. She went around careless of her appearance, always with a gloomy expression on her face. She was not treated well, mocked for her melancholy as 'Soorpnakha'—the one with overgrown fingernails. She left to live a life of foraging in the forests of a distant land like a nomad, away from the family that had forsaken her.

Right after Meenakshi's departure, Kumbakarna and Bajrajala's twin sons—Kumbh and Nikumbh—were engaged. Bajrajala's maternal family was very highly regarded. She came from a family of illustrious rulers like Virochana and Mahabali. An otherwise tense Bajrajala looked peaceful during the wedding. She had once confessed in my confidence that she loved a man other than Kumbakarna. She did not tell me who he was, but I speculated he was a high-ranking soldier in our army. She could not be blamed for loving another man, but the tragedy of her love story only made me pity her. She was loyal to her husband but he was barely there. Only women, I thought, had the strength to love like this.

A celebration heralded the completion of thirty years of Ravana's reign. Lanka had prospered under his rule; it had stronger allies, booming trade, fiscal organization, advanced equipment and weaponry and an empowered citizenry.

A grand gathering was held. I sat next to Dashaanan. Nanashri bowed to his legendary ten-headed crown. Right then, a woman rushed in with our guards behind her, a veil draped across her face. She fell unto Dashaanan's feet and wept. When she raised her face, her eyes gave her away. It was Meenakshi! She had returned to Lanka after a year.

Dashaanan stood up, shocked at Meenakshi's state. We all clambered up from our seats, the celebration in abeyance, waiting for an explanation.

Gently, Dashaanan asked her. 'What is the matter, sister?' He lifted her by her shoulders. 'I almost didn't recognize you.'

'Bhrata Lankesh, you once said that you will protect me and I have come today to seek your help!' said Meenakshi.

'I will help you, sister, but why are you in such a state? And why do you cover your face?' asked Dashaanan.

'I cannot show my face to you; I cannot even look at myself.'

'Why do you say so, Meenakshi? What has happened to you?' I interrupted.

She hung her head in shame. 'Uncover your face and let me see you,' said Dashaanan.

'I beg you to not ask this of me, brother. I have been humiliated and if you see me, you will be too,' cried Meenakshi.

'Enough, Meenakshi, show me your face!' said Dashaanan and she pulled her veil down.

There was a brief moment of shocked silence before the murmurs began. Dashaanan stared at her. I felt weak with shock. Behind the veil was the hollow of her nose. The flesh from her nose and ears was also missing.

'I knew you could not bear to see my face. I am sorry that I have come to you like this, my brother. But I seek your help; avenge me! Avenge our dead cousins Khara and Dushana!'

'How did this happen?' asked Dashaanan. He screamed at his guards, 'Why didn't anyone tell me about Khara and Dushana?'

'Two brothers portray themselves as destroyers of evil and kill rakshasa men. One of them did this to me! And that man has no guilt for what he has done. He knew I was your sister; I warned him, but he mocked you. I would have killed myself for the disgrace I have gone through, but I couldn't die peacefully either. They have insulted you too and I want them destroyed,' said Meenakshi and Dashaanan clenched his fists.

'Who are they? Who had the nerve to behave like this with my sister?' thundered Dashaanan.

'Those two brothers and a woman dwell in the forest of Dandakaranya. They have been exiled from their kingdom, Ayodhya. They are savage beings, my lord. I warned them that I was your sister and that you would finish them if you learnt about their misconduct. But they didn't care about anything, as if you couldn't stand a chance against them at all.'

'But where did you meet them, sister Meenakshi? Why would they harm you like this?' I asked her.

Meenakshi narrated in detail. 'When I reached Bharatvarsh with Khara and Dushana, we planned our journey to the colonies of Dandaka through the forest region. As we moved northwards, we heard various stories about these two manava brothers from Ayodhya who were gaining control over rakshasa and yaksha tribes by killing their men. There was a rumour that these two brothers were princes in exile, trying to finish asura rule from the north of Bharatvarsh in order to serve their kingdom in disguise. They are called Rama and Lakshmana. Some sages and devas support them in the killings too.'

Some people present in court already knew these names. They came forward to hear Meenakshi's story.

'We reached the dense forest of Dandakaranya and set our camp there for three months. I asked my son to continue his journey to Dandaka with a few guards for safety. During this time, we heard that one of our relatives had been killed by these manava brothers.' She turned towards Mama Marichan, who was present at court for the celebration. 'It was your mother Taraka, who ruled over a region in that forest.'

'Khara and Dushana now gauged that these brothers were not ordinary men. They announced a reward amongst their army to capture them. We were told that they were hiding in another part of the forest, which they kept protected from intruders. Hence, our men started looking in the regions around the area they occupied.

'Once, when I was bathing in a nearby river, I saw a woman at the other end. She was filling a pot and didn't notice me. She was as beautiful as an apsara. There were hardly any women in that region, and I was curious to know who she was. I began swimming towards her but she spotted me halfway and shouted for help. "Lakshmana, there is something in the water!"

'I revealed myself. A man hurried out at her calls. He strung his bow and prepared to shoot into the water. "Wait! That's a woman. I misunderstood her for some animal," she stopped him.

'"I am sorry if I frightened you. I saw you from the other end. Who are you? And who is he?" I asked her.

'"You tell us who you are or else I will kill you," said the man. But the woman insisted: "No, Lakshmana, wait! She is a woman." She turned towards me and said, "We mean no harm; we are in exile and he is my brother-in-law Lakshmana. Please return whence you came from."

'I returned to our camp and informed our cousins about them. Lakshmana, the name was clear and renowned. They left immediately with warriors to attack him and his brother. I followed them. Our men searched the nearby regions and found their dwelling. They lived in a protected wooden shelter inside a boundary. There were three distant boundaries set by them, which went unnoticed by our men.

Then we waited in the woods for them to reveal themselves. We saw one man trying to repair a fence, the other on guard and the woman doing household chores. As soon as our men proceeded to raid the place, we heard a crack and several of our guards hung upside down from branches. It was a trap. Our men were caught in a snare around their boundary. They heard the guards shouting from the trees and were alerted. One by one, I saw all our guards die at their hands. Khara and Dushana were slayed in front of my eyes. I screamed in terror as I watched them die. Lakshmana saw me hiding, ran towards me and grabbed my hair.

"'We saw this woman near the river. She was with them, a rakshasi, I guess,' said Lakshmana to his brother Rama. It was clear that Rama was elder to him.

"'I told you to go back where you came from; why are you here?' asked the woman, who was Rama's wife.

"'Bhabhi, she is not an ordinary woman. She must have told them our whereabouts,' said Lakshmana and pulled my hair even harder.

"'Let me go; you don't know who I am,' I told him.

"'Then tell us! These asuras that we killed, were you married to any of them?' asked the elder brother Rama.

"'No, I am a widow. The men you killed today, Khara and Dushana, were my cousins.'

"'Hmm, they said they were related to Taraka and attacked us for revenge,' said Rama.

"'You have killed our people. You have killed men with wives and children, who are now orphans. You should be ashamed of yourself,' I replied and Lakshmana slapped me. "How dare you speak to my brother like that?" he said.

'"Enough, Lakshmana, leave her on the outskirts of the forest. She is harmless," said Rama.

'"*Bhaiya* Rama, she harmed us by exposing us. I shouldn't have left her in the first place," said Lakshmana, and kicked me this time.

'"Enough, you strike me again and I will make sure my brother kills you. You behave with a woman like this! Just because I am alone doesn't mean I can't protect myself," I warned him.

'"Is that true? Then why don't you show us your talent?" Lakshmana mocked me. He bent down to face me. "You look pretty, though, you know. I would have married you and kept you here had I not been married already. You are of no use to my brother too. I pity you, with your people killed and no husband, you must be so lonely." I couldn't tolerate him humiliating me any further. I scratched his face with my nails.

'"You monster, how dare you!" he tried hitting me again but his brother stopped him. "Enough, Lakshmana, leave her now," said Rama.

'"No, *bhaiya*, not so easily. I ought to teach her a lesson first," said Lakshmana, pulling out his knife.

'"Stop it or else my brother will kill you in revenge. He is the king of Lanka," I warned him again.

'"I don't care who your brother is. If he comes for revenge, I will kill him too." He locked my arms behind my back and peeled off my nose and ears with that knife.'

We were stunned with rage. Never had we heard of a woman being treated so savagely. Meenakshi wept helplessly.

She went on: 'I screamed with pain. My ears and nose were bleeding profusely. He dragged me to the river bank and pushed me in. Night was about to fall and I somehow made it back to our camp. My four remaining guards and I fled from the forest and came back home.'

Dashaanan's face had darkened. His voice trembled as he spoke. 'I will make them repent, sister. I can't express how miserable your condition makes me feel. Your wounds are my wounds; your humiliation is mine. I swear in front of this court that I will avenge you and make them repent for their sins. You will get your justice,' he announced and stormed out.

※

Meenakshi was taken for treatment. Mata Kaikesi and the other royal ladies were informed about her return. Meanwhile, close family members gathered in the palace courtyard to discuss matters.

'They are in exile; we cannot attack their kingdom,' said Nanashri.

'We don't know their location so well. And they don't seem to be ordinary men. They are manava princes and definitely very skilled to have defeated Khara and Dushana,' said Vibhishana.

'I am not bothered if they are rakshasas, devas or manavas, I want their wicked heads off,' said Dashaanan.

'Lankesh, when I went to Dandaka a year ago, I heard various stories about these brothers who were hunting down asuras on Sage Vishwamitra's orders. I warned my mother

Taraka and brother Subahu about the threat they posed. But it is obvious that our mother couldn't escape death. I have sent a message to summon Subahu. He should be here in a few days. I suggest we plan our strategy after speaking to him as he has been in battle with those brothers,' said Marichan.

'I agree with Marichan. Subahu knows their tactics. It will be good to know how powerful an enemy we are dealing with before we attack them,' suggested Nanashri.

'Are you blind to my sister's suffering? I cannot wait a single day to finish them off!' roared Dashaanan.

'Bhrata Lankesh, we all know how mighty our cousins Khara and Dushana were. It is impossible to believe that they, along with their army of thirty-five soldiers, were defeated by merely two people of average strength. They are more powerful than we are giving them credit for,' said Vibhishana.

'Vibhishana is right. Let us prepare for the attack while we wait for Subahu,' added Nanashri.

Dashaanan stood up, thinking for a brief moment. He grudgingly agreed, 'Prepare our army in the meantime. My son Narantaka will be in charge of the mission. Inform Meghanath to take soldiers under him accordingly. Narantaka should arrest them and bring them here.'

We waited three days for Mama Subahu to reach Lanka. After his mother's death, Subahu had surrendered to Rama. He agreed to leave the forest of Dandakaranya forever in exchange for his life. Dashaanan was restless. Meenakshi's humiliation and pain tortured him. We congregated once again.

Mama Subahu told us everything he knew about Rama and Lakshmana. 'My lord Lankesh, Rama and Lakshmana are no ordinary manava men. They are Kshatriyas; they call themselves Raghuvanshi, disciples of great Guru Vashishta and Muni Vishwamitra. Skilled at warfare and archery, I have seen them vanquish the toughest of opponents effortlessly. They are the sons of king Dasharatha of Ikshwaku dynasty, and the princes of Ayodhya. I have heard that one of the three queens of Ayodhya demanded Rama's exile in order to pass the throne to her own son. They wandered around until finally settling in the western part of the Dandaka forest. Their exile of fourteen years will be over soon. While in exile, they have gained knowledge of celestial weaponry from Vishwamitra. In return, they have eliminated the asuras threatening Vishwamitra's sacred practices. Also in exile with them is Rama's wife Sita, daughter of king Janaka of Mithila.'

I saw Dashaanan's eyes widen in surprise. Thirteen years ago, the same name had caused quite a stir at her swayamwar. 'Sita, the daughter of king Janaka!' He had not forgotten her.

'Bhrata Lankesh that means this Rama is the same Prince of Ayodhya who had won that contest in Mithila. He is the one who lifted and broke the mighty bow of Shiva!' added Vibhishana.

'Sita, wife of Rama . . . are you sure she is the same Sita—daughter of king Janaka?' asked Dashaanan.

'I am most certain, my lord. She is also known as Janaki, after her father Janaka, to commoners,' said Mama Subahu.

'But, Lankesh, attacking these brothers in exile would be beneath us. Their kingdom will have nothing to do with them until their exile is over. We cannot attack them right now,' said Nanashri.

'In that case, I know another way of avenging my sister. They disgraced a woman and I will show them how it feels when a woman of one's family is mistreated,' said Dashaanan.

'My lord, what are you thinking of doing?' I probed, fearing his intentions.

'We cannot start a battle with them and, thus, must provoke them to do it,' said Dashaanan.

'And how will we provoke them, my lord? They have no purpose to travel so far for a battle,' asked Mama Subahu.

'We will give them a motive. A taste of their own medicine. I will do it myself,' said Dashaanan and turned towards Mama Marichan. 'They haven't seen you; you have to come with me. We leave for Dandaka tomorrow.'

SEVENTEEN

I probed for answers, worried about what Dashaanan would do next. Before he left for Dandaka, I had a final word with him.

'My lord, please remember that Sita is not at fault for what happened with sister Meenakshi. You can punish her husband and his brother for their deeds, but don't involve Sita.'

'Why do you think I will involve her? She is not my enemy,' said Dashaanan.

'But I know that your plan has something to do with her. What are you thinking, my lord? Please tell me.'

'Trust me, Mandodari, I haven't thought about it yet. I want to see them first and then decide.'

'If I may ask, what happened during Sita's swayamwar all those years ago? Is your revenge in any which way motivated by that?

'If you believe I want to take revenge for my own failings, you are mistaken. This is about Meenakshi. If you think I want to take revenge for what happened during that contest, then you are wrong. The resentment of losing that contest still remains but it has nothing to do with what happened to my sister. They have challenged me unwittingly. Not only have they cut my sister's nose, but they have also dared us all at Lanka. I am duty-bound to respond to that.'

'My lord, I beg your pardon, but I want to say one last thing: take no woman's wrath any more. Please don't do anything that marks you against a woman's will.'

'What do you think Rama and Lakshmana have done? And exactly how would you mark them for what they have done to my sister? Are they any different than I, Mandodari?' asked Dashaanan and I could not answer him.

'My lord, I advise you because there have been times in the past when you have mistreated women.'

'I have treated men with more brutality than women. Why do you choose to fixate on the episodes where only women were involved?'

It struck me that in my own eyes I had relegated Dashaanan to being a lecher. I had convinced myself, perhaps to reconcile with his politically driven marriages and the women he kept in the antapura that at the heart of his conduct was lust. I wanted to claim his love, be its sole recipient, and saw his adultery as debauchery.

'I will be back soon. My vengeance is towards Rama and Lakshmana; I will try not to harm Sita,' he assured. Then he took his Pushpaka Vimana and along with Mama Marichan flew across the ocean.

Seven days later, a guard reported he had seen our vimana in the air, making its way back. Along with Nanashri,

Vibhishana, Sarama, Meghanath and Dhanyamalini, I reached the landing ground.

'Lankeshwar didn't inform us about his arrival. I hope everything is fine,' said Dhanyamalini, looking for vimana in the sky.

'Lankesh shouldn't have gone. I tried to stop him but he paid me no heed. It was terribly unsafe; I am glad he is back now,' added Nanashri.

The vimana descended slowly. Dashaanan emerged first. Behind him, a young woman cowered, dressed in rough-spun clothes, taking in her surroundings.

'Oh lord, who is that woman? Is it Sita?' exclaimed Sarama.

My heart pounded. I went up to them, and although I was staring at the woman behind him, I asked Dashaanan, 'Who is she?'

'She is Sita,' came his deadpan response. He summoned the guards. 'Take her to shanti bhavan and watch over her!' he ordered them.

I froze in fear. 'Sita! You brought her here? My lord, how did she come with you?' I gaped at him, aghast.

'She didn't come here willingly, of course,' Dashaanan dodged, not giving me a straight answer.

'So how, my lord? Did you abduct her?' I couldn't help but ask.

Dashaanan looked solidly ahead. He shrugged, 'This is the only way we get our revenge.'

'No, my lord, this can't be the only way. You cannot abduct someone's wife to deliver justice to your sister!' I protested. I looked at Meghanath to say something to his father but he chose to abide by Dashaanan's wishes.

'We are not doing this for justice, Mandodari; we are doing this for revenge!' said Dashaanan and walked away.

After sometime, we gathered in the courtyard again. I was open to discussing the matter. While I was against Sita's abduction, there were some who saw it as a necessary evil. Since most council members did not want to overstep their bounds and question Dashaanan, I had to initiate the dialogue.

'My lord Lankesh, your resolution to abduct Rama's wife has astonished me. As far as I remember, we never discussed that we would take Sita hostage!'

'I have thought it through. We avenge ourselves through Sita's abduction. If Rama and Lakshmana somehow find her, which I believe they will, we will finish them. They dishonoured my sister, and I separated Sita from them. Hence, we are even now.'

'Lankesh, what happened to Marichan? Why hasn't he come back with you?' asked Nanashri in a whispering tone.

'Mama Marichan will not be able to make it back. It grieves me to inform you all that he was chased by Rama and could not escape him. He was later killed by him,' announced Dashaanan.

'Indeed, terrible news! How did it happen? And how did you capture Sita when they were on guard?' asked Nanashri.

'They were not on guard when I captured her,' he explained. 'When we reached Dandaka, it took us one day to locate them. We disguised ourselves as commoners to observe them before we acted. I hid my vimana far from their location so they wouldn't discover it. We took cover close to their quarters; they had constructed a huge hut, which was defended by a boundary around it. It was Lakshmana who guarded the boundary most of the time. I wanted to finish him off right away. But then I saw Rama, the vigilante who killed most of our people, switch duty with him. The next morning, just after dawn, I saw Sita working around the hut. She lit a fire, watered the ground and then finally walked out with a vessel in her hand. Lakshmana guarded her along the way. It became clear that Lakshmana guarded them all the time, especially Sita. She wasn't left alone even for a minute. Then we saw Rama inside the hut, he was shaping his arrows. Sita returned soon and Lakshmana went to guard the fence again. We observed them for three days. Each day, they followed the same schedule.'

'But why Sita? Why didn't you abduct Rama or Lakshmana instead?' interrupted Vibhishana.

'Try and understand, Vibhishana. I want Meenakshi to give their punishment when I get them here. They were always alert, and also merely finishing them off with an attack would not have met the demands of justice. Hence, I decided to get Sita. Rama will do everything possible to find her; Lakshmana will do everything his elder brother wishes. And if they happen to find her here, I will bring them to their knees in front of my sister.'

'She is my sister too. I am as concerned about her as you,' said Vibhishana.

'Then you better trust me,' replied Dashaanan.

'My lord, your decision to take Sita hostage has already claimed a life! How else would you explain Mama Marichan's demise?' I added.

'That was his destiny. I did not plan for all this.' He narrated further. 'I wanted to distract Lakshmana and Rama, to see if I could get an opportunity to get inside the boundary. Hence, I asked Mama Marichan to disguise himself as an animal rustling in the bushes and draw attention to himself so I may slip inside unnoticed. As expected, Lakshmana sensed an intrusion and searched the forest. But Rama stayed with his wife, foiling our attempt that day. Mama Marichan returned the next morning; Lakshmana was unable to get hold of him.

We tried again the next day, and this time Rama left for the search. I was looking for a chance, but Lakshmana would not leave Sita alone. Mama Marichan kept Rama engaged till evening and just then I saw Sita and Lakshmana arguing. She walked to and fro within the compound in front of the fence. She was clearly concerned for her husband, who hadn't returned from the search. Finally, right before sunset, I saw their dispute come to an end with Lakshmana leaving to look for Rama. Sensing the opportunity, I reached out to Sita.

I disguised myself as a Brahmin, asking for alms and cajoled her to step outside the fence. She hesitated to come outside the fence at first. I told her I would curse her for being insensitive towards a hungry Brahmin. In fear, she agreed and stepped out. That is when I grabbed her hand and hurried towards the vimana. On my way, I heard a man cry out from the same direction where Mama Marichan had gone running. I knew it was his voice. Sadly, it was his last.'

Everyone stood silent; Mama Marichan's death was unexpected.'

'That is not fair to him, my lord. He died like a prey, chased by our enemy,' I said.

'I did not expect him to die that way either, but we cannot ask destiny any questions,' Dashaanan replied.

'Bhrata Dashaanan, what will you do next? Sita is king Janaka's daughter. What if he declares war against us?' asked Vibhishana.

'What is there to fear, Vibhishana? A kingdom as small as Mithila doesn't stand a chance against us. Also, Sita belongs to Rama now. Janaka will not interfere directly. Accommodate her in the antapura. Also, inform Meenakshi about everything,' Dashaanan said and left.

Sita was like a bird trapped inside a cage. I was sympathetic to her plight; a woman abducted for no fault of her own, miles away from home. Meenakshi was not convinced with Dashaanan's scheme of justice. She had wanted him to confront and defeat the brothers directly. Mata Kaikesi forbade Meenakshi's disapproval to be conveyed to Dashaanan lest he take drastic measures and put himself in danger.

The next day, I sent my dasi with fresh robes and clothes for Sita. In order to avoid any gossip or rumour, I refrained from putting Sita up in the antapura.

My dasi soon returned with the clothes that I had sent. 'Your majesty, I'm afraid she refused to take them. She might be our prisoner, but she is still in exile, she says. She claims her clothes are made of some divine fabric that doesn't wear out or get spoilt easily.'

'Hmm . . . how is she conducting herself otherwise?' I asked her.

'Your majesty, her eyes are swollen from crying. She has refused the food given to her and now the clothes that you had sent. When I told her that the clothes were sent by you, she told me that she was obliged but it was against the customs of exile to accept them.'

'Do you think I should meet her myself? I plan to accommodate her elsewhere soon; she cannot live in a room surrounded by men. It's not safe.'

'I agree with you, your majesty. The guards, or for that matter anyone, should not treat her like a prisoner of war. She is a hostage, not a reward.'

My dasi's statement made me desperate to shift Sita to a better place. I went to meet her.

She was sitting curled up in a corner, her head between her knees. She turned towards me, dabbing her face with her sari as I walked in.

'It may seem awkward for us to talk. My gestures may not ease your pain but I am sorry for what you have to go through. You are suffering without any fault of your own. Hence, I apologize for my husband's actions.'

She stood close to me. It was the first time that I saw her closely. Her long black hair was half braided and open below the neck—it covered her waist completely. She had vermilion, which is the symbol of a married woman, in the parting of her hair, soft skin, big, expressive eyes accentuated by the perfect arch of her eyebrows, nose like a princess, and lips like a bow. Her face was pale, though, because of the turmoil she was going through. She must have been the same age as Meghanath. She wore no ornaments, just a rosary around her neck and wrist. The fabric of her rough sari rubbed against her slender waists. She tried to hide her beauty in those rags. Young, glowing and calm, she was truly a princess.

She folded her hands and bowed, 'His deeds cannot be forgiven, but it is not your fault either. Hence, I am obliged to you for your kind gesture.'

I smiled at her intelligent humility. 'I hear you have refused to eat or accept clothing. I will make arrangements for a better place for you to stay . . .'

'I don't want to stay here! Or live for that matter. I wanted to die the very moment your husband touched me. I wanted to jump out of that vimana . . . but I cannot even end this life—it belongs to my husband. So I have to live, each excruciating moment, each day, waiting for him to rescue me.'

I pitied her. The daughter of a king, brought up in luxury, married early and sent into exile right after. Thirteen years of exile with only her husband and brother-in-law. Now to be separated from the only family she had. Not only turmoil, she must be going through a crisis.

'It is not going to be easy for you. Yet, I will try and do my best to help you,' I assured her.

'Why? You are his wife, why would you help me?'

'Because somewhere deep inside, I agree that my husband shouldn't have brought you here. You are not the one from whom we seek revenge.'

'Seek revenge? Whom do you seek revenge from?'

'Your husband Rama and his younger brother Lakshmana. Rama has murdered our people and Lakshmana accompanied him. Also, Lankapati Ravana's sister Meenakshi was humiliated by them. She was brutally ill-treated by Lakshmana.'

She tried to convince me, 'My husband is not a murderer and I regret what happened with Lankapati Ravana's sister! But why did Ravana choose to abduct me?'

'I don't have answers to all your questions at this time. And I don't wish to get into any dispute with you. Our husbands might be enemies now, but we are not. I don't intend to make this more miserable for you.'

'I am sorry for Lakshmana's actions too. I wish I could go back in time to stop him from doing anything like that to a woman. He loses his temper easily . . .'

'Well, he has that in common with Lankapati Ravana . . .'

She took a moment to think. 'I agree with what you said . . . we are still not enemies. Again, I am obliged to meet you. You are kind to offer help to me.'

'Is there anything I can help you with right now?' I asked her.

'Yes, I am still in exile and as per the customs, I eat just two meals a day. I respect the food sent to me, but I don't eat anything *taamsik*—spicy or non-vegetarian food. I prefer very light meals, rice or may be just fruits.'

I felt sad for her poor appetite and customary sacrifice.'
'Certainly, I will arrange the food as per your preference.'

'Thank you! I am grateful to you. What should I call you?'

It struck me that she wasn't a commoner; she was royalty too. 'Mandodari, my name is Mandodari.'

There were rumours that Dashaanan would kill Rama and marry his wife. I was worried about the gossip. We had no news from Bharatvarsh about Rama's whereabouts. We knew he was powerful but he had no resources to mount an attack on Lanka. Also, we weren't certain if he was aware that Sita had been abducted by Dashaanan. Like me, Dhanyamalini and Nayanadini were concerned about Sita. We discussed safer housing for her while she was in Lanka.

'How can you even think about keeping her at the antapura with the king's concubines? That will only fuel the rumours,' argued Nayanadini and I agreed with her.

Dhanyamalini asked, 'Then where do we keep her? She is not a prisoner. She cannot stay in the queen's palace with us. Should we let her stay where she is?'

'I am not sure either. Personally, I am not fond of the idea of putting her up in shanti bhavan after what happened to Rishi Gritsamada but there seems to be no other place we can house her.'

'I think we should convert that place into her chambers temporarily. She is waiting for her husband, Dashaanan is waiting for his enemy . . . we don't have a waiting room in Lanka,' Dhanyamalini joked.

'Keep her in the antapura, Mandodari,' said Dashaanan who had just entered the lounge and overheard our discussion. 'Like I told you earlier, keep her in the antapura, shanti bhavan is to be used for various other purposes.'

'But, my lord, it is not appropriate for her to stay there. She is a married woman . . .'

'You want to marry her, don't you?' Nayanadini interrupted. She looked angrily at Dashaanan.

'I haven't thought about it yet,' said Dashaanan, looking at all three of us.

'My lord, don't let the rumours influence your mind like that!' said Dhanyamalini.

'You said you never wanted to marry Sita!' I added.

'I said that thirteen years ago, Mandodari. However, I haven't thought about my marriage yet. I am more concerned about her husband. And if it is destined for me to marry Sita—which I feel fate had proposed years earlier—then this time I will marry her after I kill her husband,' claimed Dashaanan and walked out, leaving us shocked with his sudden decision.

We looked at each other vulnerably, all three wives against our husband's decision to marry a fourth time. Dhanyamalini was right; the rumours had influenced Dashaanan's thinking about Sita. I went to meet Sita again.

'This bhavan seems to be the only option for your accommodation right now. If you wish, I can get this place renovated as a temporary chamber for you,' I suggested.

She smiled. 'You are too kind. But I remind you, I am still in exile just like my husband. I cannot stay here or in any other luxurious chamber. I have been living in forests for the last thirteen years. If it is not too much to ask, I wish to live in a surrounding that looks like a forest. I want to see the woods, the skies, the birds flying freely in the air. I don't want to stay under a roof.'

'But how will you live in a place like that?'

'Don't worry; I will not be living here forever. My husband will soon find me and rescue me,' she said confidently. Her belief took me by surprise.

'How are you so sure that he will find you here? He doesn't know you are in Lanka,' I tried testing her.

'He will, I am sure. He will find me towards the south. I left a trail for him; when I was taken in that vimana, I dropped my ornaments on the land below to show him a path.'

Her innocent and childlike efforts to get back to her husband concerned me. She was so hopeful to get back to him that she was thinking impractically.

I could add no more to her troubles, 'I too hope that he finds you soon.'

'You remind me of my mother, Rani Mandodari. She is as caring as you. I haven't met her for thirteen years due to the exile, but today I feel close to her.'

Her warmth tugged at my heartstrings. I was besieged with her warmth. 'Your mother . . . and your father . . . I heard he loved you the most.'

'Yes, he did. I was adopted by him, you know. I am so blessed that he found me. He once told me the story of how he found me during a yagna; he said he borrowed me from Bhoomi Mata.' She smiled remembering something, 'I later understood what he actually meant by the story. When he said he borrowed me, he meant I was buried in a pot, covered with soil by someone who didn't want me. But I believe I was destined to live, destined to meet my husband.'

Her story knocked the wind out of me. I thought back to the birth of my daughter twenty-six years ago—my child who had not lived. I was shocked at the similarities between how she was found and how Mai had buried my daughter.

The blood drained from my face; I asked her again, 'How did you say your father found you?'

'My adoptive parents, king Janaka and Mata Sunaina, had no children before me. Our kingdom was on the verge of a famine. The rains had abandoned the region for three consecutive years. My father performed a yagna, believing that it would bestow nature's blessings on the region. As part of that yagna, the king was required to plough the field. While doing so, the furrow was trapped against a rock. Still trying to push the plough, my father heard a child cry. He exhumed the soil near the furrow and found me. He asked everyone around if they knew me or my parents. He enquired for days but no one came forward to claim me as their own. And then they knew that I was probably abandoned by my parents. My father proudly said that he furrowed me from the barren land, and hence named me Sita.'

It was right in front of my eyes.

There I stood facing her, uncomfortably thinking about my past. A reality I had kept buried for twenty-six years of my life, thinking that it was over. My only daughter, whom I had considered dead right after her birth, was standing alive today with me. And why, I hadn't noticed it earlier, she resembled someone I had seen before . . . she resembled me!

I wanted to rush back to my chambers to think over everything once again and take it all at my own pace. She was waiting for me to respond, but I just stood there like a stone in front of my own daughter—I was responsible for where she was today. I took a few steps towards her. I was convinced it were true, but I wanted to be absolutely certain. I reached out to touch her right hand in what looked like a gesture to comfort her. Slowly, I touched her elbow, moved the cloth that covered her arm with my fingers and looked at her skin. There it was, the black birthmark, just like I had seen it years ago.

EIGHTEEN

Memories rushed back. The young girl was playing in a field, smiling at me. Now I knew who she was and why I saw her in my dreams. She wanted me to know that she had lived. She had taken me back to the day she was born—the day I had touched her skin, held her in my arms. I wanted to tell her I didn't abandon her, that I had wanted her enough to travel miles to give birth to her. I should have listened to my heart when it had insisted that she was destined to live.

I woke up abruptly, realizing I had slept past sunrise. Sita occupied my thoughts. The fact of her life overshadowed its consequences. I was plagued by questions—how would I tell Dashaanan? Whom do I tell first, if at all? I was a mother meeting her daughter for the first time in twenty-six years, and hoping for her to make it back safely to her husband. I had to protect her till Rama arrived.

Before I could try and convince Dashaanan to free her, I heard Sita had been moved to Ashokavanam on his orders. She was now watched over by female guards. Dashaanan had given Rama a year to find her before he would marry Sita himself. I was afraid Dashaanan's need to possess Sita would deprave him. I prayed for Rama to find her before revenge knew no reason for my husband.

An ashoka tree stood at the centre of Ashokavanam. A verandah formed its circumference, where small gatherings were held. Adjacent to it was a private garden accessible only to Dashaanan. A waterfall that merged into a stream marked its end. Dashaanan had wanted to make Ashokavanam a botanical garden for the recuperation of those who visited it.

Dashaanan's palace overlooked the verandah where Sita spent her days, seated at the crotch of the Ashoka tree. He frequently watched her. I was desperate to protect her from Dashaanan's overtures. Trijata was my only confidante. Her health indisposed her to serve at the palace; she had to be sent for whenever her assistance or presence was needed. When I told her about Sita, she was shocked to hear that my child had survived and was none other than Rama's wife. She remembered the time twenty-six years ago when I had lost my daughter to ill-fated circumstances. She had lost her child too. Thrilled and surprised to learn Sita's true identity, she took up the task of protecting her like her own daughter.

Trijata watched over Sita like a hawk. Her presence amidst the grim female guards brought some, if only a little, solace to Sita. The eight months of Sita's internment felt like eight years. My hope waned with each passing day but Sita's faith in Rama never wavered. She knew he would rescue her. Dashaanan seemed to cross off the days to a year. He summoned the navagraha deities again, suspecting time to be unfavourable to him. Also, on his mind was the question of his future sovereign stability if he married again.

Dashaanan had addressed Sita only twice since he had brought her to Lanka. I was thankful for his restraint, the cautious distance he kept from her. Sita grew to love Trijata like a mother. She told her about her life as a little girl in Mithila, about Rama and their lives in exile. I had not known my own daughter. I did not have that privilege even now; all I could do was stand by as she waited helplessly for Rama.

※

An intruder had circumvented security and made it into Ashokavanam. A gong was struck as a warning sign. This was the first time Lanka's security had been breached. Amidst the panic, a meeting of family members was convened. We had to take action. It was as if riots had broken out in the city. I went to Dashaanan; he was having an intense discussion with Meghanath and Prahasta.

'My lord, what is the commotion about? Is there really an intruder in Lanka?' I asked.

'Yes, *Matashri*, a supposed compatriot of our hostage has managed to get in,' said Meghanath.

'Is Sita safe?'

'Sita is safe. The intruder did not harm her, but he destroyed almost half the trees in that garden when the guards tried to arrest him,' said Dashaanan.

'My lord, has he been arrested?'

'Not yet, Mandodari, we will soon . . . '

'Pitashri Lankesh, I have identified the intruder! He is a vanara,' our youngest son, Akshayakumara, reported as he rushed in with guards in tow.

'A vanara! Are you sure? Why would a vanara trespass into Lanka?' asked Dashaanan.

'I am sure, Pitashri! If you allow me, I shall arrest him and get him here,' said Akshayakumara.

'Go ahead then. Get him here!' ordered Dashaanan, and Akshayakumara left for the mission.

'Bhrata Dashaanan, the king of the vanara tribe is your friend. Why would a vanara mean any harm to us? I suppose it's a mistake . . . ' suggested Vibhishana.

'A female guard at Ashokavanam saw that vanara talking to Sita. She alerted the other guards but in the meantime he escaped. We are not sure why he was talking to Sita. Vanaras are our friends but this one has caused a lot of destruction, also injured our guards,' explained Meghanath.

I was concerned about Sita's safety. Dashaanan instructed the soldiers to search for any other intruders. The palace and the antapura were under strict surveillance; the main gates were sealed until further notice and soldiers made sure that every building in the city was well searched.

While this was done, Akshayakumara was reported as injured by the guards. Reportedly, he led our soldiers at Ashokavanam to arrest the intruder; however, he was crushed under a huge tree and soon fell unconscious. I panicked. Nanashri rushed to arrange a physician for him. Dashaanan was furious about the situation. He then ordered Meghanath to arrest the intruder, alive or dead.

Meghanath followed his father's orders and took command of Ashokavanam. We witnessed his mission from the palace corridors. We saw Sita walking around unharmed, though anxious about the whole situation. On the other side of Ashokavanam, we saw a monkey-like tall man climbing the trees and trying to escape. He carried a metal mace on his shoulder; he was muscular and bulky. And as rightly identified by Akshayakumara, he was a vanara as he sported a long tail attached to his attire. Meghanath used various weapons to catch him.

This was the first time I saw Meghanath attack or fight. However, this was not a great show of his skill; the vanara dodged every attempt Meghanath made to nab him. Dashaanan grew even more furious and yelled at Meghanath to kill him at once. Meghanath took a different arrow this time, invoked a mantra to greet the weapon with respect—I knew it was the deadly Brahmastra— stretched his string and shot at the vanara. Surprisingly, the intruder did not die. He was affected by the blow, but stood unharmed; back on his feet. Then, finally he surrendered himself to Meghanath.

He was presented at court for interrogation. Everyone was keen to take a closer look at him; his arms and torso were tied together with ropes. He appeared bulky and enormous, wearing only a dhoti; he looked at us eagerly.

'Who are you, vanara? How did you get here? And how dare you trespass into our garden?' asked Nanashri.

'I am Hanuman. On the orders of my lord shri Rama, I came here searching for *janani* devi Sita. I have found her.' He answered and everyone present at court was stunned.

'You are a vanara. The king of your tribe at Kiskinda is a friend. How did he allow you to carry out the commands of Rama?' asked Dashaanan.

'I regret to inform you all that Lanka's so-called friend Vali has been defeated by his twin brother Sugreeva. King Sugreeva has now taken command,' said Hanuman and the crowd started murmuring. Some shouted, 'My lord, he is a spy!'

'So you have come to spy on us!' said Nanashri.

'I came looking for janani devi Sita who has been kept confined here! I came to deliver a message to her from my lord shri Rama,' said Hanuman.

'What is the message? Tell us,' asked Dashaanan.

'Shri Rama says he will soon slay the monster who dared to touch devi Sita! He will burn the kingdom that held her hostage and his wrath will set such an example that no one will attempt anything like this ever again,' declared Hanuman.

A chill ran down my spine. Dashaanan smirked at Hanuman. 'That is very interesting. We await your lord Rama here. If he wishes to set his wife free, he and Lakshmana can surrender to me. I am that monster who abducted Sita. I will avenge my people whom he brutally killed and ensure that no sister ever goes through this ignominy again.'

Hanuman smiled arrogantly, 'Surrender! You must be foolish to imagine something like that from *prabhu* Rama.'

'Mind your tongue, vanara! You are standing in front of Lankapati Ravana. Choose your words carefully. I will not hesitate to burn your daring tongue,' shouted Meghanath.

'I say you choose your actions wisely. There is still time; return devi Sita to prabhu Rama respectfully and ask for his forgiveness. He is kind-hearted . . . '

'Dare not utter as much as a word more or else we will finish you right here!' shouted Nanashri.

'Enough!' Dashaanan called for order. 'We are wasting time. Put him in prison.'

Hanuman let out a loud laugh. He breathed deeply. The ropes around him unspooled and fell to the floor. Deliberately mocking, he proclaimed, 'I am Pawan-putra Hanuman. I need not brag, but I would like to see who can imprison me.' He pointed at Meghanath: 'I chose to honour the Brahmastra by submitting to him. If you think you can hold me captive this easily . . . '

'I think he is *mayavi*. We should convey a warning to Rama. Let him go, my lord,' suggested Vibhishana.

'Have you lost your mind?' asked Dashaanan outraged. 'We cannot stand by and be humiliated. He injured my son and threatened me in my own court. How can we let him go?'

Vibhishana spoke softly so only Dashaanan could hear him. 'He has proven to be slippery. Meghanath employed the Brahmastra and he still stands unharmed. His looks are deceptive. He is a mayavi. If we take him captive, we may risk more destruction to our property.'

Dashaanan remained stubborn. 'I don't care. Arrest him and take him away.'

Vibhishana stood back, defeated. He turned to Nanashri and whispered something. They nodded in agreement. Nanashri intervened, 'My lord Lankesh, let us teach him a lesson. I suggest we consider him a messenger. We cannot incarcerate him then but we must punish his transgression.'

Dashaanan understood the advantage of Nanashri's suggested course. 'What punishment do you suggest, Nanashri?' he asked.

'A vanara's tail is his pride. I say we burn it. He will leave Lanka in shame. That will be our response to his people for the devastation they have caused us.' Twenty soldiers pinioned Hanuman down on his knees. He did not resist. It was a spectacle, almost like a performance put up for entertainment.

As soon as his tail was set alight, he shoved away the soldiers forcefully. The court recoiled. He took his mace, chanted 'Jai shri Rama!' and ran out, hitting the guards in the process. It was mayhem. Soldiers chased him and we all looked incredulously on. He leapt from building to building, setting ablaze everything in his wake. Soldiers scrambled after him, torn between capturing him and extinguishing the Lanka they had pledged to defend. We knew neither how he came nor how he left. We were struck with disbelief. Some claimed they saw him fly away with the help of a device around him. We hurried out. The fire was spreading rapidly. Our palaces, fountains, buildings and gardens were turning to ash in front of us, the gold that gilded them melting. Dashaanan left the scene, unable to see such destruction.

We had not anticipated the ruin a single vanara could bring.

Meghanath and the younger brothers—Prahasta, Atikaya and Trishir—took charge. They sent family and ministers indoors until the crisis was averted. The fire was doused; hurt soldiers taken for treatment and the damages calculated. Narantaka and Devantaka took care of the battalion. Borders were secured. Any trespasser henceforth was to be killed on sight. We avoided each other's eyes, at a loss for words. I stood in the corridor, watching Lanka blacken with smoke. A day of dark events, I saw the sun set into a darker evening.

The next morning, Dashaanan gave orders to repair his kingdom. He could not bear to see what he had so painstakingly built be reduced to dust. Physicians attended tirelessly to Akshayakumara but he remained unconscious. His head injury was severe. Dashaanan monitored his progress. I spent two days beside him, praying for him to wake up. He never did. He passed away in his sleep on the third day. There is no greater agony than watching your child die. Our youngest son was taken out of vengeance. I could not eat. I lay sleepless at night, benumbed by the loss of Akshayakumara. I knew people around me were trying to talk to me but I could not hear them. Three days later, arrangements for his funeral were made; the pyre set up. Akshayakumara's head lay in Dashaanan's lap and he leaned into it, howling with grief. I finally let myself cry. I touched his face, the wounds on his forehead. Dashaanan, Meghanath and the other brothers lit his pyre.

We mourned for thirteen days. We ate one meal a day. I saw the sun rise and set from my chambers. Why had the gods been so unfair to me? My daughter was estranged from me. I had left her all those years ago and she had found her way back to me. Even then I could not love her like her mother. Then Meghanath, who is more his father's son than mine. Worst of all, the loss of Akshayakumara, my youngest, in a ridiculous battle. Was this to be my fate as a queen?

It took us a fortnight to resume our duties at court. Buildings had been restored to their original condition, fountains repaired and gardens replanted. Akshayakumara's empty seat was the only, and most important, thing we could not restore. We gathered at court to honour his bravery and service. I saw the emptiness our other children felt. In my grief, I had ignored the loss Dashaanan and the other princes had endured. Dhanyamalini and Nayanadini too. In all the years of Dashaanan's reign, no other day had been mourned this way. Sita was held responsible. I stayed quiet. I did not want my firstborn to be blamed for my youngest son's death.

While others blamed her, Vibhishana held Dashaanan accountable. Something in him had changed. Amidst the condolatory remarks, Vibhishana spoke up.

'Bhrata Lankesh, accept my sincere condolences for your loss. We have mourned for our youngest prince but the grief of recent tragic events hasn't palliated. Who is responsible for this catastrophe, my lord? Don't you think the gods are angry at us for holding that woman captive? This seems like retribution!' said Vibhishana. We were shocked. The ministers started murmuring amongst themselves.

'What is wrong with you? This is not the time or place . . .' Nanashri nudged Vibhishana.

Dashaanan interrupted, 'Let him talk, Nanashri. I want to hear what he has to say.' Sarama, who sat amongst the ladies, looked frightened by the brewing tension between the brothers.

'I will not say much, bhrata Lankesh, I never have. Akshayakumara was innocent and died because of our decisions.'

Dashaanan grew grave. 'What do you have to say? Say it clearly!'

'Pardon me, my lord. Adversity followed this kingdom from the day you abducted Sita and brought her here. Nothing since then has been peaceful. Look at what that vanara was capable of. Think about what will happen when Rama and Lakshmana will reach Lanka? Are we so unworthy that we couldn't contain a vanara? No, my lord, this is because of that woman who we have held hostage. Release her or else we risk losing everything we have today.'

'I don't believe these are your words, Vibhishana. I was not the one who started this battle. They did by mistreating our sister. And it is her we seek to avenge. You think yourself wise for suggesting Sita's release? Where was this wisdom when we were planning our revenge? Where was your bravery when our sister was beating her chest with grief? You stand today to accuse me, but where was your judgement when that vanara stood in our court and you didn't let me arrest him!'

'I hold myself responsible for what happened. But I suggest you eliminate the root of these circumstances now. Release Sita and end this.'

'You speak not with wisdom but cowardice, Vibhishana!' shouted Dashaanan. 'Because you are my brother, I spare you the punishment for such violation at court. I granted you the freedom to speak, but do not forget that I am still your king.

Learn to take a firm stand, brother; had you been in my position, you would have failed this regency with your instability years ago!' Vibhishana lowered his face and remained silent.

How times had changed. After all that Dashaanan had given for his kingdom, his own brother and sister were displeased with him. His sister had pointed a finger at him for killing her husband, who had been nothing but a traitor and liability, and now his brother, who had always been sheltered by Dashaanan, had had the nerve to criticize him in open court.

※

Gradually, we learnt about other losses. The vanara had destroyed our ports, took away or scattered our devices at the astronomy tower. Shani deva, one of the navagraha gurus, went missing that day. He was not to be found anywhere, believed to have escaped when the city was burning. The other navagraha gurus assembled to guide Dashaanan as per their astrological predictions. Dashaanan was advised to initiate nothing new for the next six months. He waited impatiently for the stasis to end.

I had not seen Sita after Akshayakumara's death. Trijata conveyed her condolences. I couldn't decide on an appropriate response. She was the reason Hanuman had come to Lanka. He had been capable of rescuing Sita. Why hadn't he? The thought pressed ominously on me. Why hadn't Sita stopped him as he tore down our city and my son?

There were so many loose ends, questions left unanswered. Nine months had gone by. The deadline given to Sita loomed closer. I wondered if Dashaanan still wanted to marry her, after all that had happened. Rama's absence could not be explained. It was time for Dashaanan to know the truth. 'Your majesty, the king has summoned you to court.' My thoughts were interrupted by a dasi.

'Is everything all right?' I walked into the court. A discussion was going on. Dashaanan waited for me.

'Sit, we will know,' said Dashaanan and gestured a minister to speak. The minister, Mahaparshva, had recently been promoted as one of the chief generals of the army.

'My lord,' he began. 'We saw their army. It is huge. There were vanara people, troops of monkeys trained for labour, boats, cattle, and they have set up their camps on the southern shores of Bharatvarsh. They are certainly planning an attack,' said Mahaparshva.

'Pardon me, my lord, but whose army is he talking about?' I asked Dashaanan softly.

'Rama and Lakshmana. Our ministers were sailing back after a trade in Bharatvarsh. Near the port, they saw vanara men in a camp based at the shore,' answered Dashaanan.

'So Rama and Lakshmana are with the vanaras at their camp?' I asked the minister, trying to connect the dots.

'I am afraid it is the other way round, your majesty. We followed the vanara men without getting noticed and enquired nearby. We were told that two princes from Ayodhya—Rama and Lakshmana—along with their allies from the vanara tribe, headed by Kiskinda king Sugreeva, have set up camp at the shore, planning on ways to cross the ocean with their army and troops.'

The court erupted in whispers. Dashaanan remained silent, stoic but for a furrowed brow.

Nanashri came forward and said, 'We should probably send a spy or another army in-charge who can give us exact details.'

'The information sounds reliable; Mahaparshva knows what he is reporting,' said Dashaanan.

'Pitashri, if you allow me to, I can travel with a few soldiers and enquire further,' said Meghanath.

'No, I need you here.'

'One of us can go,' volunteered Atikaya, who stood up with the other brothers.

'I am not sending either of you there. I need you all here. I know whom to send . . . ' said Dashaanan.

I looked at Vibhishana. He had remained stubbornly mute, still offended since his spat with Dashaanan.

'How do you think they will cross the ocean, Nanashri?' I asked.

'Well, the mainland of Bharatvarsh is connected to Lanka by an indistinct narrow bridge of land. The ocean separates us from Bharatvarsh, making it impossible for any army to attack us. And the land bridge is barely a trail, eliminating the option of halting in between the ocean,' explained Nanashri.

'They can attack us if they have vessels or ships,' said Prahasta and they trailed into a discussion about the different strategies that Rama could use.

I listened patiently. They concluded that Rama could attack us if he had ships, and before he attacked, our army would destroy his ships before they could land on our shores.

Strategies were being mapped. I looked at Dashaanan. He was surprised that Rama had an army by his side. From what we knew so far, Rama seemed sufficiently equipped. 'Pitashri, we await your command,' said Meghanath.

'We can stop them before they sail. Summon Ahiravana immediately. Tell him I have a mission for him,' commanded Dashaanan.

Ahiravana was Dashaanan's cousin. He was the chief of the Patala region. He had supported Dashaanan during his battle against Indra and Dashaanan had helped Ahiravana establish his reign. He had a small but powerful army. He was entrusted to bring Rama and Lakshmana alive to Lanka.

NINETEEN

Ahiravana was convinced he could follow through with Dashaanan's orders. Dashaanan had sent soldiers with Shardula to spy on the mission assigned to him. They were supposed to relay the news of Ahiravana's victory. Three days passed with no news. Day four brought report of his death. He had been killed by Hanuman. Ahiravana and his men were outnumbered by the soldiers of Rama's camp. Attacking the vanara army with fewer men would have put their lives in danger. They decided to sneak into the camp and abduct the brothers. In the dead of night as Rama's army was sleeping, Ahiravana had got inside secretly, evading the night guards. He looked for Rama and Lakshmana and found them asleep. He used a deep sleeping draught on them. He carried the unconscious brothers out of the camp. He was to depart for Lanka with his captives the following day. Ahiravana's army had reached halfway when it was confronted by the vanara army headed by Sugreeva and Hanuman. The brothers were rescued. In retaliation, Hanuman spared neither Ahiravana nor his soldiers.

Ahiravana's fall turned the council of Lanka to cajole Dashaanan into releasing Sita. Dashaanan was steadfast, loath to give up Sita or shy away from the imminent battle. His attempt to contain Rama's army offshore had failed. Before Rama could find a way to sail his army into Lanka, it was imperative for Dashaanan to stop him. Once war was declared, there was no turning back.

The next day begot a spate of dreadful events. An alarm sounded. A ship had sailed towards Lanka. At once our thoughts went to the enemy camp. Our soldiers surrounded the ship when it reached our shore. The dead bodies of Ahiravana and his soldiers were piled up in it. The sailor offloaded the cadavers on our land and sailed back. Sambukumara, Meenakshi's son, was in the heap, a finding that chilled us to the bone.

Once again the city convulsed with agitation. Going to court felt like dipping into the past. Meenakshi was crumpled over her son's body. Apparently, Sambukumara had been taken prisoner by the vanara army on his way back. He was killed and sent to us along with Ahiravana. I could not bear another young boy dead. Our family was straining under distress. Preparations for a mass funeral were underway. Council ministers approached Dashaanan for further discussion.

We sat attentively at court. Yet again Vibhishana accused Dashaanan. 'Bhrata Lankesh, how can you live with the massacre we have witnessed today? Ahiravana defeated and dead with his men; Sambukumara, the only child of our sister, brutally killed. And here you are planning vulnerable strategies against the man who seems invincible,' said Vibhishana.

Nanashri was offended. 'Have you no loyalty, Vibhishana? Remember he is our king. You should be helping the council instead of opposing our lord's every move.'

'Have you evaluated these strategies, Nanashri?' Vibhishana raised his question boldly.

'Vibhishana, we don't have time for this right now,' said Dashaanan.

'Well then, you better clear your schedule, bhrata Lankesh, unless you want your kingdom to fall apart.'

'Decorum, Vibhishana!' shouted Dashaanan. 'I have taken enough of your criticism and ignored your insolence. You are spineless. Have you ever thought from my perspective?'

'I have always prioritized Lanka's best interests. You helped us thrive but you will also lead us to ruin. You are doomed to fail.'

'Enough, Vibhishana, do not test my patience and goodwill further. Leave this court before I expel you and suspend your position permanently,' said Dashaanan.

'This is treason, Vibhishana,' said Nanashri.

'My lord, you should suspend him. How long will we tolerate his dissent? He doesn't deserve to be seated at this court!' said the chief of ministers.

Vibhishana saw angry faces glaring at him. Sarama stood up uncomfortably. She walked towards her husband. 'What are you doing? Why are you doing this?' she asked.

'I am doing the right thing. Before bhrata Lankesh suspends me, I wilfully resign. I am leaving this court and this kingdom.'

Sarama reeled. Women stole knowing glances at each other. The council took the declaration favourably. The members were not fond of Vibhishana. He was respected for his relationship to Dashaanan but lacked his grit.

'I ask you to reconsider, Vibhishana . . .' said Dashaanan.

'I have made up my mind, Dashaanan,' replied Vibhishana.

'You moron!' began Nanashri but Dashaanan raised his hand to stop him.

'You are not being wise, brother, but I respect your decision,' said Dashaanan calmly. 'Bhabhi Sarama, your position in this kingdom is not affected by your husband's decision.' Sarama lowered her face. Her husband had embarrassed her.

Vibhishana looked at his wife. He knew she wasn't brave enough to walk away with him. He placed his hand on her shoulder and softly said, 'It is all right. I am leaving alone. I don't belong to this place now.' Sarama shook her head with tears. He turned around and walked out. It was as if he had decided to quit long ago.

'I can't believe it,' said Dashaanan. I held his hand firmly.

'He was rebelling. Had he stayed longer, I would not have been surprised if he had challenged your place as king,' said Nanashri.

I interrupted, 'Vibhishana? He would never . . .'

'I have seen brothers disputing for the throne, Mandodari. He has been sulking for ages. His incompetence made him insecure. Going against his brother's commands was a petty ploy to prove he could be a better king,' said Nanashri.

The council agreed with Nanashri's judgement. Built of the same flesh and blood, Vibhishana was genetically as gifted as Dashaanan. They were brought up and educated the same way. Dashaanan emerged exceptional. They were brothers with different destinies. Dashaanan was the king and Vibhishana a mere council member. Vibhishana had followed his brother into the dark all these years but he had been suppressed enough. He could no longer pledge obedience to his brother, especially not when, Nanashri was right, somewhere deep down he wanted to rule.

※

It broke Mata Kaikesi's heart. Her family had cracked irreparably. She refused to eat and drink. She could not comprehend the reason for Vibhishana's departure. He had not bothered to see his ailing mother before disappearing entirely from our lives.

Dashaanan visited Mata Kaikesi and shared her grief. It was not Vibhishana's absence that anguished him, but his allegations. A family that had been in power for decades saw relationships amongst their immediate family members as a matter of repute. We were struggling to bridge differences with Meenakshi after her husband's death, and now Vibhishana had struck another blow to the foundation.

Mata Kaikesi couldn't bear it for more than six days. She died of distress. It felt as if the gods had abandoned us. One by one, death snatched away those close to us. The war had not even begun, yet we mourned the many we had lost. Mata Kaikesi's death took away Dashaanan's motive for success. She was his making, his strength throughout his reign. Dashaanan asked for Kumbakarna to be woken for her last rites. He had been unwell and asleep for three months, unaware of anything that had taken place. Together, they lit their mother's pyre.

Kumbakarna was surprised to learn about Vibhishana. He knew about Sita being kept as a hostage. He was told about Hanuman and all that had followed. His condition made him incapable of participating at court. He was roused from sleep on Dashaanan's command whenever necessary. Dashaanan and Nanashri sought his advice on the forthcoming battle. Keeping all aspects in mind, Kumbakarna suggested we wait for Rama's army to cross the ocean if it could. He was not in favour of another attempt to finish them offshore. Only if Lanka got challenged for battle on its own land, would Dashaanan have the right to strike as per the rules. Hence, we had to wait and watch if Rama's army could cross the ocean.

Vigilance was demanded of us. Lanka was put on high alert. The stadium that was once a sporting arena was converted into a ground where troops were to assemble if and when we were attacked. Meghanath prepared the artillery force. He briefed the soldiers in the different war strategies that would be used and divided the army into eight equal units. Each unit had its own commander reporting directly to our sons. Atikaya, Prahasta, Trishir, Devantaka, Narantaka, Kumbh and Nikumbh were promoted as chiefs of commanders, each in charge of an army consisting of 30,000 rakshasa soldiers. The remaining soldiers were assigned to secure the city. Dashaanan also summoned other asura warriors from neighbouring regions to fight with him.

We were prepared for the war but there was no sign of Rama or any ships or boats in the ocean for days. Then almost a month later, our watch-guards reported seeing some kind of a grey lining on the ocean. It didn't look like a fleet of ships or a threat they had previously reckoned with. Meghanath immediately sent a patrol team to find out what was approaching. The patrol guards returned after their inspection. They brought us information that was beyond the limits of our imagination.

'My lord, the trained monkeys of Rama's vanara army have been gathering rocks to build a path to Lanka. The grey lining visible on the ocean's surface is in fact a manmade bridge. Rama's vanara army has constructed a broad bridge over the ocean to commute their army to Lanka. We saw a group of trained monkeys passing and gathering rocks to build the bridge,' said the leader.

This was beyond our wildest imagination. 'A bridge made by monkeys! Are you sure of what you are saying?' I asked him in surprise.

'Yes, your majesty, initially we were surprised too. Upon sailing ahead, we saw vanara men in huge numbers instructing the monkeys. They intend to bring everything to Lanka via that bridge—an army of about 80,000 vanara men, artillery machines that can fire missiles, weapons, food, tents, hardware and an army of monkeys . . .'

One of the ministers smirked. 'My lord, they want us to fight a battle with monkeys!'

'Silence! You are underestimating the enemy,' said Dashaanan. 'What else?' he asked the leader of the patrol team.

He went on: 'My lord, indeed we should not underestimate them. That bridge is well supported by layers of different rocks and designed by vanara architects Nala and Neel. We saw some rocks, probably limestone, that can float on water. Rama and Sugreeva are the leaders; and they have some brilliant minds with them. They have trained labour, warriors, skilled vanara men who are proficient in combat, and, my lord . . . ' he paused.

'What is it? Is there anything else?' asked Dashaanan.

He did not meet Dashaanan's eyes. 'And, my lord, they have your brother Vibhishana guiding them on the background of Lanka. He joined them almost a month ago.'

Dashaanan's eyes widened but he said nothing. Vibhishana had stooped to his lowest. It was still acceptable when he left, but joining the enemy was something we never expected him to do.

Nanashri was furious. 'He has stabbed us in our backs! He is a traitor! A spineless traitor!'

'Stay calm, Nanashri Malyavan,' said Dashaanan.

'Forgive me, my lord, but Vibhishana has betrayed us . . .' said one of the ministers.

'How can he go against you . . . he is your brother!' I started.

'A brother who wants to finish another brother for his throne . . . how else would you justify his decision to join Rama?' added Nanashri.

'My lord, Vibhishana is now one of the most trusted members among Rama's supporters. We disguised ourselves as fishermen from Bharatvarsh, sailing back home. We wanted to find out more but Vibhishana would have recognized us. Hence, we returned with whatever information we had,' said the leader of the patrol team.

Dashaanan could sense our hopes sinking. My mind was in disarray. I started thinking in all directions. We were going to fight a grand war. I could not believe it. What we thought would be a battle soon grew into a war. Dashaanan had fought many battles and wars, triumphed in most of them, but I had never experienced or even witnessed a war before. This was the first time that we were defending ourselves. The threat would be coming to our gates.

Dashaanan prepared to leave; he looked at us and said valiantly, 'It is good to know that our enemy is well prepared for the war. And why is everybody so surprised by their planning? Don't forget that they are coming to fight us . . . the land of the invincible rakshasas! From now on, my only family is the one with me here. I have no brother except Kumbakarna. Keep yourselves prepared . . . for the most awaited enemy to reach our gates. Har Har Mahadeva!'

※

Rama's army reached our shores in eight days. We could hardly believe that they had actually landed in Lanka. Dashaanan took me to the highest level of his palace; the shore was clearly visible from there. We saw Rama's army setting up camp far ahead of the city gates, near a mountain called Suvela. We couldn't make out distinct figures or recognize any people from that far, but we saw chariots, artillery machines and flags. Their flag was orange and blue, diagonally divided, with a conch shell in the centre. Orange represented the vanaras of Kiskinda, and blue stood for Rama. The conch shell venerated Vishnu. And the diagonal union of the colours stood for their union—Rama and Lakshmana with Sugreeva, the new king of Kiskinda.

Anxiously looking at the enemy at our gates, I asked Dashaanan: 'Is he here with their army, my lord—Vibhishana? How can he step on this land? Is he not guilty of betrayal?'

'I don't care if he is here, Mandodari. All I care about is winning this war. I have a lot to do,' replied Dashaanan.

I tossed and turned in bed that night. The sight of Rama's army had made my stomach churn. My thoughts were fraught with anxiety. There were so many things running in my mind. I wondered how Dashaanan could take so much pressure when it was wearing me down like this. I was pacing up and down in my chambers, waiting for the break of dawn. As soon as I saw the sunrise from my window, I took a dasi and a guard with me and walked to Mahanta's house, the old priest who had once predicted my future.

He had passed away eight years ago, but his son Mahantakumar still lived there. He was a healer to the commoners. He was mixing some herbs when we reached his abode. He looked at us, trying to recognize me. Before he could say anything, the guard stated: 'The queen would like to speak to you . . . she seeks your advice in private. Treat your conversation with the queen as confidential.'

'Of course, of course . . . I understand,' said Mahantakumar, clearing a place for me to sit. 'I am sorry I did not recognize you, your arrival took me by surprise. What can I do for you, your majesty?'

'Years ago, I had come to your father to seek his advice. I had seen some dreams at that time, some nightmares that had worried me about my husband and our future. Your father was concerned about my future . . . he had predicted a few things that I understood as time passed. And today, again, I seek some advice. My husband, my children and our kingdom are all under threat. A formidable enemy awaits us. I need to know what will happen next. If there is a war, then how will it end?'

Mahantakumar shook his head regretfully. 'Your majesty, I am a healer. Unlike my father, I am neither a priest nor a sorcerer. I cannot help you.'

In desperation I persisted, 'But you have the gift of vision like your father, don't you?'

He looked at the state I was in, my eagerness, and replied, 'I can try, your majesty. I am uncertain of what they mean when I get these visions. My father's voice resounds in me. My own dreams elude me sometimes. However, I will try my best for you.'

He ushered us into his house. He sat down in a corner and closing his eyes, breathed deeply. We waited as he meditated. Suddenly, his eyes popped open and he gasped.

'What? Did you see something? Anything related to the war?' I probed.

'A war between the two sects will be recorded in the history of mankind. A hero will die . . . for someone is to be elevated as god; the end of an era; a brother devoted to another brother; a boon misunderstood; the nectar of immortality; you shall reign next to him for years ahead, you shall tell him the truth; he is the real father; she will walk into fire; for fire is the reason she was born . . . ' he whispered in a trance.

A chill ran down my spine. I did not know what to make of what he had said. 'Can you say it again? What does that mean?'

'I am sorry, your majesty, I cannot repeat it because I don't remember what I said.'

'But did you see anything?' I asked him. 'What did you see?'

'Yes, I did. I saw two strong visions, only two . . . In the first one, I was standing outside the city gates surrounded by vanaras. They wanted something from me but I don't know what I was doing there as I am not a soldier. Then I saw myself mixing some herbs,' he muttered ominously. 'It's a strange vision. And in the second one, I saw you seated on your throne as the queen. You looked much older than you are now.'

I sighed with relief. A war was coming; that was certain. If I was seated as the queen, Dashaanan would have defeated Rama and would reign for years ahead. My mind went back to his mention of truth. It was time now; I could not hide Sita's identity any longer. Content with what I had heard, I thanked him and returned to my chambers.

Later that day, a vanara was presented at court as 'a messenger of peace' sent by Rama and Lakshmana. Our soldiers surrounded him. Seeing another vanara at court, the council ministers were attentively anxious. He was dressed like Hanuman, only he appeared younger. He was smiling when he was escorted in front of Dashaanan by ten soldiers. It gave him the impression that we were scared of him and his vanara army.

Dashaanan was informed about him. He dispersed the soldiers at once, furious that so many had collected against a sole vanara.

'I hear you have come with a message of peace,' said Dashaanan.

'You heard it right. We have an army waiting to crash the gates of your city. But Rama makes this last effort to prevent the war. He has sent me to convey his message of peace,' said the vanara.

'Tell us then . . . what is it that you propose?' asked Nanashri.

The vanara looked around. 'This is strange behaviour. Isn't there a code of conduct in Lanka to seat their guests? Instead, you have had me escorted by ten soldiers. Are you so threatened that you forget your manners?

'Get him a seat!' shouted Dashaanan. 'I admire your courage, vanara. You look quite young. And for a young man like you, it takes immense courage to walk inside the enemy's gates so boldly. Who are you? What is your name?'

The vanara sat down and introduced himself. 'I am Angad, son of the late king Vali of Kiskinda. My mother is Tara.'

Dashaanan smiled warmly, 'Angad! I wonder what you are doing in Rama's army . . . your father Vali was my friend. I saw you when you were a child.'

I could see that Dashaanan was delighted to know that Angad was Vali's son. He welcomed him warmly. It is my pleasure to have you here. Not as Rama's messenger, but as Vali's son. I invite you as my guest to stay with me here.'

Angad interrupted, 'I have come here for a specific purpose. I am a general in Rama's army. Sugreeva is my king now, and I follow his commands. I know you were my father's friend, but he is not alive any more. I also know that you challenged him to a duel once and he scared you to death!'

Dashaanan's smile faded. I spoke up for his honour, 'You talk about conduct, vanara. Have you no reverent conduct to talk respectfully in front of an emperor who was once your father's friend?'

'Today, he is not my father's friend but a guilty coward who abducted Rama's wife!'

'Enough, vanara, or else we will forget the diplomatic immunity you hold right now as a messenger and incarcerate you for contempt,' said Nanashri.

Angad grinned. 'Take me to prison? You can't. I bet no one in this court can even move a single limb of my body.' He stood up firmly and challenged: 'Come forward, try and move my leg off the ground!'

Everyone present hesitated to challenge another vanara. Dashaanan ignored his conceit. 'Remember that you have come as a messenger of peace, hence, do not instigate anyone from this court to some kind of a match. Tell us what you are here for . . . announce your proposal,' said Dashaanan.

'Well, Lankapati Ravana, Rama does not wish for a war. You abducted his wife through deceit, but he still extends his hand in peace. A war will cost lives. Hence, he suggests a way that can help us all live in peace. He suggests you release his wife Sita and apologize for your behaviour. Rama is merciful; he will forgive you for your actions,' announced Angad.

Dashaanan looked irritated. He replied sternly, 'Tell Rama that I agree to release Sita in exchange for his own custody. I want Rama and his brother Lakshmana captive in my court, and then I shall immediately release Sita. For I abducted his wife to drag him here; he and his brother owe my sister an apology too. They murdered asuras but I will forgive him for his actions!'

The council ministers burst into applause. They started cheering, 'Long live Ravana . . . long live his reign!'

Angad concluded that his proposal had been rejected. His voice boomed over the cheer. 'That will never happen . . . and your people are foolish to believe that they can detain Rama and Lakshmana like prisoners. I suggest you consider my proposal instead! Think once again, Ravana . . .'

Dashaanan laughed out loud, 'Oh, young Angad, they sent you here as a messenger . . . it is a pity that you take orders from them. Don't you realize that you are the rightful heir to Vali's throne? Sugreeva reigns only because Rama killed your father.' Angad looked uncomfortable and ready to leave. 'Were you not told why Rama killed your father? Didn't they tell you that Rama killed your father to crown Sugreeva as the king of Kiskinda? Go then and ask Hanuman about it. And convey what I have proposed to them. Or else I will wait for them to start a war tomorrow!' said Dashaanan. I was amazed at his confidence. Angad, the messenger of peace, left in dejection.

Asura warriors from different regions gathered at Trikota to wage war alongside Dashaanan. He and I welcomed some of the mightiest rakshasa warriors of that era—Dhumaraksha, Vajradamstra, Akampana, Mahodara, Jambumali, Makaraksha and Virupaksha. They came along with their armies to support us. Each section of the army was aligned with another division brought in by these warrior leaders. It was understood that a war would be signaled the following day. We all knew that Rama would not agree to Dashaanan's treaty and hence we were certain that the vanaras would signal us for war the next day.

Dashaanan was occupied with the army generals. He arranged a grand feast to feed his soldiers and warriors exuberantly before they set out to face the enemy the next morning. I had been restless since Angad's departure. We were the hosts, defenders and avengers. The war promised to be momentous for us. I saw Sita from the corridor. She sat under the ashoka tree; her eyes shut in prayer. My own daughter, so similar to me yet so differently destined. I went inside the garden to meet her. This was the first time I had entered Ashokavanam since Hanuman had invaded it. Barely any trees were left. Sita saw me and stepped forward.

'I have a lot to say. I am meeting you after very a long time. I am sorry for your son Akshayakumara's loss . . .'

'He was my youngest son, barely eighteen. He was protecting his land, he did not deserve to die,' I replied. She remained silent, thinking what to say next.

'It was not Hanuman's intention to cause harm.'

'If his intention was not to hurt, then why did he kill our people, including my son? You could not see the condition of our city when it was burning because we kept you here, out of danger.'

'You have kept me hostage; I am in danger all the time,' she argued.

I smiled at her innocence. She was so blinded by her love for her husband that she did not realize what a miserable life she had led with him for years.

'What about the years you spent with Rama in exile? You lived like vagabonds, wandering from one forest to another, through wilderness. Was your life not at risk then? Rama took the lives of so many, always endangering both of you.'

'How can you compare my freedom then with the helplessness your husband has shackled me to now? I never thought you could be so unfair. I have been nothing but a living corpse since the day that monster Ravana laid eyes on me . . . he is an immoral brute driven only by lust.'

'Careful what you say when you speak about him, Sita. You know nothing about him. He might have separated you from your husband but what harm has he done to you since the day he brought you here? You were in a more wretched condition with your husband than you are here. You say he is full of lust but has he ever even come close to you?'

Tears spilled from her eyes but she looked at me unwaveringly. 'Tell me Ravana does not want to marry me. The rakshasi women gossip. They say that Ravana is waiting to kill my husband and then he will drag me to his antapura. You love him too much to see that. But let me tell you this, Rani Mandodari, each breath I take is in the name of my husband. I will take my life the very moment Ravana touches me again.'

The truth in what she had said shattered my wilful delusion. She spoke the harsh reality that I had ignored for months. I was living in denial. She was right, Dashaanan did plan on marrying her eventually. He thought he could because I had kept the truth from him. When did I think I would tell him, when he was dragging our daughter to the antapura? Was it too late to tell him now? There was too much at stake. This would probably be the greatest war of Dashaanan's life since he defeated Indra years ago. I thought back; moral or immoral, my husband had never kept secrets from me. I decided to do the same and tell Dashaanan the truth about Sita.

It was almost midnight when I walked into Dashaanan's chambers. He was engrossed in playing the veena. I stood at the threshold, entranced. His fingers plucked out a soft tune. I was seeing him play a peaceful tune after a very long time. As a matter of fact, I was seeing him play the veena after years. Dashaanan liked to play music in solitude. He paused when he saw me standing at the door.

'Ah, what brings you here, Mandodari, how are you still awake? Come inside, shall I play something for you?'

'I wonder, my lord, how can you be so composed when a war is imminent tomorrow?' I asked him.

'Well then that is also a reason to stay composed now. What starts tomorrow, starts tomorrow. Why let it ruin this beautiful dark night? As for the war, I have fought many.'

'My lord, you don't seem convinced about commencing this war,' I whispered to him.

He looked into my eyes and said, 'I will be honest with you, Mandodari. I do not wish to go into any battle or war. I have ruled this kingdom for decades; nobody has ever challenged me on my land before. The revenge I seek is not worth a battle this massive. I have lost my son, my people, but I am too far gone to turn back now. My pride will not let me, my arrogance . . . you had once told me once that my arrogance made me who I was and I'd much rather sustain it than give it up now.'

We inched closer. He took my hand and kissed it.' Then why haven't you slept, my lord?'

'Like I said, of all the wars I have fought, none has ever come to me like this. My land, my own brother against me. They are right outside the gates of my city. I am bound by the laws of war or else I would have finished them off before they could have landed.'

'My lord, how long do you think this war will last?'

He smiled at my question. 'Not very long. You rest assured.'

My secret tugged at my heartstrings. I knew this was the moment to tell him. 'I want to tell you something. I know it is too late, but trust me, my lord, I have not known this very long.'

'What is it, Mandodari?

I did not know how to begin. My lips trembled in fear. It was now or never for me. 'I kept a secret from you. But before I tell you, please remember that I never meant to hide it from you. Dire circumstances and shifting priorities always made it difficult for me to tell you everything at the earliest. I'm not sure if you can forgive me for what I am going to tell you, but I have to tell you tonight, for tomorrow will be too late.'

'I have trusted you more than I trust myself. You are the only person who knows me completely, Mandodari. So go ahead and tell me what you need to. I do not question why you kept it from me. I know you would have had the right purpose for hiding it from me.'

'It happened after your marriage to Nayanadini, during the time Rishi Gritsamada was staying here. I conceived a child from you, my lord. Only I found out about it after recovering from the effects of the poison I had consumed when we had quarrelled about Gritsamada's death.' I continued, unable to look at him. 'I consulted a physician about my weakness and unusual symptoms. He told me I was with child, but it would have been affected by the poison I had consumed and the antidotes given to me. I called Mai to help me. I kept my pregnancy a secret because I knew you wouldn't allow me to keep the child. Then I asked your permission to go on a pilgrimage, and I left for Badarikasrama as soon as you allowed.

'While I travelled and offered my prayers at each tirtha, I felt the child growing stronger inside me. My body did not oppose it. There were no repulsive symptoms in my body. I observed it for seven months. Then, one night, in a secluded region of Bharatvarsh, I gave birth to our daughter.'

'You delivered a daughter! Our first child and you kept it a secret?' asked Dashaanan and I felt my heart pounding fiercely in my chest.

'Hear me out, my lord. She could not breathe, her heart was giving up. We waited till dawn to see if she would live but she did not move in my hands. With a heavy heart, I buried her inside a pot and covered her body with soil from the fields. I cannot describe my bereavement or the guilt of hiding it from you. Before I returned, I concluded that our first child was not meant to live and, hence, I made a choice to bury the secret forever in my memory.'

'How could you hide it from me, Mandodari? It was not just your child but mine too!'

'I know, my lord. I was just hiding it from you because you would have asked me to terminate the child. I was confident that the child would not be disabled.'

Dashaanan grew impatient, 'But then the child died! So after all these years, Mandodari, why are you telling me about it now?'

'Because that child, our daughter, is still alive!' I answered immediately. Dashaanan's eyes, bloodshot with rage, were now rimmed with tears. 'You lied to me, all this time . . .'

'I knew only when I saw her again. She told me how she was found in a field near Mithila and was adopted. She is the reason for this war—Sita is our daughter.'

Both of us stood transfixed. Relief washed over me but I was terrified of what Dashaanan would say. He was shaking, his fists clenched, and his face flickering between anger and shock. Unable to control myself, I broke down. 'Forgive me, my lord. I wanted to know our child and that was the only way. When you brought Sita here, I had no idea she was our daughter. Upon meeting her, I knew. She had the same birthmark as our daughter. I couldn't believe she had miraculously survived. I wanted to tell you right away but I was scared. I waited for Rama to find her but he took too long. While she stayed, you grew interested in marrying her. I should have told you then, it haunted me every minute to keep it from you, but there never seemed to be a right time.'

Dashaanan had his back to me. He hadn't said a word. 'Lankeshwar,' I begged. 'Please say something.'

'I have to fight a war tomorrow. I request you to leave, Mandodari.'

'There was no better time to tell you, my lord. There is no right time for such things. It was destined to be this way. Destined to be a secret to the world. I leave her destiny in your hands.'

TWENTY

On the third day of their arrival, the vanara army assembled outside the gates of our city. A conch shell was blown to signal the commencement of the war. Our army lined the gates, facing the enemy, and with the sounding of the conch shell, formed the famous asura *vyuha*, a defensive war formation that makes configuration impenetrable. The three gates of Trikota were secured. The only direction viable for attack was north. From Lanka, Dhumaraksha, Nikumbh, Jambumali and Virupaksha initiated the first day. Our soldiers were on standby to fight but Rama's army did not move. Instead of men, they sent monkeys to our city. Hundreds of monkeys swarmed through Lanka, tumbling over the iron barriers of asura vyuha. They were uncontrollable, in massive numbers, leaping over gates and racing across the city. We were soon besieged by monkeys. It was chaos. They carried no weapons nor attacked us but the racket they made left us at a loss.

They plundered the queen's palace like thieves, terrified the women, climbing in from everywhere—doors, windows, corridors. Dhanyamalini and I were sent to a safe room; Nayanadini and others soon followed. Our soldiers chased the troop, seizing one monkey occupying three men.

While they were parrying the attack, we remained unaware of the situation outside the city gates. The queen's palace was firmly safeguarded. Dashaanan watched from the topmost corridor of his palace. He used various magnifying devices to view all directions of the war field. The soldiers lit torches to scare the monkeys out of our buildings. Along with the other women of the palace, I waited impatiently for some news to reach us.

A guard finally reported to us.

'Dhumaraksha and his army attacked the vanaras as soon as the war started. The number of casualties on both sides is equal.'

'Nikumbh? Where is Nikumbh?' asked a concerned Bajrajala.

'He is guarding the western gate with his army. His unit may not fight today,' answered the guard and left her in peace with the knowledge that her son wasn't fighting. She told us she had noticed several bad omens around her and had wished that her sons delayed their entry in the war.

It was almost twilight when we heard from the guard again. 'Hanuman broke Dhumaraksha's chariot into pieces. Dhumaraksha fought valiantly but was sadly defeated and killed by Hanuman. Lankeshwar has sent the mighty Vajradamstra and his army next, towards Angad and his unit, who are proceeding towards the eastern gates.'

After sunset, the conch shell sounded again. Battle drums were beaten inside the city. The day's war was over. The guard gave his final report.

'Your majesty, the number of casualties on both sides remains equal. A fierce battle was fought between Vajradamstra and Angad. Sadly, Vajradamstra was killed in combat.'

We lost two great asura warriors on the first day. Their armies were almost ineffective without their leaders.

'Where is Lankesh? I need to meet him,' I asked the guard.

'I am sorry, your majesty, but Lankeshwar is occupied with the generals in the stadium.'

'I would like to request an audience with him at the earliest.'

'I shall convey your message, your majesty.'

I longed to meet Dashaanan privately. Since the war had started after I had told him about Sita, I had been unable to meet him. Throughout that evening, I kept sending him requests to see me and he kept denying them.

Vigorous drum beats marked the second day of war. Akampana and Mahodara, two great asura commanders, were sent to fight along with Prahasta. Nayanadini waited with us at the palace, praying for her son's victory and safety.

The guards soon reported to us. 'On the field today, Akampana fights a duel with Hanuman, and his army has attacked the vanara *sena*. Mahodara formed the vajra vyuha and attacked Sugreeva. Lankeshwar has asked Prahasta to attack from the eastern gate.'

I tried to calm Nayanadini and her daughter-in-law's anxiety. 'Prahasta will do well; he is a great warrior.'

'So were the warriors who were killed yesterday . . .' Nayanadini replied impulsively.

'You can watch him fight from the tower, if you wish,' I suggested.

'No, Mandodari, I don't want to see my son on that field. We're terrified. I know you understand, you lost Akshayakumara, but our children are too young to fight in this deadly war.'

At that very moment, another report from the warfront reached us. Nayanadini grew more restless. 'Prahasta has killed many important warriors of Sugreeva's army with his unique combat skills. He was attacked by a vanara called Neel. Lakshmana is trying to move into the formation to rescue the army suffering at Prahasta's hands.'

'Lakshmana! He has to fight with Lakshmana now?' Nayanadini turned towards the guard. 'Call my son Narantaka and tell him to help his brother on the field.'

Dhanyamalini tried to placate her. 'Gather yourself; the war field cannot be ventured into at random.'

She cried back, 'Then why don't you tell Lankesh to fight his own battle . . . '

I grabbed her shoulders, 'No one wanted the war, Nayanadini. We got dragged into it and so did Lankesh. Compose yourself for your grief will not help your son on the field.'

Like clockwork, our army retreated at sunset. The second day was over. It was reported that Akampana was killed by Hanuman and Mahodara slayed by Sugreeva. We received no news about Prahasta. Nayanadini ran outside the palace hoping to see Prahasta. A chariot brought in his body, soaked in his own blood, an arrow pierced through his throat. He had been killed by Lakshmana. His body was presented to his mother and wife.

※

The palace echoed with the howls of the bereaved. Nayanadini was devastated; she sat with Prahasta's head in her lap, not ready to let his body be taken for his funeral. Meghanath came forward to take his brother's body for the last rites; he had lost another beloved brother today. Dashaanan waited near the pyre, his eyes reflecting a deep sorrow on losing another son. Meghanath lit Prahasta's pyre along with Narantaka and Devantaka. They pledged to avenge their brother's death. Meghanath declared that he would finish Lakshmana off the next day.

I returned to my chambers. I had lost another son, not born of my womb but still my own. It was past midnight when a dasi knocked. 'Your majesty, Lankeshwar would like an audience with you in his chambers.'

Dashaanan had finally sent for me. I had wanted to hold him at the funeral, share his grief, but he had not even looked at me. This time, when I entered, he did. 'My lord, thank you for seeing me, your silence has tortured me. You distanced yourself from me at a time when we needed each other the most.'

'I needed time to think, Mandodari. I was angry with you, very angry. I trust you more than life itself and you betrayed me. However, I have broken your trust in me more than you have. My crimes remain larger than yours.'

Dashaanan moved closer and I wept in his arms.

'My lord, hiding it from you is my greatest regret. I should have told you at the beginning itself.'

'Quite the contrary, Mandodari. You did the right thing by not telling me then. I would have asked you to terminate your pregnancy at once. I wouldn't have risked a disabled heir. You did what you had to do; you fought your own battles as I did mine. It was probably destined to be this way. But one thing is for sure, you could have told me the truth earlier. Knowing it at this hour shattered me.'

'Forgive me, my lord . . . '

'This is unforgivable; like a few deeds of mine you cannot forgive. Look at what we have lost. I have a daughter that I so longed for, whom I have held hostage. My own daughter curses me every day. It is her husband I am to fight. What if I had won the contest at Mithila? What if I had married my own daughter? Then I carried her here and planned to marry her if Rama didn't come for her. What if I hadn't given her a year?' Dashaanan groaned, a man repenting for what he had done unknowingly.

I tried to comfort him. 'You didn't know, my lord. Even I came to know only after I met her. Something forbade you from marrying Sita. Don't you think that is destiny? Some supreme power favours us and prevented it.'

'Prevented it to what end? This day? My daughter is a prisoner in her own home. Like a nomad she wandered with her husband at his service. Is this her destiny? Was she born to suffer? If a supreme power kept me from marrying her, why did it keep my daughter from a life of happiness too?'

'We can never know why it had to happen this way. What do we do next? Should we tell her?'

'We can never tell her. She wouldn't believe us if we did. What kind of father imprisons his daughter and plans to marry her? I cannot see her as my daughter even now that I know who she is. It tears me apart, the state I have put her in.'

'We will not tell her then, but we cannot stop this war, we have to win it.'

'If that is what it takes to make Sita stay, then we will win this war.'

'We will build her a palace. You may declare that she is like a daughter to you; we will find her a suitable husband . . . '

Dashaanan smiled at my plans. We shared a moment of tenderness that we could not afford otherwise. War precluded vulnerability. We had already lost another son and one more was headed to war come daylight.

※

On the third day of the war, Virupaksha, Makaraksha and Meghanath attacked. Dashaanan and I saw Meghanath fight. He was a dexterous warrior, quickly eliminating the army guarding Sugreeva before calling Lakshmana out to fight. The vanara army attempted formations to distract him from Lakshmana but Meghanath outsmarted them. Dashaanan explained the events to me and I prayed for Meghanath's safety. A chariot emerged from the western flank of the vanara camp. Lakshmana was mounted on it, answering Meghanath's call for battle. Another chariot, we speculated Rama's, tailed his.

As soon as Meghanath saw Lakshmana's chariot, he signaled for his men to train the weapon in Lakshmana's direction. A warhead in it exploded into poisonous gas used to obstruct the enemy's vision and breathing. The soldiers' first shot coloured the air dark green. Right then Meghanath and his men shot arrows at Lakshmana's army. Soldiers were falling everywhere, disabled by the green gas.

'Nagapash, a weapon as poisonous as the venom of a hundred snakes,' explained Dashaanan. Nagapash was not only a weapon, but a trap set for the enemy. It was a strategy to reach Lakshmana and Rama even as they stood guarded behind their men. The gas was so powerful that Rama and Lakshmana fell unconscious in their chariots.

Dashaanan was thrilled; he applauded his son's intelligent strategy. He kept cheering his name from the tower even though he knew his voice would not reach Meghanath. We waited for our men to reach the spot and surround the brothers, but before they could, the vanara army formed a garuda vyuha to save Lakshmana and Rama. It looked like a huge bird from above. Chariots with orange flags, led by Hanuman, surrounded the spot and saved the brothers from getting detained.

We emerged victorious on the third day. We waited for Meghanath at court. Virupaksha and Makaraksha returned victorious too, but it was mainly because Sugreeva's army was too busy fighting off Meghanath's attack on the western side of field. Meghanath returned with a humble smile, and Dashaanan embraced him at once. Now, we waited for further reports from the warfront soldiers to confirm whether Lakshmana and Rama would fight the next day.

Failing to get a validated report, Dashaanan prepared his next set of warriors for the fourth day. Atikaya, Trishir and Mahaparshva were asked to fight. We were told that Rama and Lakshmana had recovered from the effects of Nagapash, and had regained their stance on the field. Concerned about his brothers, Meghanath asked permission to join them but was denied in accordance with the laws of war. The frontline commanders and generals could not enter the field on the same day or at the same time. In order to function with continuity, commanders and generals were grouped as per rank and sent out on the field periodically.

Dhanyamalini waited for the day to end. Both her sons were fighting. Their wives waited at the lounge for the soldiers to report the scene. I observed the war with Dashaanan again. We waited for Atikaya and Trishir to end the day victorious. Atikaya attacked Lakshmana, Trishir went for Rama, and Mahaparshva fought with Angad. Atikaya fought heroically, his skill in archery at its best. Lakshmana fought a duel in archery with him. Dashaanan kept explaining the weapons they used. Lakshmana's parvata baan, an arrow named after the mountains, was defused by Atikaya's pavan baan, an arrow named after the wind. Atikaya's naga baan, which was shaped like a serpent, was defused by Lakshmana's crescent moon-shaped arrow.

While Atikaya and Lakshmana fought in the west, Trishir fought his battle with Rama's army near the eastern gates. The day was about to end. Our army had fewer casualties than the vanaras. As the day was about to close, Mahaparshva retreated to the city gates without concluding his battle with Angad. Trishir drove his chariot to cover Mahaparshva while Rama chased Trishir. Hanuman's army attacked Trishir and his unit from the other side and trapped him in between. Frustrated at not being able to defeat Atikaya, Lakshmana invoked the Brahmastra and finished the job. Dashaanan and I rushed down. Dhanyamalini, along with Bajrajala, came towards us. They did not know yet. I stopped in my tracks. She looked hopefully at Dashaanan. 'It ended, didn't it? The day is over . . . no major casualties I was told.'

Dashaanan could not break the news of Atikaya's death to her. Mahaparshva entered the city, and Bajrajala lightened. Dhanyamalini's eyes searched for her sons, 'Where are they?' Atikaya's chariot was brought inside, followed by Trishir's chariot. They stopped in front of Dashaanan. Dhanyamalini knew; she walked to the chariots and fainted at the sight of her dead sons.

*

Piles of bodies burnt. Hundreds of women mourned for their sons and husbands. Children wept for their fathers. We cursed the day Rama's army had stepped on our land.

Dhanyamalini was barely conscious. I stayed indoors with her, unable to see or attend any more funerals. Atikaya's wife, pregnant with his child, was now widowed. She stepped inside to check on her mother-in-law's health. War had made us all suffer; the living and the unborn. The carnage I had seen spattered my dreams with blood. I could not sleep. From that day onwards, I withdrew indoors, avoiding watching the war.

Meghanath's strategy was conveyed to me. Narantaka and Devantaka were to accompany him. My will was broken; all I wanted was for Dashaanan to return Sita to Rama and end this war. I could not bear the thought of losing more children. Meghanath visited me after midnight. He walked into my chambers, clad in armour.

'Have some pity on your poor mother, Meghanath. Why have you come to me in armour? I don't want to see you fighting any more; I don't want to see any of my sons fighting any more . . .'

'What are you talking about, Mother?'

'I am going to ask your father to end this war. He has to return Sita and end this ridiculous war.'

'How can we give up now, Mother? What of the lives we have lost, our martyrs, how will we do justice to their sacrifice? This war is not about Sita any more. It is about all we have lost. They started this war with a purpose—to defeat the reign of rakshasas.'

'I don't understand what you are saying. You talk just like your father, Meghanath!'

He smiled and took my hands in his. 'I seek your blessing, Matashri. I will fight Lakshmana again tomorrow.'

I kissed his forehead. 'You have always been your father's son. You never obey me like you do your father. Tell him there is a way to stop the war. If you tell him, he will try to stop it; he will listen to you.'

'I cannot do that, Matashri. The only way to end this war is by winning it.'

His valour amazed me. I smiled and blessed my son. 'Go on then, may you end this war by winning it.'

Come dawn, Meghanath entered the field again to fight Lakshmana. A protracted battle was fought between them. Narantaka and Devantaka aided him. Meghanath used all his force; he knew by now that Lakshmana was not an ordinary warrior. He perplexed him with deceptive disappearing acts, repeatedly vanishing and reappearing in front of him. Their fierce encounter lasted for two days. The sun set and rose again and they kept fighting. Neither would yield. Meghanath's illusions finally led Lakshmana out of his defensive formation to face him alone. He employed the deadliest weapon he possessed, the Ghatini Shakti, deposing Lakshmana off his chariot. He fell unconscious, poised to die precisely before sunrise.

Meghanath returned exhausted from his two-day battle. Against all odds, Lakshmana survived. Rumours of a disloyal healer helping the vanaras spread. Dashaanan asked Meghanath to perform Nikumbhila yagna, which would enable him to ride the invincible celestial chariot he had been gifted once. Kumbakarna was summoned to fight. He feasted before the battle and met his wife and sons. Although of mammoth proportions, his military prowess had been compromised because of his boon. He, however, did not give marching into the battlefield second thoughts. Bajrajala and her sons were prepared to not meet him alive again. Meghanath started his yagna to please Goddess Prathyangira. He sat inside the temple cave to attain siddhi over the celestial chariot and weaponry. On the field, Kumbakarna kept the vanara army occupied for two days with the havoc he wreaked. The commanders of the vanara army tried to contain him, but they were all defeated one by one. As a last resort, Rama took to battle on the second day. He wounded Kumbakarna with numerous shafts; disabled his arms with shots and crushed him with the Indrastra. Kumbakarna fell like a great hill into the sea. Death was inevitable in war, as was deceit. While Meghanath meditated, vanaras attempted to distract him from his yagna. Only Vibhishana knew the purpose of this yagna and he had undoubtedly cued the vanaras about it. Lakshmana went to the extent of attacking Meghanath while he was unarmed inside the cave, injuring him. They succeeded as Meghanath had to abandon his quest.

Some nights, monkeys would loot our temples and granaries. Their supposed morality had been reduced to farce. They assaulted our women, beating them, tearing their clothes, sometimes even dragging them out of their chambers. A wounded Meghanath entered the field with his brothers. Narantaka took a javelin and killed several vanara men. He fought a duel with Angad, while Devantaka fought Hanuman. Both parties sustained grave injuries. Meghanath continued his battle with Lakshmana. They fought with various weapons trying to knock each other down. I barely understood the effect of the weapons they used; unwilling to see the war unfold, I waited for explanations.

'Meghanath fired a Yamastra, a weapon named after Yama, the god of death, that Lakshmana destroyed with Kuberastra. Lakshmana launched a Varunastra, but Meghanath destroyed it with Raudrastra, the weapon of Shiva,' reported our guards.

The battle continued, culminating in news that sent tremors across our city. 'Narantaka has been defeated by Angad. He has been brought to the city but he suffers deadly injuries. Lakshmana fired an Indrastra at Meghanath, destroying his chariot and . . . ' one of the guards trailed off. I needed to hear no more.

Three more sons taken by the enemy. Dashaanan lit their pyres. Nayanadini, Dhanyamalini and I sat frozen. Their wives wept with grief, cursing their killers and Sita. Sarama bore the brunt of many taunts because of Vibhishana's disloyalty. The sky thundered at Meghanath's death as it had upon his birth. Sulochana, his beloved wife, handed her four-year-old son to me and became sati on her husband's pyre.

TWENTY-ONE

A day after mourning, a broken-hearted father and a shaken king prepared to fight. Nanashri, Dhanyamalini, Nayanadini and I talked to him through the night. We said everything but what was on our minds. We wanted him to come back alive. We wanted him to come back to us.

Sister Meenakshi's arrival was announced. It was for her that Dashaanan was fighting this war, but except for attending funerals, she had severed her connection with us.

We thought we would express our resentment but Dashaanan welcomed her warmly. 'Bhrata Dashaanan, I have come to wish you luck.'

'My sister . . . I will fight for your honour. I may not have been the best brother but I tried making it up to you. I will deliver Lakshmana's head to you by dusk. But in case I fail to do so, I hope you will not hold it against me.'

Meenakshi fell on his feet with regret. 'Bhrata Dashaanan, I am sorry for being so cruel to you. Long before asking for revenge against Lakshmana, I wanted revenge from you. I held you responsible for my agony; you killed my husband and I blamed you for my misery. After Khara and Dushana's death, I came to you for justice and vengeance because I wanted you to fight for me, but more than that I wanted you to repent for my despair. I don't know why, but I wanted to see you fail somewhere. In order to prove yourself, you started a conflict by abducting Sita. When my son was sent to me dead, I thought my only family here was Vibhishana and Kumbakarna. I was still angry with you. Vibhishana disgraced us by joining our enemy. He took refuge under the same rival who had assaulted his own sister. But you kept your word and gave everything to this war, even your children!'

Dashaanan stood still. He looked at our enraged faces. Dhanyamalini and I were irritated with the futility of what she was saying. Nanashri was eager to condemn her selfishness.

'So, today you admit to your real intention of provoking your brother to war!' Nayanadini yelled at her.

Dashaanan gestured for her to stop. He held Meenakshi's shoulders and raised her up and accepted her confession.

'I knew you wanted more than just revenge. You wanted me to repent and compensate for your misery, and I hope you are satisfied now. In order to fulfil your thirst for vengeance, our kingdom had to bear the brunt of this war. I hope you realize what is at stake, dear sister. When the widows of Lanka were cursing Sita for all the fatalities, they forgot to mention you,' said Dashaanan.

'Please don't say that. I never thought it would start a war . . . I never thought it could take so many lives!'

'Then how did you think a war is fought? A war costs lives; it claims the throne, causes destruction and leaves a kingdom deprived of food, wealth and sometimes even the right ruler.'

'So I request you, brother, please don't fight. Don't go. Give them Sita and put an end to it.

Nanashri interrupted, 'You think it is that easy to stop the war? You really think they are here only for Sita? They want to conquer this kingdom, Meenakshi. Our community, our people and our land is at stake. Rama and Lakshmana are on a mission and they want to conquer Ravana's Lanka. While they were slaughtering rakshasas and asuras in Bharatvarsh, thereby deteriorating our strength, they were always backed by the devas. They may not directly involve themselves in this war, but they extend their support to Rama and his army.'

'So in between their mission, I just happened to encounter them . . . '

'Yes, but your desire for revenge provoked your brother to abduct Sita, and Rama's mission got a new dimension wherein he had reason to attack one of the greatest rakshasa kingdoms. It was for you that Dashaanan took Sita captive and lured her husband out to war, thereby marking Lanka as a possible target,' answered Nanashri.

'The only regret I have, dear sister, is that although we fought for your honour, you considered me your adversary. While we were fighting the war for you and also for my people, I had my own brother Vibhishana and you wanting to see me fail. Now you can leave, at ease after your confession, yet I have to fight this war today for my people and my kingdom,' said Dashaanan. Meenakshi bowed deferentially and exited.

Dashaanan bowed before Nanashri. 'I have so much to say, Lankesh,' Nanashri said, blinking back tears. 'I am grateful to have served you. No matter what happens today, you will be a hero and the golden era of your reign will have a place in Lanka's history.'

'Nanashri, you have been the keeper of the throne from the time my grandfather Sumali sought to win Lanka. I have relied upon you for guidance throughout.' His voice cracked. 'In case I don't return, promise me you will mentor my heir, and along with Mandodari, let him claim his rightful position.' He walked towards the corridor. He wanted to see Sita before he fought, in case it was the last time he saw his daughter. Hesitantly, I asked, 'Should we tell her before you go?'

'We can never tell her. I could not bear pity for me in her eyes. Let her hate me for what I have put her through, but not as her father. Right now, it feels like the last time I will see her.'

'You are not being yourself, my lord. You are Ravana, a mighty emperor, a formidable conqueror . . .'

Dashaanan took my hands in his. 'I am nothing today, Mandodari. I have nothing. I have lost my sons, my family and my compatriots. I have watched them die, set fire to their pyres. Tell me what remains now.'

I was struggling to give him hope so he would live, for his sake as much as mine. 'My lord, you cannot lose this war, you are invincible!'

Dashaanan shook his head. 'I was arrogant, Mandodari. I thought I was invincible. I asked to be indestructible by all beings except vanaras and *manavas*. Never could I imagine them attacking my kingdom. I face Rama as a mortal man. Today, I am not invincible.'

My heart sank. I did not want to believe what Dashaanan had somehow made his peace with. He would return safely. He would rule and I would sit beside him like the old days. Mahantakumar had seen it happen. Dashaanan would triumph and Lanka would thrive again. 'You will come back to us. This is where all your life's work has led you to. Deliver us, my lord.' I was crying as I reassured him. It was meant more for me, I realized.

Dashaanan looked at me earnestly and cupped my face. 'You are a queen, Mandodari. This kingdom is as much yours as mine. If I am gone, you have to lead our people.' He kissed me gently. 'You are the same as you were when I first saw you.' He held me close. 'It's time. Give me my Chandrahas and bring me my bow. I will fight them with the might of Bhairava. Wish me luck.'

※

Nanashri and Mahaparshva watched the battle from the tower. We waited inside on tenterhooks. I prayed to Shiva to favour his parambhakt.

A narrator visited me thrice during the day to narrate events that took place on field.

Mounted high on his parasol, Lankeshwar Ravana entered the battlefield with his mystic missiles. Rama and Lakshmana attacked Ravana together. A tumultuous battle broke out between the two entities. The ground was covered with the black flags of Lanka; Kumbh and Nikumbh had destroyed most of the vanara army with their power. Rama repeatedly charged at Ravana different astras, thereby injuring his sky-borne ambari war elephant and bringing him down on a chariot. Both Rama and Ravana made full use of their knowledge of warfare. Rama charged deadly weapons at Ravana—Varuna astra, Surya astra, Trimurti astra, Bhumi astra, Garuda astra, Deva astra, Sudharshan astra, and many more. But the lord of Lanka defused all of Rama's attempts with his miraculous retaliation.

The first day of the battle between Ravana and Rama came to an end at sunset. After an arduous battle, Ravana proposed to Rama to dismiss his falling army for the day and gather his dead from the field. Thousands of vanaras were dead that day. It was too much killing for one single day. Hence, it was decided to continue the battle next day. Soldiers of both sides returned to their camps. Ravana too returned to his camp, which was set up outside the gates of his city. A young and impressive warrior like Rama couldn't have imagined the incomparable prowess of an aged king like Ravana, until he experienced his sagacious and strident aggress on his own. That day they had fought like they would bring the sky down to earth, inflicting severe injuries on one another, brutally killing soldiers of each other's army.

The next day too there was a similar sight on the field. Ravana was unstoppable. The warrior princes from Ayodhya set a different strategy today. They made a crescent moon formation to separate Ravana's army. Sugreeva led his army behind Kumbh towards the western gate and Hanuman challenged Nikumbh on the eastern side of the gate. Thus, the unbeatable duo was separated from each other. Ravana saw his army drifting in opposite directions and knew it was a trap. He doubled his force and went straight for Rama and Lakshmana, without letting anything distract him. What looked like a crescent moon formation was soon eclipsed by Ravana's wrath. Seeing their emperor Ravana fight with such valour and ability—nothing of the courage and strength of a Veerbhadra or Bhairava from Shiva—the rakshasa soldiers cheered in high spirits. The fierce battle did not conclude that day, it continued throughout the night till dawn.

Tired and separated from the rest of the army, Kumbh decided to fight a single combat with Sugreeva. He stepped down from his chariot, an iron club in his hand and charged towards Sugreeva. But his blows did not impact the vanara who was an expert in martial combat himself. One after the other, Sugreeva lifted his fists to strike a blow and shattered the armour worn by Kumbh. The strong rays at sunrise hit Kumbh's weary eyes, blood oozed from his body and he fell on the ground, thus defeated by Sugreeva.

Seeing his brother fall in another part of the battlefield, a distressed Nikumbh hurried towards him. But the powerful and swift Hanuman was behind him—he pounded his mace on Nikumbh's shoulder and Nikumbh fell from his chariot. An angry Nikumbh leapt towards his enemy, roaring horribly in irritation, but Hanuman landed another blow with his mace and tore off Nikumbh's head at once.

While his brother's sons were being mercilessly slaughtered on the same field, Ravana fought an exceedingly terrific round of archery with Rama and Lakshmana. He kept the brothers engaged in responding to his splendid compilation of celestial weaponry. He bombarded them with the Shakti astra, Shiva astra, Kali astra, Yaksha astra, Parvata astra and Maya astra. By afternoon, due to the non-stop pace of the battle since the past two days, Rama and Lakshmana were exhausted. Ravana's charioteer too was tired. Lakshmana started to succumb to the pain of his wounds; his injury was not completed healed. Hence, this time Rama proposed to discontinue the battle. He raised a flag to propose a halt and call it a day. Ravana looked at the state of his charioteer, now failing to cope with his pace, and signaled him to lower the flag on his chariot, accepting the proposal. Hence, they mutually agreed to continue the next day.

It was the fourth day of Rama and Ravana's battle, and the thirteenth day of the war. Rama and Lakshmana were now concerned about their multiple failed attempts to beat Ravana. On this day they had a familiar face among them; standing with his newly formed alliance was Lanka's enemy, Vibhishana. He had joined Rama on the field to guide him. As if his betrayal of his own land wasn't enough, he stood beside our enemy, without any guilt or regret, to defeat his own brother.

Seeing his deceitful brother come out of hiding, Ravana's eyes must have turned red with anger because the first arrow he pulled on his bowstring was the deadly Mangal astra. Rama defused it with a Yama astra, which not only destroyed the approaching Mangal astra but also injured the person firing it. Although Ravana was injured—he fell inside his chariot from impact—he stood up momentarily to fight Rama again.

I was walking across the courtyard. An ominous disquiet had settled in the pit of my stomach. My dasis were trying to ease me but I was disconsolate. Dashaanan had been fighting for four days now. I awaited his return. Nanashri came looking for me. 'I am afraid it is not good news; Dashaanan has been gravely injured.'

I stumbled and Dhanyamalini and Nayanadini rushed to sustain me. Disoriented, I asked him, 'I was told he was still fighting?'

Nanashri looked at the reporter with him and nodded. He began, 'Your majesty, after the Yama astra failed to do what it was meant to, Rama and Lakshmana consulted Vibhishana. Vibhishana gestured towards his lower abdomen and pointed at Lankeshwar. Wasting no time, Lakshmana handed his brother the Brahmastra, a weapon that makes the earth quiver. Rama immediately pulled it on his bow and pierced Lankeshwar's naval with it.'

The shadow of Dashaanan's past fell over the courtyard, stifling every sound till it was completely still. Years ago, Dashaanan had created amrita. It had been administered intravenously, via an incision behind his naval. The antioxidants accelerated his cell growth, allowing his body to heal rapidly. Vibhishana had known this and chosen the right moment to use the knowledge against Ravana.

'How is he now?' I asked breathlessly.

'We are not sure. Rama sent a messenger to inform us. Dashaanan was knocked off his chariot,' replied Nanashri.

'I want to see him right now!'

Nanashri tried to convince me otherwise but I paid him no heed. 'My husband has been wounded, this kingdom has almost collapsed. How do you expect me to sit here and wait?'

'Rani Mandodari, it could be a trap to get to you. Let's bring Dashaanan inside our compound.'

I was already running towards the field. Guards clambered behind me as I ran through the gates into the heart of the battlefield. It was a sea of bodies. They lay in pools of blood, viscera scattered everywhere. Dashaanan's chariot gleamed in the sun. Beside it, he was sprawled on the grass. I prayed to find him alive. If he were to die today, I'd die tomorrow.

'What brings you here, Mandodari?' My knees buckled with relief at Dashaanan's bemused remark. I laughed. Tending to him, I asked, 'How did this happen?'

'It was bound to happen. I braced myself for it. I put up a good fight, though, didn't I?'

I smiled. 'We'll take you inside now and you can make a full recovery.'

'It is of no use. The nectar has been ruptured. My body will slowly decay. I lived this long only to see you one last time.'

'I will die with you.'

'Don't you even think about it. You are Lanka's queen; it needs you. Promise me you will do whatever it takes . . .'

I held him and wept. 'Don't cry like I have failed you, I die written in history.'

He took his last breath. His eyes closed. I held Dashaanan's body for a long time. The sun blazed and extinguished into night. Eventually, Nanashri tapped my shoulder. 'It's time to go inside.'

While I cried and moaned over my husband's dead body, other women were howling in grief too—Dhanyamalini,

Nayanadini and a number of concubines from the antapura. Some of them, who had never crossed my path, screeched and yelled on losing the man we shared. Beside Dashaanan's chariot, Angad, Hanuman and Sugreeva stood with Rama and Lakshmana.

'Devi, your husband was a great king and warrior. Accept our condolences.'

'You must be Rama,' I said.

'I am.' He gestured to the man beside him, 'This is my brother Lakshmana. We have learnt a lot from your husband during this battle. We pay our respects to him.'

Lakshmana added, 'We would not have harmed him had it not been righteous.'

'And you decide what is righteous and what is not,' I snarled.

'Devi, it is time to give Ravana his last rites. Take him inside,' said Rama, avoiding any further conflict.

We rode inside in chariots. Everybody gathered around Dashaanan, chanting his name. I looked around, dazed. Lanka was lamenting the king who had given his life for this kingdom. We had fallen apart. The vanara leaders followed us, Vibhishana on board their chariot.

Aghast they should desecrate Dashaanan's last rites, I took Nanashri aside. 'Why are they here?'

'This kingdom is now theirs.'

His reluctance to continue made my blood run cold. Finally he said, 'These are the norms of war. The defeating army gains right over the defeated kingdom. Lanka is at their mercy now.'

I had been so preoccupied with the events of the war that I had disregarded the consequences of losing it. We had no warriors left to challenge the *vanara* army and reclaim our kingdom. It was only the women who had lived. Rama and Lakshmana, after all the blood they had shed, stood amidst us, indomitable.

※

Kings and leaders of neighbouring regions poured in to pay their respects to Dashaanan. His other lands had now fallen into Rama and Lakshmana's command. The funeral was arranged for the next day. Lanka's streets spilled over with ministers and dignitaries who grieved for Dashaanan. Songs of his valour reverberated across the city. The reign of rakshasas was over—the golden era of Ravana's empire dimmed into the twilight of history. While I prepared for my husband's funeral, Vibhishana invited Rama and Lakshmana to live in our guest mansions. Vibhishana's return had plunged him into lower depths than his departure. He had no place in the very land he had betrayed.

Dashaanan's body was placed on the pyre. I relived the first time our eyes had met. My father's introduction had muffled, the courtroom ceased to matter—it had been only Dashaanan's gaze holding mine. This is where I loved him now, in memory. Nanashri climbed the pyre to light it. Vibhishana stood with him. 'What is he doing up there?' I protested. 'He has no right to touch him!'

Bajrajala, Meenakshi and my mother looked pointedly towards Rama. I continued, 'Who is he to direct my husband's funeral? We stayed silent when they entered our city, but no more. They have no business here and neither does Vibhishana. That traitor!'

The council stepped forward and stood beside me. People joined in, taking a stance of defiance. Rama gauged the shaky ground he was treading on. He walked up to me, cloyingly humble. 'Devi Mandodari, we are not in a state of war any more. A blood relative is required to give burial rites to the deceased. Vibhishana has the right to do so. He belongs to this kingdom like you do,' Rama cajoled.

'You may have the right to rule this kingdom, Rama, but I will not allow as much as Vibhishana's shadow to fall on my husband's pyre!'

'Devi, I implore you. Let your king depart peacefully. We can sort out our disputes once this funeral is over,' Rama insisted, joining his hands.

I looked around. We were gathered to venerate Dashaanan's death. There would be time to resolve personal conflicts. I lowered my eyes and agreed. Vibhishana looked broken but I could neither believe nor sympathize with him.

Dashaanan burial rites were administered by Nanashri and Vibhishana. After the funeral, Rama and Lakshmana performed a yagna in our courtyard. They worshipped Shiva and started a penance to cleanse them of brahmahatya dosha—killing a Brahmin was a sin and as Dashaanan had been half-Brahmin, it was mandatory for them to atone.

The next day, I stood in court as a widowed queen. One by one, the ministers and dignitaries came up to me and expressed their condolences before departing. When my parents came, I whispered to my father, 'Pitashri, take me with you.'

'Putri Mandodari, you have a duty towards your kingdom. You cannot come with us. You have to stay here and serve your people. It is time to overcome your grief. Your people need to see the throne stable,' said my father.

'We can only extend our help if you really need us. But you have to stay here and justify your position as a queen,' said my mother, who had unwaveringly held that my loyalty belonged to the kingdom I was married into.

The council left after the war was meagre, the court barren.

Rama, Lakshmana and Vibhishana entered the court. I was enraged but powerless.

'Rani Mandodari and esteemed council ministers of Lanka, I have an important announcement to make. I would like to crown Vibhishana as your rightful king. He is noble, wise, pious and the lawful holder of the crown. The throne belongs to him now.'

I looked at Rama in disapproval. 'How can you do that to us? Can't you see that we can barely stand being under the same roof with him, and you want him to ascend the throne? You are wise enough, Rama. Do you think he is capable of stepping into Lankapati Ravana's shoes? Our people will never accept him as their king. The council too will never accept him. He has betrayed us.'

'Think rationally, devi. Vibhishana joined us to follow the path of righteousness that Ravana was not on. The right to govern this kingdom lies with me and I enthrone

Vibhishana. I wanted to place someone from among you all on the throne,' said Rama.

Lakshmana came forward to add. 'If you change your perspective, you will find Vibhishana being loyal to the new leader of Lanka. How is that a betrayal, then?'

They were unrelenting. Vibhishana was to be our king in spite of our many protests. In the eyes of Rama, we needed Vibhishana more than he needed our support.

'You may have proved your point, Rama, but our people will never accept him . . . ' I tried, still adamant.

'Yes, I agree. I took the liberty of discussing our options with Nanashri. We reached the conclusion that only with you as their queen will Vibhishana be popularly accepted. Lanka needs a king. Hence, under the acts of statesmanship, your marriage to Vibhishana will favour him as king.'

I was reeling under Rama's proposal. Vibhishana, Nanashri, Mahaparshva and the council members looked at me eagerly. I turned to Vibhishana. 'Have you no morality? How could you even imagine such a thing? And you,' I faced the council. 'You, our trusted advisers, are amenable to this solution?'

'I understand how you feel, Mandodari, but this is the only way. I am the keeper of this throne; I will do whatever is best for the person who occupies it. Our motive is to keep the throne stable by passing the crown to a rightful and reliable heir,' replied Nanashri.

'We want the same thing but in different ways. I will never agree to marry Vibhishana. He will never be my king or my husband!' I stormed out.

I isolated myself in my chambers for several days. Lanka was mourning for Dashaanan and so was I. I missed him terribly. I was torn between sustaining Dashaanan's legacy and protecting his kingdom. I did not know what to do. On the twelfth day of mourning, Vibhishana requested an audience with me. I denied at once but he was persistent. I grudgingly agreed. I asked my dasi to make him wait in the lounge. When I entered, he stood up to greet me like he used to earlier, as if nothing had changed. I remained stubborn, unwilling to agree on anything that he had to offer.

'I have made it clear I do not wish to be in your company. What is it that you have to say?'

'Rani Mandodari, tomorrow will be the last day of mourning. I have come to you to ask for forgiveness and your consideration,' said Vibhishana. I noted he addressed me differently and not as his brother's wife.

'Your treason cannot be forgiven. You have been disloyal to your brother, this kingdom and to this land. And I wonder how you do not have any guilt or remorse for what you have done!'

'Why should I feel guilty when I don't think I have done anything wrong? I tried to warn bhrata Dashaanan. His stubbornness made him incapable of governance. The results are laid out in front of you.'

'He made mistakes like the rest of us. I agree he was stubborn but it was also his stubbornness to succeed that led this kingdom to glory.'

'Abducting a woman of high prestige as bait to lure her husband . . . how was that right for the kingdom? We were on the verge of a war and yet bhrata Dashaanan didn't give her up. The Lanka that remains today is only the wreckage of what it used to be. He did that to it. All because he lusted after Sita.'

'Enough! How little you knew your brother! Have you forgotten what Lakshmana subjected your sister to and our people whom Rama murdered? How can you be so ignorant? What would you have done to deliver justice to them?'

'If all he did was right, would we have been here today?'

I had no answer to give him.

'We can either choose to argue about it or resolve it. I saw my brother mishandling a situation I was certain would culminate this way. I respect your decision to support him. Why can't you accept mine?'

I was still silent.

He sighed, 'Sometimes, I imagine what would have happened if I had stood by him. I am not exceptional. I would have died in the first two days of the war. I chose the winning side—I was wise—and now I claim the throne that belongs to our dynasty rather than losing it to some other ruler.'

'They won only because you betrayed us to them—everything Dashaanan had entrusted you with, you chose to trade with them. It must have been because of you that they knew every gate, every commander and every strategy beforehand. You must have warned them about the Nikumbhila yagna, and definitely told them about the weakest part of Dashaanan's body to attack.' It was Vibhishana's turn to be silent. I questioned him further. 'Do you think Rama and Lakshmana would have survived the war if you hadn't disclosed all our secrets to them? You were the closest to your brother, you shadowed him, his wish was your command . . . then why be so cruel? Eventually, you wanted more than his kindness, you wanted his throne.'

His swallowed, looking away. 'I was not cruel to him but there were times when he was. I don't blame him; he had too much on his mind to be patient with an ordinary brother. I didn't want the throne then but I want it now. I want to continue his legacy on my own terms.'

He prepared to leave and joined his hands once again. 'Like I said before, our argument will never conclude without a negotiation. Our kingdom is in dire need of a king. You cannot rule the kingdom alone, and I will need your cooperation to work within my office. Together, we can piece together what is broken. I am not wrong but I still ask for your forgiveness. I am married already but I ask for your consideration to marry me. Accept the proposal and our union will give hope to our people.'

He handed me a scroll before leaving and said, 'I leave this with you. It states the terms of our marriage in accordance with the act of statesmanship. It is an agreement. Kindly consider the proposal and if you decide to agree to it, send it to me with your seal.'

Brahma's Boon

Vibhishana had asked me a question I wanted to dismiss at once. Yet I kept thinking about it. What answer could I give when I was looking for answers myself?

'A war between the two sects will be recorded in the history of mankind. A hero will die. You shall reign next to him for years ahead. I saw you seated on your throne as the queen. You looked older than you are now.'

What had that prophecy meant? Its ambiguity tormented me. Had it meant Vibhishana's proposal all along?

The designated thirteen days of mourning were over. Lanka anticipated its new king. Rama couldn't crown Vibhishana until he had majority approval. My council of ministers awaited my decision. I remembered Dashaanan's wish for me to serve Lanka. I had made up my mind. We were married in a small ceremony witnessed by notable council members and relatives. Sarama was absent. I had not seen her since the funeral and would not see her thereafter. Nanashri was pleased with my decision. The ceremony brought back the day Dashaanan and I had got married. I quelled those memories.

My marriage with Vibhishana was a political necessity. Thinking about Dashaanan's many wives that I had envied and he had claimed to be 'political necessities' made me laugh now. For the first time, I was a queen before I was a wife. I had braced myself for the women to look at me differently after my marriage to Vibhishana, but nothing changed. If anything, they respected me. Bajrajala, Meenakshi, Dhanyamalini and Nayanadini and I were bound by the same grief. We had all lost our husbands and our sons. We had all survived to live a life of sacrifice.

On the sixteenth day after Dashaanan's death, Vibhishana was coronated by Rama. The ceremony was not grand. There was barely any applause or any people.

Nobody announced a grand feast and nobody celebrated. Vibhishana bowed to the ten-headed crown that had belonged to Dashaanan and expressed his gratitude. He sat on the throne and Hanuman blew a conch shell to mark a new beginning. It was Rama's support that had turned Brahma's boon into reality.

'Vibhishana's era of reign will observe peace, and righteousness will be established.'

On the first and auspicious day of his reign, Vibhishana returned Sita to Rama. I saw them meet from the corridor of Dashaanan's palace, now Vibhishana's. The vanaras rejoiced. I was happy for Sita. Her suffering had finally come to an end. She bid farewell. Before she left Ashokavanam, she turned and took it in one last time. She embraced Trijata, who had become like a mother to her. Fleetingly, I felt envy slither in me. After Sita was introduced to the vanara army, she walked towards my chambers.

This was the last time I would see my daughter. I hastened to meet her outside my door.

'Rani Mandodari, I wanted to meet you before I left. Thank you for your kindness.'

'I am happy for you. May god bless you.'

'You are the most virtuous woman I have ever met. Forgive me for what I said to you.'

'It does not matter now. I have forgiven you, Sita. I wish you a happy life with your husband.'

'We are going home to Ayodhya. Our exile is over. I would like to invite you, please visit someday.'

I nodded. She took dust from my feet and I trembled at her touch. I held her shoulders and embraced her for the first time. I could not help but cry. Hurriedly saying goodbye, I rushed inside my chambers.

Vibhishana and his council escorted Rama, Lakshmana, Sita, Hanuman, Sugreeva, Angad and a few other commanders from the vanara army to the airport outside the city gates. He gave them the Pushpaka Vimana to fly across the ocean in order reach Ayodhya faster. Later, my dasi told me that Sita had been asked to walk through fire in a ritual. It seemed more of an assessment of her chastity to me. Her captivity in Lanka had raised doubts over her purity—and Rama sought to know by putting her through this test. I cursed Rama. How could he doubt his wife for whom he had doomed a kingdom? I was furious but again helpless to change the order of things.

Sita passed and they climbed into the vimana and left for Bharatvarsh. A few days later, the invitation for Rama's coronation arrived. I declined, but Vibhishana took a few council members with him to attend the most prosperous event of Bharatvarsh.

AN AFTERWORD—BY MANDODARI

The new beginning that dawned on Lanka was stable. It may not have been prosperous but that is how it was destined. The war between Rama and Lankapati Ravana soon became folklore. Some saw Ravana as the heroic emperor, while some deigned him an immoral villain. Rama's defeat of Ravana had elevated him to the position of a god in the eyes of his followers. He was now called 'Maryadapurushottam' or the supreme being. He was considered an avatar of Vishnu. For the people of Lanka, Rama would forever be the man who took their beloved king from them. They never wanted a new beginning; they simply had to live with it when it came.

Four months after Sita left for Ayodhya with Rama, she was abandoned by him. It was said that Rama sacrificed his wife for the morality of his kingdom. It was shocking news; unbelievable at first, but our sources confirmed it. He gave away some of his valuable possessions for a penance, including his wife. She was escorted outside his kingdom by Lakshmana. Did this really make him an ideal man? The killings, rituals and sacrifices were all thus justified. This was the fate of a pious and innocent woman after fourteen years of exile—walking through fire and yet being banished by her own husband. The gods did not favour her; estranged from her mother, given in marriage to a man who would eventually disown her and abducted by her own father. What had she done to deserve this misery?

No one asked about the other wives of Ravana, nor did anyone bother themselves with the occupants of his antapura. Dhanyamalini resisted her father's insistence to take her back to Trikota to keep me company. Nayanadini returned to her family home overseas. Nanashri, the most trusted keeper of the throne, guided Vibhishana, just like he had guided Ravana. As for me, I devoted myself to bringing up Meghanath's son for the future of Lanka.

For ages to come, my story may not be told as it occurred, my name may not be mentioned, but my voice will be heard forever—in this story that I write as the queen of Lanka.

ACKNOWLEDGEMENTS

My deepest thanks to:

—Gurveen Chadha, Penguin Random House India, who has been equally passionate about 'Mandodari' as I.
—My husband, Jeetu Anandani, who backs me in whatever I choose to do.
—My parents, Nisha Singh and S.S. Thakur, for their unconditional love and encouragement.

GLOSSARY

Antapura	Women's quarters, mainly for wives and concubines
Ashram	Dwelling of a hermit
Atimaharathi	A warrior capable of fighting many warriors at the same time
Bhabhi	Brother's wife
Bhavan	A multipurpose building with hall
Bhojan	Meal/Food
Chanwari	A porch or platform built for weddings and ceremonies
Guru	Spiritual teacher
Kundli	Horoscope
Mantras	Chants and hymns
Navagraha	Nine (nava), planets (grahas)
Putri	Daughter
Rajsik	Overly tasty and lavish meals
Sena	Army
Siddhi	Enlightenment
Taamsik	Spicy or non-vegetarian food

Tapasvi	An ascetic
Tapasya	Ascetic period of fasting, prayer and meditation
Tirthas	Sacred pilgrimage, holy places
Upanayana	A sacred thread worn across shoulder and torso
Vyuha	War formation
Yagna	A ritual sacrifice performed in front of fire
Yogi	A hermit